Tom Benjamin grew up in the suburbs of north Lond and began his working life as a journalist before bec spokesman for Scotland Yard. He later moved

wife was offered a job in Bologna he came along the rest of the baggage, learning Italian while mind the door at a homeless shelter and, during the quieter oments, creating Bologna-based sleuth Daniel Leicester.

Quiet Death in Italy is the first novel in his Daniel Leicester me series.

A QUIET DEATH IN ITALY

TOM BENJAMIN

CONSTABLE

CONSTABLE

First published in Great Britain in 2019 by Constable
This edition published in 2020 by Constable

A CIP catalogue record for this book
is available from the British Library.

ISBN: 978-1-47213-157-7

Typeset in Adobe Garamond by Initial Typesetting Services, Edinburgh
Printed and bound in Great Britain by Clays Ltd, Elcograf S.p.A.

Papers used by Constable are from well-managed forests and
other responsible sources.

Constable
An imprint of
Little, Brown Book Group
Carmelite House
50 Victoria Embankment
London EC4Y 0DZ

An Hachette UK Company
www.hachette.co.uk

www.littlebrown.co.uk

For my father

L'erba cativa l'an mor mai
Bad grass never dies

Emilian proverb

Chapter 1

Like much else in a city that had once been governed by the Catholic Church, the old morgue was a muddle of the sacred and profane. The brick-domed room with its crucifix above the doorway felt as reverent as any crypt, the corpses were stacked on marble shelves in white body bags that could have passed as shrouds. The strip lights suspended from the ceiling and capital-lettered ordinances of the secular authority reminded us that God had since died and we would all end up in this place or somewhere like it one day, tagged and bagged in white if we were lucky and no suspicious circumstances were associated with our passing.

But we weren't stopping here. Doctor Mattani unlocked the door to the autopsy room and paused. 'Better that we allow a moment,' he said, opening it halfway. He meant to acclimatise. Not a hint of the macho humour that usually bludgeoned you in places like this – if one of us threw up, the doctor would probably have to dispose of the mess himself. This was not an official visit, after all.

'They found him attached to some fencing,' said the doctor. 'Apparently, that was what alerted the authorities in the first place – some kind of blockage in the canal system. He went missing two weeks before, and the state of decay would be consistent with this timeframe.'

That peculiar hybrid smell – from the butchering and the pickling – exited the doorway. Not so disagreeable until your imagination got to work. That was when your stomach would begin to tighten and you were glad you had had a light breakfast. But it wasn't the anatomy that really troubled me, it was the entropy. The toll time took on an abandoned body; the reminder that death was not only an event but a process, and a progressively ugly one.

Standing outside that room alongside my boss, the Comandante, and our friend the doctor, I began to sense its presence: insinuating itself behind the blood and chemicals like the base note to a particularly sickly perfume.

The doctor opened the door fully and we stepped in. This room was like a smaller version of the 'crypt', only white-washed and with a pair of gleaming stainless-steel tables plumbed to sinks. Lying flat on the first was a black body bag zipped to the top.

The extractor fan came on and a weary rattle began to escape from the vent. I turned to the Comandante. 'A black bag,' I said. 'Didn't our guy at the Questura confirm it wasn't being treated as suspicious?'

The Comandante shrugged. Doctor Mattani shook his head. 'I don't know anything about that.' He stepped forward and positioned himself beside the corpse. 'If you wouldn't mind closing the door.'

I felt it click behind me. The doctor took hold of the large plastic zip and, walking the length of the table, opened the bag from head to toe. Despite having adjusted to the stink, the accumulated gasses caused us to step back and place our hands across our faces. We stood observing the corpse for some time, each, I think, unwilling to make the necessary effort to speak until our senses had sufficiently recovered and the ventilation system had played its part.

Death had utterly claimed Signor Solitudine, who was unrecognisable from the photo I had stored on my phone – the sinewy, clean-shaven older man with windswept hair and bright eyes marching behind a protest banner – unless, that is, you were looking for the Man on the Moon. A fortnight in the river that ran beneath the centre of Bologna had done its damnedest to swell his features to comic proportions. He had assumed a flattened, almost two-dimensional appearance, bolstered by the silver-grey patina that always came with corpses that had spent too long in dirty water. His eyelids and mouth were bloated closed, his fingers swollen together like fins, and from his collarbone to his pelvis there were broad post-mortem stitches, as if he'd been sewn up in a hurry.

'There was evidence of trauma to the cranium,' said the doctor, 'but we are unable to say whether this took place before or after he was submerged, or what caused it. There is water in the lungs—'

'River water?' I said. The doctor smiled.

'Yes, Daniel, river water – he was not drowned in his bath-tub and dumped, I can tell you that at least.'

'The bang on the head, though,' I said, looking at the Comandante, 'baton?'

'It certainly could have come from human agency,' said

the Comandante, 'but equally a boat or even the debris in the current . . . isn't that so, Matteo?'

'In those conditions,' said the doctor, 'it would be impossible to say for sure.'

'Anything else?' said the Comandante.

'We scraped his fingernails and so on but nothing.'

'River water . . .' said the Comandante. The doctor nodded.

'Remarkably corrosive. I always say that if I was to commit a murder, that would be how I would dispose of my victims. River water doesn't just wash any evidence away, it scrubs the corpse clean.'

'And you'd be the perfect murderer too,' I said, 'being the one to examine the bodies.'

'If we are ever asked to hunt an elusive serial killer,' added the Comandante, 'who dumps his victims in the Reno, we will know where to come.'

The smell had now almost disappeared, although that had as much to do with mankind's faculty to adapt to new odours, no matter how unpleasant, as the efficacy of the ventilation system, and we found ourselves smiling over the mouldering corpse. Looking back down at it sobered us up.

'Done?' said Doctor Mattani. The Comandante looked at me. I took in Paolo Solitudine's body one last time. Thought of the handsome older man he had been, of the woman who had sent us here.

'Done,' I said.

2

If morgue time was set to perpetual midnight, back in the land of the living it was past midday. Despite our grisly encounter, I wasn't surprised the Comandante and Doctor Mattani headed straight to Diana's – it would take more than a soggy cadaver to get in the way of an Italian's lunch. I was not invited. Here, old men ate with old men and the young grabbed sandwiches, although because I was close to Mercato delle Erbe I headed for the fish place where they had a cheap menu. I was not that young, after all.

I had bought a copy of *Il Carlino di Bologna*, which I propped against the bar, the only spot that still had seats available. Ever since a British TV chef had visited the eatery on a tour of the lesser-known Italian cities, Banco's regular clientele had been bolstered by tourists cooing over its top-notch grub. Today our *primo* was *tortelli* filled with potatoes, capers and mint on a crab bisque, no less, which the locals were wolfing down as if this was nothing more than their due, while the foreigners oohed and snapped photos.

Solitudine featured on pages three and four of the *Carlino*. Apparently the rag was still running with the official line and hadn't yet got wind he'd been 'black bagged', so there was none of the usual *SOS CRIMINE* that ran above crime stories. Instead they were using the space to rehash events of forty years past, when the country had been consumed in a maelstrom of political violence and our man had found himself in the centre – sent down for a seven-year stretch after a botched robbery. It was mostly 'End of an Era' stuff featuring various ageing gents opining about the old days, among them one Mario Cento, described as a former cellmate and co-founder with Solitudine of 'Civil Action', the current moniker of the local squatting movement. I made a note to look him up.

'It's a shame,' said Niccoló as he lay down my bread.

'You knew him?'

Niccoló shrugged. 'Everyone knew *of* him. The old guard. Those days . . .' He looked misty-eyed even though the events Solitudine had been caught up in must have happened long before he was born. 'They got him in the end.'

'Who do you mean "they"?'

Niccoló arched his eyebrows. Wasn't it obvious?

'The cops, authorities . . .' He gesticulated as if to evoke the invisible hands everyone knew were pulling the strings. 'Fascists.'

'I heard there was trouble in Via Zamboni,' I said. 'Some kind of demonstration.'

'If they think they can get away with this, they're crazy.'

I thought about saying – what do you care? You're hardly a radical, you're minting it as a partner in this restaurant. But as soon as anyone put on a black t-shirt in this city they seemed to feel instantly connected to its revolutionary past. And black was *de rigeur* for the staff at Banco.

A British couple were placed beside me. Late-middle aged empty-nesters who began trying to decipher the menu as they might clues in the *Telegraph* crossword.

'*Scusi?*' The guy called Niccoló over. He asked what was what in his phrase-book Italian. Niccoló played along – he could speak English fluently, but gamely replied as he might to any local.

Watching the couple in the bar mirror I clocked the incomprehension behind their smiles. They thanked him anyway and he went away presuming he had been perfectly understood – for the moment, tourism remained a novelty in the city and waiting staff had yet to lose patience with visitors, which was great if you wanted to learn the language, less so if you couldn't actually speak it.

'Did you get any of that?' said the man. The woman shook her head.

'Not a clue,' she said. The man took out his phone, presumably to try and translate. I reached around the bar for an English menu and handed it to him.

'Oh!' he said. '*Grazie!*'

I nodded. 'You're welcome.'

The man looked at my *Carlino* and frowned. 'You're . . . English?'

'Guilty,' I said.

'But . . .' He looked at the paper again. 'You're not a tourist.'

I shook my head. 'I live here.'

'Nice?' said the man, clearly trying to get the measure of me. There are few things more suspicious to an Englishman abroad than another Englishman abroad.

'It's all right,' I said.

'Better than just all right, surely,' said his wife, who clearly didn't share his apprehension. '*Such wonderful food.* You're so lucky.'

I smiled. 'So I've been told.' In the mirror I noticed a flat-fish at the fishmongers behind us, lying like a grey puddle upon the ice. The Image of Solitudine on that slab flashed before my eyes.

Niccoló plonked down my pasta and the lady nodded her approval. What else could I do? I scooped up the *tortelli* and turned back to the *Carlino*.

Chapter 3

Marta Finzi lived in the old Jewish Ghetto. When we arrived at the entrance, a line of riot police was blocking our way. Chatting, resting against their shields, smoking. Beyond them, it sounded like a carnival of drunks – the thud-thud-thud of an amplified bass drum, angry Italian rap, whistles, cheers and chants bouncing off the Renaissance porticoes on either side of Via Zamboni, the thoroughfare that ran through the university zone.

A megaphone screeched some slogan, a smoke canister popped and sent vanilla wisps of grey drifting our way. They sounded like thousands down there but I knew there were probably just a few hundred.

'Where do you think you're going?' A riot cop, his visor raised above his navy blue helmet, stepped in our path.

The Comandante pointed to the archway. 'We just need to go through there.'

He shook his head. 'Not today,' he said, 'you'll have to go the long way around.'

'Officer,' the Comandante smiled through his tidy grey

beard, 'we are a little late for a business appointment. I can assure you, we are not here to make trouble.'

Another *carabinieri* came up and pulled the first one out of the way. 'Stefano,' he said, 'don't you know who this is? Please –' he waved us through '– Comandante.'

'Thank you, Corporal.'

'You're welcome, sir.' He saluted.

'What would we do without you?' I said as we passed beneath the arch.

'Take the long way around,' said the Comandante. It must have been almost twenty years since he had taken early retirement but his reputation, along with his former rank, still preceded him.

The archway marked the entrance to the Ghetto, which dated back to the days when Bologna's Jewish community had been confined to cramped quarters close to the market. Once through it, the city shrank to medieval scale: narrow, cobbled lanes, low porticoes propped up by reclaimed Roman columns.

The quarter's official title suited it better: Ex Ghetto, as the signs rather emphatically proclaimed. What would have once been an overcrowded, ramshackle area with Via Inferno – Hell Street – running down the middle was now one of the most sought after addresses in the city. The second-hand clothes shops were strictly vintage, the *osterie* featured fine wines and artisanal beer. The shoemaker's immaculately crafted wares bore no price tag. This was the home of professors at the nearby university, youthful beneficiaries of old money, successful filmmakers. And the Finzi-Manzis.

We walked along the low-hanging portico until we came

to their door, perfectly nondescript, even down to the white, blue and green graffiti tags that covered it from top to bottom. This was par for the course: the closer you got to the university area, the denser the graffiti became.

I rang the Finzi-Manzi bell. There was an immediate response, as if Signora Finzi had been waiting by the intercom.

'Come through the building and into the garden at the back,' she said. 'I'll meet you there.' The door buzzed open.

Inside, I switched on the hallway light and we began to walk down a gloomy corridor. There was a metal and stained-glass door at the end. Deprived of any other options, I tried the handle.

The door opened onto a small park. I shouldn't have been surprised – the city was built around its hidden spaces – but even by Bolognese standards this was impressive. Stepping out of the dark passageway onto a gravel path, nature expanded around us. Ancient trees towered above an expanse of uneven lawn. Islands of plants and shrubs studded the grass, while closely cropped vines were garlanded around copies of Roman and Greek statues (at least, I presumed they were copies). Old red brick walls rose, some way distant and partly camouflaged by flora, on either side.

The path led us toward an age-smoothed fountain decorated with the fauna of the Renaissance: cherubs, cupids and other chortling child-creatures, while beneath them sea nymphs spouted from their upraised breasts.

'It's Giambologna,' said the Comandante. 'After he'd finished the statue of Neptune in Maggiore, the owners commissioned this. Ah,' he said, 'there she is.'

A woman was coming toward us between a trio of gnarled

pines, tall and slender, her long frizzy hair streaked with grey. Behind her, partially screened by the trees, stood a three-storey palazzo.

'Marta,' said the Comandante, clasping her hand.

'Giovanni,' she said. She looked at me.

'My partner, and son-in-law, Daniel.'

'Of course,' she said. She held out a long-fingered hand. Despite her even gaze, her palm, I noticed, was damp. 'In fact, we've met before. But you probably won't remember me. I was at the funeral – Lucia had been one of my students.'

She was right – I didn't remember her. I couldn't, in truth, remember much from those times.

Signora Finzi gave me the smile I hated most – of pity. It may have showed – in any case, she changed the subject: 'How's your Italian these days?'

'It puts my English to shame,' said the Comandante.

'But then in our day, Giovanni, we were taught only French, no?'

'So were we,' I said. 'And my French is terrible.'

'But your Italian seems okay.' She looked around the garden.

'An oasis,' said the Comandante, 'as ever.'

'We should go inside,' she said.

Despite its venerable façade there was little inside the palazzo that appeared to have fallen under the auspices of Bologna's notoriously strict department for the preservation of historical monuments. Abstract art hung from the otherwise feature-less whitewashed walls; a modern, wood-burning stove took centre-place in the living room, its flue suspended from the ceiling so a glass-fronted oblong bulb hung half a metre above the dark-stained parquet.

I passed an Antonello Ghezzi mirror with *guardami ancora* – look at me again – etched across it in illuminated script, and was momentarily surprised by what I saw on second glance: in my dark overcoat and suit, my neatly cropped hair with that widows peak about to fall off the cliff, I caught the reflection not of an Englishman, but an Italian.

I evoked Lucia's spirit – *not bad*, she was laughing, although I didn't doubt that on closer examination no matter how well I dressed, from the shape of my skull to the size of my feet, my origins would speak of the East Anglian Fens and London smog rather than the Po Plain and Bolognese guilds.

We stepped into a modern, industrial style kitchen that had been created out of only the most expensively distressed materials.

Signora Finzi made us a coffee. She opened the window looking out onto the garden and produced a pack of cigarettes. She offered one to the Comandante, who accepted. I declined.

'I presume Carlo is in Rome,' said the Comandante, 'for the conference?'

'Hm. Rome, yes.' Marta Finzi's eyes swivelled around the kitchen as if she was worried her husband was about to come sauntering in.

'The PD these days is quite a mess.' The Comandante meant the political party to which her husband, Carlo Manzi, belonged.

Signora Finzi made another strained smile. She took a

sharp drag on her cigarette and expelled a short plume of smoke in the direction of the window. 'Isn't it,' she said.

There was a boom from outside, so loud it rattled the window. We watched a smudge of black smoke rise against the Mediterranean-blue sky.

'You know what it's about,' said Signora Finzi, 'this protest?'

'The man they found dead in the canal,' I said. 'The man we've just paid a visit, at your request, Signora Finzi.'

She nodded, contemplating the cigarette smouldering between those long fingers. 'That man,' she said, looking first at me, then at the Comandante, 'Paolo Solitudine, was my lover.'

Neither I, nor the Comandante, was exactly bowled over. We had not needed to discuss it to assume, I was sure, it would be something like this – it seemed unlikely the lady would have gone to the trouble for her window cleaner. On the other hand, there was certainly novelty about the coupling: Marta Finzi, wife of Bologna's Mayor, Carlo Manzi, PD bigwig synonymous with the affluent Leftist consensus that had ruled this town for more than half a century, carrying on with a leading light of their sworn enemy, the anarchists, who hated everything the PD stood for and were wont to demonstrate it by smashing up the city on a regular basis.

But although it didn't come as much of a surprise, I wondered whether it was my imagination or the Comandante had turned a shade greyer than usual. Certainly his cigarette had grown a pyre of ash that now balanced precariously above his knuckles. He cleared his throat. 'My condolences,' he said, and tilted it into the ashtray.

'I'm sorry,' said Marta, 'after everything you did for us.'

The Comandante shook his head. 'That was a long time ago. But tell me, Marta, what it is we can do for you now.'

'The police are treating it as an accident,' she said. My thoughts returned to that black bag – *officially* he should have been in a white one. Yet there he was, dressed in black. Had they just run out of white, or was someone playing silly buggers?

'But you don't believe them?' said the Comandante.

She looked out of the window again, gazed at that dark stain against the sky. She shook her head.

'You believe the anarchists, then?' I said. 'That it's somehow connected to this raid on their squat?'

She scoffed. 'Who would you believe?'

Only in Italy, I thought, would the city's very own Marie Antoinette, ensconced in this elegant palace, place more store in the judgment of a rabble than the forces of law and order.

'There's more,' she said. She took another cigarette out of the box and was about to light it when she realised she still had one on the go in the ashtray. She tried to place the unlit cigarette back in the box but her hand was trembling too much, so she left it on top. She picked up the lit one and lifted it to her lips. She looked back out into the garden.

Her features slackened as if her real face was emerging from behind the mask. Then tears began to run down her cheeks and splash upon the work surface.

'Come,' the Comandante took her arm, 'come, Marta, darling, let us sit down.' He guided her to the burnished-metal island in the centre of the kitchen and pulled up a chair, sitting beside her and placing an arm tentatively around her shoulders.

When Signora Finzi spoke again, the strength had drained from her voice. 'It's . . . Carlo,' she said. 'His behaviour. He's changed. These past few weeks, no, that's the thing – months –' she shuddered '– I've noticed . . . it's like this: it's as if he's been watching me. I don't mean like . . . like *you* do, like spying and so on, but it's like he's really been paying attention.

'You know, Giovanni, in every marriage . . . in every long marriage there's always a sense of complacency, but with him, these past years, especially since the kids have left, it's been . . . it's been like I hardly exist. Once I went to a conference for a weekend and when I got back I realised, well, he didn't say anything, but I just realised – *he hadn't even noticed I'd gone*. But now, recently, that's all changed. It's as if . . . as if, suddenly, he's zoomed in on me.

'It's . . . unnerving,' she said. 'At first, you know, I was flattered . . . I began to feel guilty . . . about Paolo and me, but then, after what happened, to Paolo I mean, I began to think –' she raised a hand to her mouth '– my god, that's it – he found out.'

I caught the Comandante's eye. Not only did we have an accusation of murder on our hands, but one involving Bologna's first citizen.

'With respect,' I said, 'there might be any number of reasons why Signor Manzi has begun to pay more attention to you, *signora*. Perfectly innocent reasons.'

'It's not like him,' she said, 'not like him at all.'

'Things like flowers,' I said, 'dining out?'

'Oh, nothing that obvious,' she said, 'you think he's so stupid? No, he's just more attentive, questioning, *interested* . . . it's the little things . . .'

The little things – a wife would know, I had to admit, and that phrase would be enough for us to take on an adultery case, but murder? 'Is there any *hard* evidence you can provide us with? For example, has Signor Manzi ever threatened you,' I said, 'been violent?' She shook her head, looked at me with a mixture of pity and contempt.

'He doesn't understand,' she said to the Comandante.

'What don't I understand?' I said.

She was still shaking her head. 'What he's capable of.'

'I presume you had no reason to believe Signor Manzi had found out about your relationship with Signor Solitudine *before* his death?' I said.

'None. We were very careful.'

'Could someone have told him?'

'No one knew. *No one.*'

Somebody always knows, I thought. 'Did Signor Solitudine have a wife, girlfriend?'

'There was no *wife*, no *girlfriend* . . .' She sat back in her chair and undid her hair. She gave her head a rigorous shake, running her fingers through the frizzled mass before winding the scarf – a Chinese dragon design which danced between her fingers as she whipped it into shape – and tying her hair back, tight.

Marta Finzi straightened up. Gone was the anguished, grieving adulteress. Despite the red eyes, that tear-stained face, Bologna's First Lady had returned to the room. Only the tremor at the tips of those long fingers gave anything away. She laced them together.

She looked across the table at me, then remembered the Comandante sitting beside her. 'Will you do it?' she said. 'Can you help me?'

The range of vested interests, never mind the paranoia that was a constant factor in every Italian equation, meant that this was not an assignment anyone would take on lightly. Signora Finzi knew this as well as we did. Italy had once been dominated by city states, after all, and it could be a short step from mayoral office to prime minister. Certainly the financial rewards of taking the job had to be offset by the price of getting on the wrong side of the Mayor. Still, I didn't have any doubt about the Comandante's response, even had the lady been unknown to him. He nodded solemnly.

'Yes,' he said, 'we will look into this, Marta.'

'You will find out if Carlo was involved?'

'We will.'

'And if he wasn't . . .' She reached for the unlit cigarette still lying on top of the packet but didn't light it. 'Find out who was . . . I mean, whether it really was the police, or whoever.'

'That is certainly something we can look into,' said the Comandante.

She nodded, pushed back her chair. Stood up. The audience was over.

As we parted company Signora Finzi seemed cool enough. It was only when I took a final backwards glance that, seeing her standing there at the front door lost in her thoughts, she struck me not so much as Marie Antoinette but an exotic bird in a cage. I felt a sudden urge to go back and take her with us, usher her through the darkness of the corridor, and out, into the world.

I wondered if Paolo Solitudine had felt the same way.

We stepped onto the street. 'We should speak,' I said. The Comandante looked up and down the empty portico.

'I had dealings,' he said, 'with Carlo and Marta many years ago . . . We were all young. They were murky times, you know, the 1970s—'

'The Years of Lead,' I said. 'Political terrorism . . .'

'Murky times,' he shrugged, 'they were involved in politics. It was my business to know what was going on.'

'She said you helped them.'

'Which is why she approached us, I presume,' he said.

'Do you think the Mayor could actually have done it, murdered this radical, or had him killed?'

'Marta believes he may have. Our role is to place her mind at rest.'

'She said he wasn't a violent man,' I said, 'but she did seem scared.' The Comandante didn't respond. 'Giovanni,' I said, 'you dealt with him. Should she be afraid?'

A pair of traffic cops turned the corner and began ambling toward us.

'She should,' he said.

Chapter 4

An English detective in Italy has certain advantages. For a start, Italians adore the British – or rather, at least before they made a hash of Brexit – deeply admired them for representing everything they believe they are not: sober, pragmatic and trustworthy. Those are pretty good credentials before you've even walked through the door. Add to that, from the nation that invented the *giallo*, an enduring affection for Agatha Christie and Arthur Conan Doyle, and you've got much the same reputation for detective work any random Italian visitor to the UK might have for cookery.

The disadvantage is, of course, Italy. The Comandante had said the 1970s was murky, but although the days of political terror were no longer with us, the country remained much as I imagined it always had been, only with a change of clothes and sprinkling of new technology. So if you'd told me I'd be a gumshoe when we'd arrived all those years ago, I'd have been on the first flight home. No, Lucia sold it as a chance to finally deliver my long-commissioned book on north London gang culture. What I had failed to take into account, of course, was *Italian* gang culture – families. *Why rent when there's so much room here? We're a bit short-handed, could you help out?* Little by little, I became drawn in and, before I knew it, there was no going back. But it wasn't just about Lucia, or my reluctance to wrench my daughter, Rose, from the world she knew following the accident – anywhere else, not least my old stamping ground, would have seemed infinitely less vivid.

I crossed Piazza Maggiore, a tour de force of the Italian centuries. To my left, the baroque copper-green dome of Santa Maria della Vita rose behind the porticoes of Palazzo dei Banchi. Ahead, the bulk of San Petronio, a church so large its construction was halted by a pope worried it was set to dwarf Saint Peter's. I turned right into the courtyard of Palazzo d'Accursio – once the home of bishop princes and now the headquarters of the Comune, or city council.

I made my way toward a confetti-speckled corner where newly-wed couples would emerge following their ceremony in the wedding salon; where Lucia and I, in fact, had stood more than a dozen years before.

I could have taken a lift up to the second floor, but that would have felt like cheating – it was our corner, our memory, albeit one shared with all the other couples who had come down that broad stairway with its steps so shallow the bride was obliged to cling to the arm of her husband as she teetered toward waiting family and friends, as it had obliged Lucia to cling to me.

Now I made my way briskly upward, alone.

A speech from the event above echoed around me. I found the foyer busy with caterers and business people on phones. *Sala Farnese* was packed. There was a guy at the entrance with a clipboard, but when the crowd rose to applaud the Mayor, and he turned too, I took my chance and slipped in.

'Look around you, and what do you see?' Carlo Manzi was standing behind the lectern in the foyer of the town hall, every inch the Leftist politician in his tailored navy sports jacket and open-necked, man of the people shirt. Along with everyone else, I dutifully looked at the frescoes – a parade of soldiers, bishops and potentates, proceeding through Maggiore.

'When the Comune commissioned these works from Cignani and Taruffi,' the Mayor continued, 'they set out to record a source of tremendous municipal pride. Bologna had been chosen by the Pope as the venue for the coronation of Charles the Fifth, the new Holy Roman Emperor. Why? Because our city was second only to Paris in its reputation for learning and culture, and this was a reputation that persevered for centuries: that drew the young Copernicus, Cervantes, Michelangelo and Mozart to study here.

'Friends, we may have the oldest university in the world, but we also have one of the youngest populations in the country. Students from all over the globe come here to study: tomorrow's Mozarts, tomorrow's Michelangelos, even if –' he paused and we could clearly hear the demonstration outside '– they can sometimes be a little exuberant.' The mainly silver-haired audience laughed.

This election event was as much for the TV cameras behind us as the audience, and the Mayor was clearly in his element. I had at first been surprised to see so many old folk at a speech about the future of the city, but I shouldn't have been – 'future' hadn't meant digital start-ups, Carlo Manzi was preaching to property developers.

'We have successfully secured funding to expand the airport and build the high-speed rail link. We are opening up the old canal system. And yet there remains much work to be done in the competition for the tourist euro, dollar, yuan. A mere fraction – five per cent or thereabouts – of Italy's tourist "foot fall" passes through our fine city, and that means, ladies and gentlemen, that despite our high-speed link, the money train is passing us by. Partly, this is unavoidable – while Michelangelo may have studied here, he went to practise his trade in Florence and Rome – but there is still much we can do.

'Not everything must be preserved. The zoning and planning regulations, for example, restricting development within the city centre: we're not going to attract more tourists if they can't sample our famous *gelato* because some functionary in 1977 decided a grocer's store should go there instead. They're not going to come if they simply have *nowhere to stay* – the shortage of hotel rooms, ladies and gentlemen ... well, frankly, it's a scandal ...'

That explained the protesters' placards I had glimpsed on my way in: WE WANT A LIVING CITY, NOT A DEAD ONE, TO HELL WITH BOUTIQUE BOLOGNA. I was also quite taken with GIVE US BREAD, NOT ICE CREAM, but I avoided lingering outside for too long – I didn't want to be associated with the rabble.

'We cannot continue to preserve our buildings,' said the Mayor, 'our by-laws, in aspic. Just like our esteemed predecessors, ladies and gentlemen, we must celebrate the past but plan for the future.'

Cue further applause. The Mayor joined in and began to gesture for earlier speakers to come up to the stage. But his enthusiasm faltered when he saw a hand raised among the sea of grey. He returned to the microphone.

'Roberto,' he said, 'do you have something to say?'

'Carlo,' said a distinguished voice, 'I'm sure all of us here salute your sentiments, but the reality, well, it's somewhat different, isn't it. The old hospital, for example. What are you going to do about those troublemakers?'

The Mayor looked pained. 'As you know, Roberto, we have been making every effort to remove the squatters, every effort, but then there was . . . the incident.' I leaned forward: he meant the death of Paolo Solitudine. 'We hope, however, to get things moving again as soon as possible.' The Mayor's tone was more aggrieved than grieving, but it seemed to strike the right note with the audience. Then, as if remembering the ones watching at home, he said, looking directly at me, although he would have actually been focusing on the TV camera above my head: 'But we should never forget the *human* dimension to all of this. From now on we must work together – all of us – to explain ourselves better, to reassure, and to be reassured, that we are working for the best interests of the whole community, so there can be no doubt, no doubt about that at all.'

He was good, I thought. I believed him, in as much as I believed any politician, which was as much as I believed any decent actor. Barring special circumstances, he wouldn't have a problem getting re-elected – Bologna was not only *La Grassa*, the fat, and *La Dotta*, the learned, but also, *La Rossa*, the Red. The Communists had ruled this place after the war until, like all the other parties, they had dissolved following the scandals of the 1990s. Now the PD, or *Partito*

Democratico, its politically tepid successor, ruled the roost. It wouldn't be so much an election as a coronation, and I found it hard to imagine this manicured, gym-thin fox with his immaculate head of (dyed, presumably) dark hair wrestling Paolo Solitudine by the side of a canal. But ordering someone else to do the job? Wasn't that, ultimately, in the ambit of every politician? And the trouble with orders – perhaps to give the old radical a warning, a fright, or even a roughing up? – was that they could easily be misunderstood.

Then I found the person I was looking for: a girl with stars on her neck. She was one of Manzi's staff, one of his hangers-on. Somebody's niece, somebody's daughter, a bourgeois brat with a salon tan and a string of tattooed stars rising up from the nape of neck into her hairline. When she wasn't causing havoc on her Vespa she would be double-parking her mum's SUV in front of the *pasticceria* with one hand on the wheel and the other on her mobile. Manzi was pointing the well wishers in her direction and she would take down their details on her iPad while they glanced surreptitiously at her breasts.

I waited until the Mayor had drifted far enough away before approaching her.

'Hi,' I said, 'I'm from Bologna Welcome.' That was the Comune's tourism website. 'I'm sorry for my poor Italian, I deal with foreigners.'

The girl gave me a charming smile. 'Your Italian is excellent! Are you German?'

'No,' I said, 'English, actually.'

'Really?' she said. 'I'm sorry, it's just that you don't expect the English to be able to speak Italian . . .'

'That's my secret weapon,' I said. 'Look, you're in charge

of the Mayor's diary, right?' She nodded with some pride. 'I thought so. I saw you here, and wondered if I might take the opportunity to check something? We had an event a few weeks ago and the Mayor was invited but he wasn't able to attend because he had something else on. A colleague of mine was dealing with it, but they're off sick, and my boss has just asked me why he couldn't make it. I see you've got his diary open, could we have a look?'

'Certainly,' she said, eager to help. I mentally crossed my fingers. I was hoping the Star Girl would provide me with a meaty all-day council meeting with plenty of witnesses that would at least place the Mayor away from the scene at the time Solitudine went missing.

'Ah,' she said, 'yes, here it is. Between twelve and four o'clock he had a "private appointment". I'm sorry, I can't tell you any more than that.'

'That's fine.' My smile masked my frustration. 'That's all I need to know, thank you, you're very kind.'

'You're welcome, Bologna Welcome!'

I drifted away from the girl but lingered in the room for a while and continued to watch the Mayor from the fringes of the crowd. Despite the awkward question, he was a man very much at ease, full of familiar greetings and jokey confidences. This lot, I thought, would have grown up together – had probably gone to the same schools, universities, bars and restaurants; had the same girlfriends, wives, lovers . . . spent summers together at the beach in Riccione, or now Miami, as I believed was the fashion. And grown wealthy together, too, if they weren't wealthy already, *especially* if they were already wealthy. This was old Bologna *par excellence*. Regardless of anything the Mayor might say – the team may have changed but the game was much the same.

Goons with transparent coils of wire in their ears scanned the crowd. One with a goatee beard beneath his gleaming bald dome seemed to clock me. I looked down at my brochure. As soon as he had turned the other way I got to my feet and ducked out.

More frescoes loomed above the crowd availing itself of canapés, fruit juice and Prosecco. I headed toward the staterooms, preserved much as they would have been when the Pope had been in charge.

The gallery stretched before me. It may have once played house for a bishop but it was kitted out, in fact, for royalty. With its coffered ceilings and portraits of the city's great and good, punctuated by the odd masterpiece, it was dressed to impress. I made for an opening closed by salmon-coloured drapes, parted them and stepped into a musty room decked out in ornate Regency-era wallpaper, its gold still glowing after all these years. A kind of reception room, with a plumped-up eighteenth-century sofa, a portrait of a scowling fellow in a tricorne hat and dark oak furniture. Opposite was another set of drapes that led to another room decorated much the same, only this time with throbbing deep-crimson walls, then another in silver . . . I passed along the wing, through rooms that had once hosted nervous courtiers or card-playing cardinals, until I arrived at a cool, spacious chamber with a *Veneziana* floor and painted, parkland scenes. At its centre stood a statue of Apollo by Canova.

I crossed the chamber and gave a section of the wall a sharp shove. It transformed into an open door.

Luca looked up at me from behind his computer. 'I should never have shown you the secret entrance,' he said. 'If you get caught I'll get into trouble.'

'Isn't the point of a secret entrance not to get caught?'

'So –' he pushed himself back from his desk '– how did it go? Did you see Chiara? She's a looker, no?'

I had to smile at Luca's irrepressibly good humour even if, in this case, it was directed at undermining his ultimate boss, the Mayor. Although he didn't directly blame Manzi for condemning him to this office job instead of running the homeless shelter where he'd taken me on as a doorman when I was still trying to get to grips with the language, any small thing to undermine the hegemony of the PD was all right in his book.

'So?' he said.

'So, what?'

'So, are you going to tell me what all this is about?'

'That,' I said, 'you know I can't do.'

'You could at least offer me a bribe. Isn't that what you guys do?'

'I might if you'd accept one.'

He grinned. There was no one more honest in Bologna than Luca Monza.

I noticed a brochure poking from his overflowing in-tray, pulled it out. *Future-proofing Bologna* it proclaimed on the cover, *the Comune's five-year plan*.

'Five-year plan?' I said. 'I thought the Communists were a thing of the past.'

'That's about the only communist thing about it.'

'I saw the demonstrators outside. I hadn't realised this

zoning thing was such a big deal. I may be more in the dark about local politics than I thought.'

'Then you've finally become a proper Bolognese.'

'You've got some kind of discussion group, haven't you?'

'Well, I would hardly call it that . . . but yes, it has been said the still-beating heart of Bologna's radical political scene can be located at the back of the Osteria della Luna . . .'

'Of course.' If there was one place in Bologna synonymous with politics, it was la Luna. 'Would you mind if I came along?'

'Dan,' he said, shaking his head, 'you hardly have to ask. After a few drinks, I have to stop them pulling people off the street.'

I left Luca's office the official way, via the corridor in the ugly eighties building that had been grafted onto the old palace and where most of the drudge work of the Comune took place – a kind of purgatory reserved for awkward types like my friend.

I took the lift down. The door opened onto another dull, age-worn corridor. A couple of orange plastic benches were pressed against a wall, partially filled by dead-eyed folk in the process of being masticated by municipal bureaucracy. Notices lined the walls. There was a cloudy, Perspex-fronted reception desk, but no receptionist.

I headed toward the glass-fronted exit but stopped before going through. I stepped back. Outside was the Star Girl – Chiara Delfiori – in deep conversation with Carlo Manzi. He made some kind of reply and she shook her head, rattling back a response. Her gestures spoke of frustration, impatience.

She stood there waiting with her hands on her hips. Manzi resignedly reached into his jacket and produced his wallet. He handed her two, three, four fifty-euro notes. Chiara said something and he gave her another two, or three, in any case he wryly opened his wallet toward her as if to demonstrate it was empty. She unclasped her Miu Miu handbag and tucked the notes into an envelope, I noted, instead of a purse (and a *fighetta* like Chiara would never go out without her purse). Who was that envelope destined for, I wondered.

The pair went their separate ways: Manzi headed back into the Bishop's Palace while Chiara walked across the courtyard and onto Via Ugo Bassi.

I began to follow her. She was going in the direction of the two towers – the looming medieval fortifications that marked the city centre – but before she reached them, she crossed the road and turned down a side street, entering a supermarket. I went to the portico opposite and called my brother-in-law.

'Jacopo, what are you doing?'

'Having lunch.'

'Where?'

'dell'Orsa.' He was around the corner.

'Great. I need you in Via Oberdan in . . . five minutes.'

'You're kidding!'

'It's important, Jac.' I stepped back into the shadows of the portico and monitored the glass front of the supermarket. Fortunately it was busy and Chiara, when I spotted her wandering up and down the aisles, didn't appear to be in any hurry. Jacopo arrived, panting, in ten minutes.

'Bravo,' I said. He glared at me, but he was a good kid and knew I wouldn't ask for no reason. 'You see her? The pretty girl in the queue for the cashier? We're following her. She's already had eyes on me – I had to speak to her earlier – so I need you to do it.'

'Is she expecting a tail?' I shook my head. Jacopo relaxed. 'I'm on it.' I watched him lollop into the supermarket. If there was a perfectly inconspicuous Bolognese twenty-something it was Jacopo Faidate with his slack jeans, scuffed trainers, ironic t-shirt, nose stud and mop of unruly black hair. He could have been any one of a hundred binge-drinking kids in Piazza Verdi.

I watched Chiara load up the bags while Jacopo stood innocently behind her in the queue. As she left, Jacopo replaced a jar of Nutella and slipped out after her. I watched them wander down the street, away from the centre. I checked my phone and was pleased to see Jacopo had activated his app; designed to enable anxious partners to track their loved ones via Google Maps, we used it to keep an eye on each other from a distance.

A couple of minutes later I set off myself, following Jacopo's course with my phone, until it stopped in Via Pallone, a non-descript street riddled with graffiti that bordered Montagnola Park. I could see Jacopo in the distance, slouched against the park railings opposite a residential building. I messaged him.

'Has she gone in? Did she use a key or was she visiting?'

'Visiting, she buzzed. I got the name.'

'Great. Wait until she comes out, then meet me in the park.'

It was about half an hour before we hooked up again. He sat down next to me on the park bench. 'Been shopping?' He nodded at my bag.

'That's right. So, tell me.'

'The name on the buzzer was Bellidenti.'

'Good work,' I said, 'and she bought?'

'The normal. Women's stuff, I would say. A couple of tubs of yoghurt, fruit, bath cream – you know, that gooey white stuff girls use. Oh, and coconut oil moisturising cream, no less.'

'She's not shopping for her granny, then.'

'Maybe,' he said, 'who knows what grandmothers moisturise with these days.'

I took the clipboard out of the bag and attached the swathe of garish broadband plans I had swiped from a phone shop. 'Look after this.' I took off my jacket and, holding the clipboard, headed down the hill toward Via Pallone.

I rang every bell except Bellidenti until someone answered. 'Who is it?'

'Comune information, open the door, please.' The door buzzed.

I had worked out that the Bellidenti apartment should be on the second floor, so I didn't bother with the lift.

Although the building was pretty grim on the outside, it was reasonably smart and tidy once you got in – a typical post-war block, presumably occupied by working- and lower middle-class families. Although I had seen some pretty rough housing estates in Bari and Naples, I had never seen anything approaching that in Bologna – despite the graffiti, Italians kept up appearances on the inside. You'd never encounter the taint of urine in a lift in a place like this, or even down south for that matter.

I paused on the stairs and took out my phone, switching on the video, then slipped it screen-first into the breast pocket of my shirt so the camera would see everything I did. I rolled up my sleeves and placed a pen behind my ear. I found the Bellidenti door and, taking a deep breath but not giving myself too much time to think, rang the bell three times in quick succession.

'All right! I'm coming . . . I'm coming . . .' I couldn't tell if it was an old or a young woman's voice. In any case, she sounded tired.

The door opened. I looked down at my clipboard. 'Signora Paola Bellidenti?'

The young woman, her hair tied back, dark rings beneath her eyes, said, 'What? No—'

'You mean you're not Signora Paola Bellidenti? It says here "Paola" . . .'

'No, I mean, I am Bellidenti, but Anna. Why?'

'Ah! Anna! Please excuse me. Do you realise, Signora Bellidenti, you are entitled to three months free broadband connection if you change your supplier to—'

'No,' she shook her head wearily, 'no, do I look as if I care about broadband . . .' We both looked down at the huge bump pressing against her black cotton dress.

'Congratulations!' I said. 'But a new arrival is the perfect time to economise—' She was shaking her head, she was closing the door.

'I'm sorry,' she said, 'that's all taken care of . . .'

'If you would be kind enough to direct me to the person—' The door closed.

Chapter 5

Faidate Investigations had once occupied two entire floors of a nondescript sixties office block on Via Marconi, but it now amounted to little more than a reception and a few back rooms.

When the Comandante had set the agency up, it had quickly attracted the patronage of the rich and powerful, content to entrust their secrets to the famously incorruptible ex-Carabiniere. But over time, like many an Italian family business, things had begun to unravel. His old contacts in the police (Carabinieri, Polizia di Stato, Guardia di Finanza, Polizia Municipale, plus the seemingly infinite number of lesser branches of Italian law and order) began to retire. The Comandante sold off the security side which, given his reputation, had been one of his greatest assets. Until Jacopo joined us, he had never really got a hang of the potential of the internet and his competitors got a lead on him.

But although the agency's floor space had long since shrunk, the reception still had a spacious feel with a marble floor and a nineteenth-century desk at the far end. A large pair of abstract canvases dominated, all scrambled, murky swirls and dollops of red and brown (*the shit storms*, Jacopo called them) opposite were waist-to-ceiling windows, venetian blinds splicing the room into Noirish shadows.

'Why are you two looking so pleased with yourselves?' said Alba, the Comandante's niece and company administrator, sitting behind the desk.

'Cracked the case, cuz,' said Jacopo.

'The Comandante was asking for you, Dan . . . Hey, what do you think you're doing?' Jacopo was leaning over the laptop.

'Who's this handsome chap then?'

'Never you mind . . . Jaco!' Jacopo had swept the computer up.

'Marco, thirty-five, works in finance . . . likes fast cars and slow women . . . come on!'

'Give it back!' Alba began trying to wrestle the laptop from him.

'Jac . . .' I said. Alba wrenched it away but it slipped out of her grasp and clattered onto the floor.

'Hey, be careful with that,' Jacopo said.

'*Me* be careful? You stole it!'

'Now what's all this?' It was the Comandante, standing in the doorway. Jacopo and Alba both looked down. Alba bent to pick up the laptop. Jacopo inspected his nails. The Comandante shook his head, gestured me toward his office.

'They've always been like this,' he said, 'ever since they were little.'

In contrast to the office Jacopo and I shared – basically a mess of tech, stray wires, old newspapers and Styrofoam cups

– the Comandante's was old school. It had a glass-fronted bookcase, an oak desk, framed certificates and photos of his time in uniform, receiving awards, meeting dignitaries, and so on, along with his late wife, Angela, when she was in her prime; Rose as he undoubtedly still viewed her – about four years old and dressed as a princess for *Carnevale* – and Lucia, his daughter, and I, as we reached the bottom of those stairs in Palazzo d'Accursio. I looked away.

The Comandante was surveying me across the green leather surface of the desk. His eyes were almost completely obscured by their lids, his lips creased around a cigarette – he was certainly no pin-up for smoking. He let out a long plume and tapped the cigarette into the glass ashtray.

'I hear congratulations are in order,' he said.

'Excuse me?'

'Haven't you "cracked the case"?'

'Well,' I said, 'we have dug up something pretty interesting about Carlo Manzi.' I showed him the video.

'And you did this . . . how?'

I explained.

'The future never ceases to astonish me,' he said.

'It's not the future, Giovanni,' I said, 'it's the present – perhaps we've touched upon the problem?'

That smile again. 'That I live in the past? Well, that much we know. That's why I have you here.' It was a very Italian arrangement – an implicit understanding that I was to gradually take control of the firm while he, rather like a constitutional monarch, would remain titular head. In due course, his son would become an equal partner, and so on, in the event that Rose one day wanted to get in on the action, although I hoped she'd choose a different path – this wasn't the kind of career you dreamed of, but ended up in.

'Jac did good work today,' I said.

'If you say so, Daniel,' he said.

'He's more use here than at university,' I said.

'Well, obviously,' said the Comandante, 'as he was *no use* at university at all.'

I felt sorry for Jacopo, but let it drop. 'So,' I said, nodding at the phone, 'this could explain Signor Manzi's unusual behaviour: he's been acting so oddly around his wife because his girlfriend's about to give birth.'

The Comandante looked at the image of Anna Bellidenti frozen on the screen. 'Yes,' he said finally, 'it could explain his behaviour if – as we are both assuming – he is the one responsible for placing that bun in the oven. Good work, although I think we will need a little more than that . . .'

'Jac was just joking about "cracking the case", but it's a promising lead.'

'And of course, a revelation of this kind,' said the Comandante, 'well, it could have repercussions of its own. We will have to consider very carefully what we say to Signora Finzi, and when.' He pressed his hands together in front of his mouth as if in prayer. 'And, equally,' he said, 'just because it seems that Carlo Manzi may have been having an affair, it doesn't mean he was not aware of, and disturbed by, his wife's . . . dalliance.'

'What's good for the goose is not for the gander?' I said. The Comandante gave me a puzzled look. 'An English expression: what's okay for him is not okay for her.'

The Comandante nodded. 'Human emotions do not abide

by rules, do they, my boy. And then, of course, there is the financial aspect: divorce is an expensive business in Italy.'

'Divorce is an expensive business everywhere,' I said. 'I suppose he wouldn't be the first husband to commit murder in order to avoid a hefty settlement, but it's usually the lady, not the lover, that gets it.'

The Comandante puffed on his cigarette. 'Problem solved, nonetheless? After all, who really cares about a dead anarchist, other than the living ones? A dead mayor's wife, on the other hand, might be a little more difficult to explain. And if Carlo Manzi is anything,' he said, 'he is a man who, in my experience, is cold-hearted enough to think like that.'

'The Mayor as a murderer, though, Comandante?' I said. 'It seems a leap. What makes you believe Signora Finzi is right to be so afraid of him?'

'The Carlo Manzi I remember, Daniel, was a very ruthless, self-interested individual. We were able to use these tendencies for our own purposes when we were combatting terrorism. He had some influence in radical circles, and he went on to use those talents for his own climb to the top.

'I am not necessarily saying he pulled the trigger, so to speak, but I can understand why Marta might be afraid. And Carlo has the power now. We will have to be careful about our dealings with the Mayor, Daniel. Very careful indeed.' The Comandante seemed about to add something but think better of it. He reached under his desk. 'In the meantime, I have been successful in my research at the Comune archives.' He produced a large, yellowing scroll of paper and unrolled it across the table. It looked like a blueprint for some kind of complex industrial design, except that it wasn't in blue and was apparently a plan of underground Bologna.

'What we have here,' the Comandante said, pointing at the map, 'is Paolo Solitudine's destination – the place where his corpse was discovered. What we need to see is if we can establish his point of departure.

'This is where the body was found, attached below the water line to fencing that serves to filter debris from the river flow.' He planted his finger on the map. 'Unfortunately, or perhaps, predictably, it is a point of convergence for a number of tributaries. Here.' He pointed to one bold line. 'Here –' another '– and here.'

'So, basically,' I said, 'he could have floated down from half the city. And what are these?'

'Major access points. This one here, for example, is in Piazza Minghetti.'

'These?'

'Minor – manholes, that kind of thing.'

'These?'

'Ah,' said the Comandante, 'I believe they indicate where buildings still have access to the canals, from their basements, and the like.'

'But there are dozens of them – he could have been dumped from any of them. These?'

'Sewers. You know, it's quite interesting, as many of them were constructed by the Romans . . .'

I tracked the lines with my fingers. 'That's Via Mazzini, right?'

'That's it,' said the Comandante.

'Which would put this –' I put my finger on the

upside-down triangle that indicated access to the canals '– in the grounds of the old hospital building occupied by the anarchists, the one raided by the police.'

The Comandante leaned over the plans, holding his glasses to the bridge of his nose. 'It's some way from where he was discovered,' he said. 'And you see – this canal does not join with the one in which he was found. In fact, if I understand these arrows correctly, the water would be flowing in the opposite direction – he would have ended up on the other side of Bologna.'

'Which makes the anarchists' case that the police were behind it, at least at the time of their raid on the squat, weaker; if the suggestion is that they simply threw his body in the canal. On the other hand,' I said, 'this sewer, or tunnel, or whatever it is, seems to connect up the two.'

'It would seem like a lot of trouble to go to,' said the Comandante, 'to transport the body . . . too thought-through – even if the police were responsible, I can't see them having the presence of mind in the heat of the moment.'

'Unless it was premeditated.'

The Comandante shrugged. 'Even less likely.' I looked at him. 'Yes,' he said, 'it is no secret that there were examples of unwarranted violence during my time in the service, but the sort of characters who carried out that sort of thing were not the type you would expect to think more than one step ahead.'

'And the fellow in charge of the raid, Sergeant Romano?'

'Nothing new – a local lad, unblemished record – but I want to hold off on the police until I have seen Umberto.' I looked at him questioningly. 'Ispettore Umberto Alessandro of the Special Operations Group. He used to be my subordinate, now he's in charge. He's been out of the city but we're having lunch later this week.

'Clearly, Daniel,' he said, 'this is a matter that needs to be handled with the utmost sensitivity – I suppose we could consider it a good result, for our client, if we discover the authorities *were* actually behind the death. Either outcome, however, could have profound implications for the future of our company.'

'That's the problem with having a reputation like yours, Comandante,' I said, 'people forget we have a business to run.'

'It would certainly be doing us all a favour,' said the Comandante, 'if you were to discover it really was an accident, or someone else was behind it.' He looked down at the map and his finger began tapping on the location of the squat. 'The anarchists are calling for a proper investigation,' he said, 'so they can hardly complain if it begins to be treated like one.'

Chapter 6

I was on my way to the squat when I came across them, filling the narrow passageway: a woman and a dairy cow surrounded by a group of riot cops.

The Friesian had a red sheet tied around her neck, creating a giant bandana, and was harnessed to a rope held by the young woman, a student almost certainly, whose head was piled high with dreadlocks, her face full of piercings.

She was trying to coax the creature along the passageway but the cow was having none of it, rooted to the spot and looking up at her with scared, stupid eyes. Although perhaps not so stupid – who wouldn't be freaked out by a group of hard nuts in body armour blocking the way?

The cow let out a bellow and the cops jumped back.

'Will you look at that – have you got a shovel, girl?'

'Jesus, what a stink!'

'You'd better have a bag. You know the city ordinance for shit – not only dog shit. If you don't pick it up, we'll pull you in!'

'You *and* your cow, anarchist bitch.'

'A few sides of steak on that one, eh?'

'More than a few, Silvio . . .'

I knew that if the police weren't keen on arresting beggars with dogs (which predominated in the city to the extent they had developed their own moniker: *punkabbestia*, 'punk with a beast') then they weren't about to pull in an anarchist with a cow, whatever they might say. On the other hand, I also knew it wouldn't do me any harm to get in with the in-crowd rather than simply turning up at the squat and firing off a list of questions.

The woman spotted me herself, and stared so intently that even the cops turned to look. I couldn't tell what she was playing at – it certainly wasn't pleading I saw in those eyes, nor fear. Was she looking for a witness? Or was this a cry for help after all? Either way, I decided to bite the bullet, although as I ambled toward them, I couldn't help wondering if I would exit with all my teeth.

I nodded to the woman. 'I didn't expect to find you here.'

A cop stepped in my way, his visor half raised so it covered his eyes. 'What's this young lady to you . . . sir.'

'I'm her English professor,' I said. In Italy you are what you wear so I was glad I'd remained in my suit. 'Problems?'

The cops bristled.

'With your cow,' I said, looking at the woman, 'getting her to move?' She nodded cautiously. 'Well, I might be able to lend you a hand with that. If you don't mind, gentlemen?'

The cops made way. As I stepped between them I noted the gap close behind me. If this turned nasty, no one would be any the wiser. 'There, there,' I said to the cow. Through her flank I could hear her big heart racing. For the first time the woman gave me a look that was a little less than bold.

I turned to the cops. 'Gentlemen,' I said, 'if you'll just give us a little space.' The cops hesitated, then the circle around us widened, though not by much.

I felt behind the cow's neck for the muscles between her shoulder blades, and pressed hard. The cow bellowed and now the cops jumped back, afraid of getting mess on their boots. Instead, like a temperamental automobile, the cow lurched forward.

'Bloody hell,' said one of the cops, jumping aside, 'it's the bloody cow whisperer.'

'Signori,' I said, my fist still bunched between the cow's shoulders. The line of cops opened up, and with it, the empty lane ahead.

We moved off at a trot, the woman jogging beside us, hanging limply on to the rope.

We reached the end of the lane.

'Are they coming after us?' I said. The woman looked behind.

'No.'

I relieved the pressure as we turned the corner and the three of us slowed to a walk.

I held out my hand. 'Daniel,' I said.

The woman looked at it suspiciously. 'Dolores,' she said, taking it.

'And who's this?' I guessed they would have given the cow a name.

'Desdemona,' said Dolores. 'How did you move her like that? Did it hurt?'

'I grew up on a farm,' I said, which wasn't strictly true – I'd once gone undercover in a slaughterhouse, 'and no, it doesn't hurt. But what were you doing with her here? This isn't a place for cattle – she was terrified.'

'That was why I was in the alley – we were at the demo and she got scared. But then I couldn't get her any further. Anyway,' she said as we steered Desdemona down a lane filled with shops and gawping pedestrians, 'who are you? You're not my English professor!'

'How would you know, Dolores? You never attend your classes.'

'Because I'm not taking English, I'm taking ancient civilisations.'

'Is that why you look like a Celt?'

She shrugged. 'Who are you then? An English teacher, touting for work?'

We began to cross Maggiore. While the Comune's campaign to boost tourism was evidently beginning to take effect – a group decked out as if they were about to climb Machu Picchu were tramping indifferently behind a blonde with an up-raised pennant – the piazza was mostly abuzz with ordinary Bolognese. Despite the best efforts of Bologna Welcome, Maggiore still remained the centre of a bustling city with business on its mind.

Except, as the girl and the cow and the English professor, by all appearances, crossed the square, business ground to a halt. The people stopped, the people stared. The tourists swivelled their cameras and clicked. This wasn't necessarily a bad thing considering the forces of law and order were out in strength – a dark-blue Carabinieri van and light-blue Polizia di Stato Range Rover were parked in front of the Bishop's Palace, the Guardia di Finanza – the fraud police, in grey – were positioned at the top of the steps of the church, while the actual army – in khaki, naturally – were sauntering outside the shops. They had no reason to stop us, *per se*, but this being Italy, there was presumably some by-law specifically prohibiting the passage of cattle across the square in daylight hours.

'I'm a private investigator,' I said.

'A what?'

'Keep your voice down,' I said, 'people will look.' I reached over Desdemona and handed her my card.

'Daniel Lie-chest-er. Faidate Investigations. What do you want with me?'

'Don't worry,' I said, 'this isn't about you – but, as it happens, you could help me out.'

'Help you out?'

'In exchange for some animal husbandry tips? I was wondering if I could take a look in the basement of that building you're occupying.'

'Why would you want to do that?'

'I've been asked by the coroner to see if there's access to the canal.'

'The coroner?'

'He's looking into the death of this guy you're making such a fuss about. Paolo, is it?'

'Oh,' said Dolores. We walked on, past a busker belting out Bob Marley's 'Redemption Song'. Without missing a beat he called out in a faux Jamaican accent: 'Yo, Dolores, yo, Desdemona . . .'

'I don't know . . .' said Dolores.

'Come on,' I said, 'it's in your interests, isn't it? I'm on your side.'

'On my side?' Dolores scoffed. 'Hear that, Dez? He's on our side!'

'Don't you want to learn the truth, Dolores?'

'The truth?' Dolores looked amused. 'Well, that would be a first.'

The three of us headed up Via Mazzini until we arrived at the abandoned building the anarchists had occupied. It had served as the city's main hospital for three centuries until being closed down a few years before. It had had a patchy existence ever since, its largely impractical spaces variously taken up by light industrial workshops, arts co-ops and fashion shows. A quick google had told me it had now been snapped up by the Omega Group, presumably among those investors Manzi had been presenting to. The only trouble was a black and red banner currently hung above the old building's entrance that read: TIME TO TAKE BACK WHAT'S OURS.

A youth was sitting on a seat outside, smoking. 'Who's he?' he said.

'With me,' said Dolores. We headed through the hallway, battered benches lining either side of the high, cracked walls, then passed through a small courtyard, complete with a well. I knew where this was heading – straight into the past. Sure enough, after another nineteenth-century corridor, we emerged onto a large courtyard constructed at least a couple of hundred years earlier, and beyond that – green, presumably some kind of makeshift biological farm. Dolores let the rope drop and Desdemona automatically trotted toward it.

'Very nice,' I said, looking around, 'very pretty.'

'They want to turn it into a hotel, of course,' said Dolores, 'because it's so "pretty". Don't worry about the people, don't worry about their health.'

'I'm sure they have a good reason,' I said, 'I mean, it can't have been very practical.'

'But practical enough for a hotel?' She looked at me despairingly.

A portico ran around the courtyard and from the shadows, like Amerindians appearing out of the depths of the Amazon jungle, figures dressed mainly in black, but with splashes of red – a bandana, a neckerchief – began to emerge, and close in upon us. I looked around – suddenly we were surrounded.

'Who's he?' said a skinny young man with a bushy jet-black beard and moist, Jesus eyes. Dolores left my side and wrapped herself around him.

'*Amore*,' she said, 'what happened to your cheek?' She touched a swelling just above his beard line.

'Nothing,' he said. 'Pigs. I looked around and you had gone.'

'Desdemona was scared.'

'I told you not to bring the cow.'

'It was important, to demonstrate we're about more than—'

'More than what?' He let her go.

'I didn't mean it like that! I meant that we've got an alternative, a—'

'And now you've brought this suit here,' he said. 'Have you any idea who he is?'

'He says—'

'I'm a private investigator,' I said, holding out my hand, 'Daniel Leicester.' The anarchists were crowding around me now, and I felt the Beard's hostility radiate through them.

Some of them were pretty knocked up, and it looked like they wouldn't mind meting out a beating themselves.

The Beard looked down at my outstretched hand. I let it drop. 'I've been asked by the coroner, who is looking into the circumstances surrounding the death of your compatriot . . . er . . . comrade, to—'

Those Jesus eyes hardened. 'What do you know about what happened to Paolo?' he said.

'Not much,' I said, 'but I've been asked to take a look in your basement, see if there is access to the canals.'

'Why should we help you?'

'Don't you want to know what happened to your friend?'

'What's there to know? He was killed by the cops.' I felt the circle close menacingly around me.

'Look,' I said, 'let's try to start off on the right foot.' I didn't think that under ordinary circumstances these kids would try to harm me, but they did have the taste of blood in their mouths. 'You're the good guys,' I said, 'and I'm not so bad myself.'

'Says you.' A man's voice. He stepped in front of the Beard. 'But aren't all you private eyes former cops?' He was an older guy with a grey waistcoat over his black shirt. He lacked the urban cool of the kids, looked instead as if he'd come straight off the fields. A squat, podgy son of the soil, with neck-length, swept back grey hair and bushy eyebrows like a Bolognese Brezhnev. I recognised him from the *Carlino*: Mario Cento.

'Not all of us,' I said, 'I used to be a reporter.'

'A journalist, Mario,' one kid piped up, 'they're just as bad.'

'Reporter?' said Mario. 'What kind?'

I shrugged. 'Investigative.'

'But what would a . . . where are you from? Germany, is it?'

'England.'

'You don't expect...'

'I know – an Englishman to speak Italian.'

Mario drew closer and the crowd compressed around us accordingly. I could smell whisky on his breath and, despite his advanced years, felt an edge of recklessness, perhaps fuelled by the liquor, perhaps all these angry kids, probably a bit of both.

'What would a *British* reporter be doing in Bologna?'

'Like I said, working as a private investigator. It's my father-in-law's agency.'

'Wouldn't you be happier being a reporter, son?'

I smiled. 'Look, I think we're getting this the wrong way around – I should be asking the questions. If you'd be prepared to help me, and I can't see why not, maybe, together, we can get to the bottom of this.'

'It's true,' Dolores was holding her smartphone, its screen splintered and cracked but still, apparently, working. '*Daniel Leicester uncovers sweatshop conditions at sports retailer. The price of a human life – Daniel Leicester with the people smugglers. Among the middle-class drug dealers, by Daniel Leicester. Daniel Leicester goes inside the north London crime cartels.*'

'So you are what you say you are. Or were,' said Mario. 'Well, don't expect any prizes for selling out.'

'Don't you want to know what happened to your pal?' I said.

Mario's face turned red. 'I know what happened,' he said.

'Mario,' the Beard laid a hand on his shoulder.

'This is not England,' said Mario, 'this is not fair play and bobbies and Miss Marple. There's no mystery – not to us. Not to any Italian you meet in the street. They'll know, we all know "whodunit".'

'The police, you say,' I said.

'But that's not the problem,' he said. 'The problem is – how to prove it? Now this is where we Italians are beyond compare – *fabrication*. *Manufacturing* mystery every bit as fine as our clothes, so even the most obvious facts become obscured, most evident truths remain just out of reach.

'You, Englishman, might imagine the coroner is asking you to discover the truth, but what are they really trying to achieve? What interests do they *really* represent? Not us, the people, I can tell you that!

'Instead of making things more transparent, you might simply be being used to muddy the waters. Have you considered that? Take care, son. You're a stranger in a strange land.'

'All right, Mario,' I said, 'point taken, but look, I've still got a job to do—'

'And he *was* an investigative reporter,' said Dolores. 'He was on our side.'

'In my experience,' said Mario, 'the only side journalists are on is their own.'

'Let me just try to get some facts straight,' I said. 'Tell me, first of all, what makes you so sure it actually was the police?'

Bitter laughter rippled around me.

They had been mid-way through rehearsing a play in the courtyard, they told me, the day Paolo had disappeared. Riot police forced their way through the main entrance, and at the same time another group broke down the gate at the back and came in through the farm. They stormed into the courtyard, hitting out at the squatters indiscriminately. They scattered but were pursued through the building.

'They smashed up everything, they smashed up everyone,' said the Beard. He pointed out the pile of broken placards, chairs, a portable TV.

'They threw it out of the window,' said Dolores.

'They threw it *through* the window,' said Mario, looking up at a gaping hole in the glass.

'And Paolo,' I said. 'What was he doing?'

'He was with us,' said Dolores, 'rehearsing. He was one of the actors.'

We headed inside the building. 'We've cleaned up most of the blood now,' Mario said, 'but look.' A smear of red upon a radiator.

'We uploaded it,' said Dolores. Through the shattered glass of her phone was a shaky film. Someone was breathing heavily, the sounds of sobbing, moaning.

I realised that the shape on the floor, dragging itself towards the camera, was a person. Then the footage jolted upwards. The corridor – this corridor – was full of similar shapes: slumped, lying down, crying, bleeding upon a bed of broken wood and glass. It looked like the aftermath of a bombing.

'Why?' I said. 'I mean, was there some kind of provocation?'

'They don't need provocation,' said Mario.

'*We're* the provocation,' said Dolores, 'just by existing.'

'And I suppose you are occupying this place illegally,' I said.

'And you think *that* excuses *this*?' she said.

'I didn't say that,' I said. 'And what happened to you?'

'We were arrested,' said Dolores, nodding at Mario. 'They had me standing up at the Caserma all night. If I touched the wall they would scream at me.'

The Beard peeled up his t-shirt to reveal a string of fading bruises running up his rib cage.

'And Paolo Solitudine? Did anyone see what happened to him?'

The Beard shook his head. 'We thought he had managed to get away,' he said, 'but we never saw him again.'

'No one saw him being arrested, running in a particular direction . . .'

'You had to be there,' said Dolores, 'it was chaos. Everyone was focusing on the police, trying to protect themselves . . .' She shook her head. 'It was horrible.'

'Apparently a canal runs directly under this building. Did you search the basement at any point, looking for Paolo, I mean?'

'Not until a few days after the raid,' said the Beard. 'At first, as Dolores said, it was all confused. We didn't know what had happened or to whom. We had people locked up, people in hospital, people who had just got away. It was only later, when we realised he hadn't shown up, that we started looking . . .'

'You declared him missing?' I said.

'To who?' said Mario as if it was the stupidest question I had yet asked. The others looked at me with the same bemused expression. Poor Paolo, I thought: no wife, no girl-friend, apart from Marta Finzi, who was hardly about to log an official enquiry, and his fellow revolutionaries too para-noid to go to the police.

'Can I have a look myself, then?' I said. 'I'd like to see if I can gain access.' Mario and the Beard exchanged a glance.

'Come on,' said Dolores, 'I'll show you: these two, they don't trust a soul.'

Chapter 7

To get to the basement we had to go through the old hospital kitchens. Much of the equipment had long since been ripped out and the gaps were now covered by boarding, with cabinets and shelves made from reclaimed materials. I was impressed by the anarchists' ingenuity. Pots of herbs and plants – both edible and decorative – hung from crafted baskets. Those elements of the original kitchen that had survived – principally metal sinks, worktops, pots and pans – had been meticulously refurbished. Vegetables and glass jars full of beans and grains were lined up along the surfaces ready for a self-evidently organic and vegetarian communal meal. Although still, in fact, semi-derelict, the space had the kind of feel hipsters in London, Milan or New York would pay thousands for. Marta Finzi probably had.

'Are you sure you wouldn't be happier being a journalist?' said Dolores. 'You could write about our struggle.'

'And what would you want me to say?'

'What do you mean?'

'Do you think anything I wrote would change anyone's

mind?' I said. 'I've seen plenty of coverage in the *Corriere* and *Carlino*, and on the TV. Has it made any difference?'

'Is that why you gave up being an investigative reporter, detective? Because you became so cynical?'

Dolores led me down some steps to a closed fire door. She pushed it open. 'You've got a torch app?' she said. 'It's dark down here.' We switched on our respective apps and went down a spiral staircase. 'There's no electricity, obviously, although they managed to hook something up for some of the rooms upstairs . . . oh . . .'

'What?'

'I probably shouldn't have told you that. Don't tell Mario or Beppe.'

'Who's Beppe?'

'My boyfriend . . . the one you were talking to, with the beard.'

'Don't worry, Dolores, your secret is safe with me.'

'This is it,' she said. 'It runs beneath most of the building.' Huge metal tanks lined the passageway with batches of pipes running off into the darkness. We followed them until we turned a corner into an open space littered with trash, blankets, scorched bottles . . .

'When we came here, this was used by druggies.'

I took out the plan and had a look at it. 'I think it must be this way.'

We crossed the space into a section that appeared to have been occupied by storage units, but most had had their doors removed and, at points, the walls too. I cast my mind back to the structures I had glimpsed on their 'farm' and understood where the materials must have come from. My torchlight fell upon a discarded blanket. A coiled, dark-stained sleeping bag.

'Some of them used to sleep here,' said Dolores.

A sweet and musty smell began to grow stronger. Too sweet to be a corpse, I thought, at least a human one. As we made our way through the ravaged former storage space and found ourselves once again in the realm of abandoned plumbing and heating machinery, I began to look out for rats.

'You're not squeamish?' I said.

'Why?'

'Not worried by . . . mice, that kind of thing?'

'No, not at all.'

I checked the plan again. 'It should be somewhere around here.' My light followed the pipes into the darkness, at the same time tracking across the floor to make sure there were no unexpected obstacles or holes.

Could Solitudine have come all the way down here, perhaps pursued by the police? Yes, making a getaway during the raid, I could see that. Coming to the end, cornered by a couple of cops, cowering as the blows rained down . . . In this darkness it would be hard to know who you'd caught, be it a healthy young bloke who could handle a dose of 'unwarranted violence' or an old revolutionary, who couldn't.

'Dolores,' I said, swinging my light around, but only as far as the family of vermin nestled upon a crown of regurgitated wood and shredded paper inches from my face. I jolted back, hitting the opposite water tank with a heavy clang and dropping my phone.

'*Damn*.' I bent down, bathed in Dolores' light.

'What's the matter, detective?' she said. 'Squeamish?'

I scraped my phone off the floor. I couldn't see if it was damaged, but at least the light was still working.

'Can you hear it?' I said.

'What?'

'Water.' I pointed my light ahead. Adjacent to what appeared to be the dead end, behind the final tank, I could see a dark space. I pointed the light around the corner. There were three steps down, leading to an ancient, oak door, black with dirt. I could feel the rush of water reverberating through the wood. I gave it a shove. It was stuck fast. I pushed harder. Still no movement. I shone my light down at the oversize keyhole. Tried again.

'Locked.' I felt in my pocket for the slim set of picks I habitually carried. Technically, this shouldn't have been a big deal compared to a modern lock but I couldn't help feeling a certain amount of pressure as I bent over the keyhole and began twisting the pick inside the cavity like a demonic dentist while Dolores breathed down my neck.

'What's the problem?' she said.

'If you will just give me a moment . . .'

She gave me a moment.

'What's the problem?'

'The problem is, Dolores, that I need to move the cylinder, but it appears to be stuck. It's probably rust.'

'Do you want me to have a go?'

'No, I do not want you to have a go.'

'What if I give it a kick?'

I straightened up. 'All right,' I said. 'Go ahead.'

Dolores took a few steps back then took a running kick at the door with the sole of her boot. The door shrugged her off and she fell backwards onto the floor. I helped her up.

'He had them,' said Dolores.

'Who's "he"?' I said.

'Him,' she said, 'Paolo. He was in charge of the keys.'

We retraced our steps through the basement and into the kitchen, exiting via a back door that opened onto the cultivated land I had glimpsed earlier.

The land had been turned into strips with the intention of growing a range of produce: stakes were driven into the ground to support trees and vines, and the soil had been dug over for vegetables. The structures I had glimpsed earlier were serving as sheds, stills, or some kind of renewable energy source (at least that's what I guessed the tiny windmills sprouting from their roofs were all about). There was a half-built greenhouse with a roof apparently crafted out of bottles and cans. Chickens were clucking about outside a generous, solar-panelled coop. A rainbow flag with the word *PACE* – PEACE – was hanging from the branch of a tree. There was an air of bucolic calm and quiet industry. I was touched by their optimism: they were, literally, putting down roots, when all the signs were they'd be booted out within the month.

'He kept them in his office,' said Dolores as we headed toward Mario and Beppe, who were messing about with some sort of wooden contraption.

'Is that here?'

'Oh no,' said Dolores. 'It'll be in his apartment.'

'Look.' I checked my watch. 'I've got to go and pick up my daughter. Would you mind if we went there together tomorrow? I'd be interested in taking a look.'

'If you like,' she said, then her eyes narrowed, 'but what's that got to do with the canal?'

'Just curious,' I said. 'You never know, I might notice something that could help you build your case.'

'For a cynic,' said Dolores, 'you seem awfully helpful.'

'You mentioned the raid took place during a rehearsal,' I said. 'What was it, the play, I mean?'

'Oh,' she said, 'we do a performance every year, to mark the murder of Pinelli.' She looked at me as if I knew what she was talking about. '*Accidental Death of an Anarchist*,' she said. 'Ironic, no?'

'Of course Dario Fo, the playwright, won the Nobel Prize for it.' The Comandante was sitting at the head of the dinner table with Rose and I on one side, and Jacopo and Alba on the other. 'But then, they also gave one to Obama.'

'You're not a great fan then?' I said.

'Of the play? They say that the winners write the history. Well, in Fo's case, the losers wrote the comedy, only, it seems, that the comedy has now become a kind of history – the young people study it in school, in fact it is the only thing they study about the Years of Lead, so it has become a kind of official record – and a Nobel-winning one, no less – in which the anarchists and their ilk were all innocents, and the police were all terrorists and buffoons. History turned upon its head.'

'But it's based on a real-life case, isn't it?' I said. 'They pushed this guy, Pinelli, out of the window, during the interrogation.'

'That's why it's a comedy,' said Jacopo, stabbing his remaining *tortelloni*, 'a black one.'

'There we have it,' said the Comandante, 'a prime example. You take the allegation in the satire – that Pinelli was pushed – as a fact. All that is known is that the anarchist fell to his death – he could have jumped, for example – and the police officers involved were all subsequently cleared of any wrongdoing.

'Of course Pinelli himself was no innocent,' the Comandante continued, 'he was a well-known troublemaker. Remember – he was picked up after a bombing in Milan that claimed a dozen lives. And two years later, the officer who led the interrogation was murdered in the street. He left behind a wife and three children, I seem to recall.'

'And Pinelli,' said Jacopo, still not looking up, 'how many kids did he leave?'

'It was a very troubling time, Daniel,' said the Comandante. 'Even this one here –' he nodded across the table toward Jacopo '– who of course wouldn't remember, even he used to tell me, Daddy, come straight home.'

Jacopo finally looked up. 'I don't remember that,' he said, 'but I do remember all those bolts across the door, and the guns, and how Mama would stand on the balcony and wait, even after the gates had closed, as you walked down the street. I guess, yes, I guess she was waiting for the sound of a gunshot.' He glanced at the picture of his late mother, which sat, among a clutch of happier family memories, on the credenza next to a picture of his late sister.

'Why a gunshot?' asked Rose.

'That's ancient history,' I said, 'from the olden days when your mum was your age and Uncle Jac was even younger.'

'But why a gunshot?' Rose now asked in English, even

though I had told her not to use it in front of 'The Italians', as she called everyone else.

I gave her a look. I was increasingly at odds about how to deal with my girl, who had just reached her thirteenth year and was seesawing between artless child and snarky teen. 'She was afraid he would get shot,' I said, in Italian, 'but I think you worked that out.'

'But why would someone want to shoot Grandpa?' Now she looked genuinely confused.

'If you had been paying attention,' said Alba, 'instead of playing on your phone, you would have heard what they were talking about.'

'Dad was playing on his phone,' she said.

'I was working,' I said, pushing it aside.

'Anyway, I wasn't *playing*, either,' she said, 'I was working too. *Explaining.* To Stefania. English.'

'You were helping her with her homework?' the Comandante asked hopefully. Rose laughed.

'Sort of,' she said.

'What's so funny?' I said.

'Nothing,' she said.

'*Rose.*'

'It's just . . .'

'In Italian,' I said.

'It's just Stefania. She only hangs out with me so she can improve her English.'

'I'm sure that's not true.'

'She only wants to talk to me in English. Her mum, too! They use me as a free lesson.'

'Well, they'll never be as good as you, think of it like that.'

'They sure won't. I teach them the wrong words.'

'What does that mean?'

'Don't get kertup.'

'*What?*'

'*Kertup*. It's another word for angry I've been teaching them.'

Jacopo laughed out loud.

'Cool, huh?' said Rose.

'Shouldn't you be less reckless with your friendships, Rose?' I said. 'You remember how upset you were when you fell out with Rita . . .'

'By the way,' she said, ignoring me, 'I forgot.' She produced a form from her school. 'I suppose I can go on this trip?' She waved it at me.

'Another one? What is it?'

She read it. 'Permaculture,' she said.

'What's that?'

'*Environmental*,' she said as if it was obvious.

'Ah,' I said.

'I'll take that as a yes.' She got out her pen and began writing with some concentration along the dotted line.

'What are you doing?' I said.

'Saving you the trouble.'

'Is that what you call it?' I said. 'Does this explain why I haven't seen any report cards recently?'

'What do you think?' She held her forgery up.

'Not bad,' I had to admit, then remembered who was supposed to be in charge. 'But if I don't see a report at the end of the month I'll be speaking to your teacher.' Rose nodded as if she was humouring me. 'I mean it,' I said.

'Daniel?' The Comandante nodded toward the balcony.

We lived, as the Bolognese put it, 'inside the walls', although the walls that had surrounded the city for more than half a millennium had been torn down a century before, an act lamented even then as municipal vandalism. However, the city planners were not too bothered about pretty: they wanted to keep up with the motor car and turn Bologna into an industrial powerhouse to rival Turin and Milan. The outskirts at any rate. 'Inside the walls' the city largely retained its medieval character; its palaces, tenements, courtyards, churches and towers were built along a web of large boulevards and small streets that for hundreds of years had confused and confounded the not infrequent armies of invaders. Its kilometres of porticoes masked the buildings and lent the streets a daunting uniformity. They had been built to accommodate hard-up scholars back when the University of Bologna had competed with Oxford and Paris for the Fresher purse, and come nightfall the covered walkways would have been lined with the poorest students bedding down on the pavement. They still provided shelter from the sun and rain and snow, although the only invaders they now confused were tourists stepping into the traffic as they tried to get their bearings, and the only people you found asleep under the porticoes were drunk, homeless, or on drugs.

Home, or The Faidate Residence, as it was called, was a fairly typical family compound dating from the late middle ages: basically a mini fortress in a city street, although its battlements, while still visible, had long since been bricked together, and the double doors, wide enough to accommodate a horse-drawn carriage, were now operated by remote control.

The courtyard was home to my Fiat, the Comandante's black Lancia limo and a patch of uncut grass. It was overlooked on three sides by balconies, their ceilings still enlivened by traces of frescoes. Nymphs chased after disembodied winged-feet, a sooty sun peaked out behind clouds that had once hosted heavens but were now held together by cement. Much of Bologna was like this – placid façades concealing the historic and mundane, beauty and decay. A place with its back turned to the world – what mattered was family.

I watched the Comandante take out a cigarette, produce his gold-plated lighter. His face flared grey in the gloom like a half-glimpsed gravestone in headlights. In the courtyard the rain was falling to a steady beat. Inside, I could see Rose watching *X Factor* between dabbing at her phone. Not for the first time, I wondered what Lucia would have thought and, not for the first time, noted it was becoming increasingly harder to tell – I could still picture Lucia the young mum, with Rose, the toddler. Then how she had been when she had returned to work. No different, really – she had only been thirty-seven at Rose's tenth birthday. Then . . . a jumped light . . . She hadn't been wearing a helmet (no one here did and by that time I'd given up pleading with her – perhaps I had believed the same invisible hand that pulled the political strings also plucked unfortunate cyclists from danger).

They said she was dead before she hit the ground, but that was crap. I knew how these things were. At least she was unconscious – I was able to establish that – *after* she'd hit the ground.

In England you really have to go looking for trouble; in Italy it seems to seek you out – shoots across a bike lane and sends you flying.

But what kind of mum, what kind of *woman*, would she be now, three years on? What kind of dad, what kind of man, would I be if she had still been here? What kind of girl would Rose be, if her mum was still with us?

That was unknown territory.

'What's your take on these people?' said the Comandante. 'The "anarchists", I mean.'

I turned away from the window. 'That you're no fan?' I said. 'Well, that's hardly news.'

'I suppose they have your sympathies,' he said. 'You might not think so if you had encountered them from the wrong end of a gun.'

'I don't think this lot are that bad, Giovanni. They're all ecology, peace and biological farming, blah-blah.'

'They're the same people,' said the Comandante. 'The times may have changed, but the people have not. And if circumstances change, so will the people.' He drew on his cigarette through the petrified forest of his beard. 'Perhaps the circumstances have already changed, which is why their erstwhile comrade now lies on a mortuary slab.'

'Maybe,' I said. I thought about Mario and Beppe. That glance they had exchanged when I'd asked to go down to the basement. It could have signalled guilt, or they could have simply been suspicious of having a stranger sniffing around. As Dolores had said: *These two: they don't trust a soul.*

'What are you smiling at?'

'Just a girl I met, one of the anarchists.'

'Oh?'

'Not like that, Giovanni, she's young enough to be my daughter. Well, almost. But I like her spirit.'

'And this other girl,' said the Comandante, 'Anna Bellidenti.'

'Alba has done a search of her publicly available information,' I said. 'She's twenty-two, a local. Graduated from technical school at eighteen then went into bar work and promotions. There's a whole list of them on LinkedIn. You know the kind of thing: hostess for stands at exhibitions, bars, nightclubs. Her public social media presence has fallen pretty quiet over the past eight months, presumably for the obvious reason. She's lying low.

'Considering how difficult it will be to mount a frontal attack on the Mayor's official online accounts, we've been looking for the weakest link. We would usually go after Anna, but she now seems more or less housebound, so instead our best bet is to target the woman linking the pair of them – Chiara Delfiori.

'It's our guess that a fair amount of traffic will pass between the three of them. Young people these days don't use phones to talk but to type. We want to get into Chiara's messages, see what she's saying to him, what he's saying to her and what Anna's saying, too. It should also provide us with details of his private messaging accounts, and could even help fill in his movements.'

'Provide an alibi, you mean?'

'Maybe,' I said.

'And how do you plan to do this?' said the Comandante.

'The Nonnies,' I said. The Comandante exhaled a plume of blue smoke that twisted in the wet air.

'Careful with them,' he said.

There was a scream from inside. We both looked – but it was only Rose bouncing up and down on the sofa to some boy band.

'I always check my pockets,' I said, 'if that's what you mean.'

Chapter 8

From outside Rose's room I could hear her iPad blasting some *X Factor* after-show. I knocked lightly on the door.

'Rose?' She was probably asleep. I hoped she was asleep. 'Rose,' I knocked again and cautiously opened the door. 'I'm coming in.'

Sure enough, she was out cold. I lifted the iPad from her bedside and switched it off. She turned over with a sigh, dreaming of boy bands, no doubt.

I closed the door.

'They're the same people. The times may have changed, but the people have not. And if circumstances change, so will the people.'

I walked back down the corridor. I was all too familiar with law enforcement's articles of faith, number one of which was: people never change. The bad guys remain bad, whatever they might claim, while the good – well, that's them. So where did that leave me? I hadn't always been a reporter in the UK – my path to 'print', as it was still quaintly termed, had been unconventional, to say the least. I was even something of a poster boy for the power of restorative justice.

The Comandante had never mentioned my less than lily-white past, but I didn't doubt he knew all about it. Yet despite that, he had not only given me a stake in his business, but the hand of his daughter (although I doubt he would have actually had much choice in that matter). I suppose if it ever came up he would say I was the exception that proved the rule, and he might even believe it. But there would always be the doubt, the throwaway phrase – *The times may have changed, but the people have not* – we would both have to live with.

Chi l'ha visto? – Who Has Seen Them? – Italy's version of *Crimewatch*, was on the TV, the difference between this and its British counterpart being that the venerable three-hour show was dedicated solely to missing persons. Once a week, the nation – or at least a sizeable proportion – sat down to see if they had spotted some poor bastard who had had enough and decided to decamp to Milan, Turin, or, who knew, Bologna. But their family – and the barking blonde presenter backed by a wall of muttering housewives – was not giving up that easily . . . I usually followed it myself. I used to put it down to professional duty, although in reality it filled the hours between Rose going to bed and midnight when I felt qualified to turn in myself.

But not tonight. I switched it off and put on my coat. I looked down into the dimly lit courtyard. It had stopped raining.

Out there somewhere in the slumbering red and black city – *Chi l'ha visto?* – who had seen it? The truth.

Even if Solitudine had somehow made his way underground alone, slipped and fallen as the police were suggesting, the truth existed as a fact. It was there somewhere – it was just excavating it that was the tricky bit.

I shut the front door behind me. I had few qualms about leaving Rose alone – we lived in the family fortress, after all – and slipped into the night.

The city was still, yet felt strangely alive, like a sleeping animal. A haze of wood smoke hung in the damp streets, cloaked on either side by dark porticoes. The steady drip from a leaky gutter, the lonely chime of a distant church bell. A pair of shutters slammed closed. If it hadn't been for the parked cars, it could have been any time in the past half a millennium.

I wandered along one portico after another contemplating bodies bloated by water, ladies in secret gardens, philandering politicians . . . Bologna as it had been, as it was now, as it would always be.

I passed the Bastardini, an impressive, columned edifice that had been built to house the city's orphans but which now, too, was up for sale. But the Bastardini hadn't been occupied by the anarchists, or anyone else, and I knew why, having been to a couple of events there: it was too inhospitable even for them. And that was the Comune's problem: it had a load of listed buildings that couldn't be sold off, but the Berlusconi era had left local authorities with few other ways to raise cash than to flog the family silver. I experienced a somewhat unwelcome spark of sympathy for the Mayor: the solutions weren't always as simple as some folk would have you believe.

I tried to picture Paolo Solitudine on the day of the raid. I imagined him as the police arrived. Had he slipped away or been bundled out? Truth – where were its traces? I circled the old hospital in my mind, retracing the steps I had taken after I had left Dolores that afternoon.

The riot police had entered through the main entrance and the garden. What else was there? As I walked the perimeter all I found had been a boarded-up doorway. I tested it. The wood partition came away in my hands. Behind, a heavy brown door decorated with graffiti, bird mess and grime. I gave it a push, but it was either locked or stuck fast.

Apart from those two openings and the door, I couldn't see any other ways out. The windows were either barred or too high up to drop from without the risk of serious harm.

The basement then, I thought, Paolo must have gone through the basement and into the canals. Under his own steam or someone else's.

I arrived at the Osteria della Luna, easing myself through the crowd of smokers standing outside. Inside, a group of semi-alcoholics cackling at the bar; youngsters celebrating a birthday with a picnic spread out across a couple of tables. It didn't look like it, but this was one of the oldest *osterie* in the city: the Bolognese had been drinking, arguing (especially arguing), fighting and probably dying in this vaulted space for hundreds of years, although there was little evident respect for the past, or the present, for that matter. The cracked, filthy walls were crowded with bad art, old photos, yellowed newspaper clippings, warped postcards, Bologna FC paraphernalia and even the odd municipal announcement, ranging from calls to prevent violence against women to volunteers for the Mayor's regeneration programme.

I bought a glass of wine and spotted Luca at a packed table

toward the back. Some space was made for me and I squeezed in next to him. The group, ranging from the young to the very old, was, as expected, talking politics.

'They like to present it like there's no going back,' Luca was saying. 'that there's no alternative to their hegemony.'

'*There's always an alternative,*' said his on-off girlfriend, whose name escaped me, but who always looked angry. She cradled her glass of wine and scowled at Luca, although it may have been affection. And now she was scowling at me. 'Look at England,' she said. Everyone else looked at me too.

'Apologies,' said Luca, 'let me introduce my friend Dan.' I raised my glass to the assorted oddballs, who went from about seventeen to seventy.

'You're English?'

'What is it with England?'

'How is Brexit island?'

'Freer!'

'Poorer!'

'Ah, but more democratic . . .'

'Democratic? *Palle* . . .'

Happily, the conversation spun off without my actually having to make a contribution. In the Osteria della Luna, as in the nation as a whole, no silence was ever knowingly left unfilled.

'How are you doing?' said Luca. 'Any updates from your latest –' he grinned '– *investigation*?'

I shook my head. 'Sadly, no. But I did stumble across a rather surreal scene this afternoon.' I told him about Dolores and Desdemona. 'What do you make of it all? This business with the anarchist . . . Paolo . . . something.'

Luca raised his eyebrows. 'Solitudine,' he said. 'Who knows what they were thinking?'

'Who were thinking?' I said.

'The police.' He shook his head. 'Now *there's* a state organ that still acts like it did in the past, yet the politicians are conspicuously quiet on reforming *that*. Ironic, don't you think?'

'Could there be other suspects?' I said. 'Everyone seems to be jumping to that conclusion – except the police, obviously – but how about in-fighting among the anarchists, or even their enemies on the right? Solitudine was in the thick of it back in the old days, wasn't he? Could one of them have been behind it? Some of them are still about, aren't they?'

Luca shook his head. 'Not like before. Even our modern Mussolinis, well they're just a bunch of kids really – like a Doberman without any teeth – and in any case, the ones that used to carry out killings were backed and funded by the secret services, the CIA. I don't think there's any evidence of that these days.' He looked around the table. 'Despite what some of this lot might read online.'

'*Of course it was the fucking police,*' said his girlfriend. 'They beat him up, realised they'd gone too far, and threw him in the water.'

'But come on, Vanessa,' another one of the group said, 'you never really know: maybe it was a jealous husband—'

'Or a jealous lover!'

'A mugging! There's more of it about, you know—'

'Maybe he owed some money—'

'To whom? He always said property was theft!'

'Maybe he got caught stealing.'

'Maybe by his own hand, it could happen, you know. Or an accident.'

'I saw him here, only the night before.'

'Really?' I said.

The old guy was shaking his head. 'Arse,' he said.

'Come on!'

'That's no way to speak about the dead!'

'I'll speak how the hell I like,' he said. 'He was an arse, and his mate, that prick . . . what's his name.'

'You mean Mario,' said Luca with a smile.

'That's right, fucking bum brothers—'

'Woh!'

'I can't believe he said that . . .'

'Who knows what they got up to in gaol,' he said. The man looked like an old sea dog with his chianti-stained white bristles and fisherman's cap, although in Bologna we were about as far from the sea in Italy as it was possible to be.

'I read something about that,' I said, 'but it was a bit vague. Something about a robbery. Do you know what happened?'

'They got nicked, that's what happened. Attempted robbery, to fund "the cause". Amateurs. Cretins. Still, they did their time, won their badge of honour, their "place at the table".'

'So . . .' I looked at Luca.

'Franco,' he said.

'Franco, I'm getting the impression you don't think much of them and their cause?'

'Now he's done it!'

'Don't get him started!'

Franco leaned forward and almost knocked over his wine.

'Before they were "anarchists", they were "communists", you know.'

'Wasn't everyone in Bologna a communist back then, Franco?' I said. He ignored me.

'But not *real* communists, like us,' he said. 'Who understood that discipline was everything, who toed the party line. Who accepted the decision of the central committee that, in Italy, a democratic front was the way forward.' He looked around the table at the indifferent and sardonic faces. 'And it was. No, not that lot, Paolo, Mario, all the rest. They called themselves *Le Brigate Rosse*, "Red Brigades". *Red bollocks*. Bunch of narcissists. It was all about them — they were the opposite of communists, the opposite of working for the good of the people. It was all about the buzz for them, shagging the gorgeous women.'

'Not much wrong with that,' said a young bloke.

'Snigger all you like, young buck,' said Franco, 'but it was your type that got their heads blown off while they were getting the blow jobs.'

'Franco!'

'He's so coarse.'

'He's just jealous.'

'Maybe I am,' said Franco, 'but I'm sitting here and, well, one of them finally got what was coming to him.'

'Why do you think that, Franco?' I said. 'I mean, it's all just history, isn't it? Why should anyone care about them now?'

Franco shrugged. 'Look, lad — while me and my comrades had our heads down trying to improve the lives of the people in this city, that lot, they were gallivanting about, murdering—'

'You don't know that,' said Luca, 'like you said – they were convicted for attempted robbery.'

'And how many lives did that affect, eh? It was *only* an attempted robbery. Listen to yourself, Luca. How many robberies have you *attempted*? And their team – *Le Brigate Rosse* – they killed hundreds, all right, including fascists, but also cops and innocent bystanders too, even the fucking prime minister himself – Aldo d'Oro . . .'

'Moro.'

'd'Oro, I always called him. For gold.' He rubbed his thumb and index finger together. 'See? And who's to say who actually did what. Only a handful of the bastards ever went down for the serious stuff. So, *who knows* what Paolo and Mario really got up to and were never collared for. Maybe the "court of public opinion" convicted him, maybe a relative or victim decided to settle an old score, before it was too late.' He grinned. 'I bet that prick Mario is watching his back, that's for sure.'

'Well,' I said, 'that widens the list of suspects to half of Bologna.'

'That's right,' said Franco, 'and I'd keep an eye on the other half, too.'

A pensioner was moving among the tables and laid down a handful of red and green election leaflets for the PD.

I picked one up. Manzi was waving from the front cover while behind him stood a crowd of supporters in various stages of ecstasy. Chiara Delfiori was among them, but no Marta Finzi. Perhaps that was par for the course or perhaps, I imagined, that afternoon she had made an excuse and even as Manzi and his cronies manufactured enthusiasm for the camera she had been lying with Paolo Solitudine.

I looked at Manzi's photoshopped image, tried to divine if behind those touched-up eyes was a man who would care. And how far he would be prepared to go if he did.

Chapter 9

'You knew Paolo spent time in gaol?'

'Of course,' said Dolores, 'seven years! They didn't even steal anything.'

It was a beautiful morning. Despite the rain the night before, Italy had graced us with good weather, almost like an apology, or an excuse, for her other shortcomings. I met Dolores in the square outside San Francesco – a minor church that would have done as a cathedral in most English cities. Some kids were playing football and their game continued around us as if we were no more substantial than phantoms.

'And you hadn't heard anything,' I said, 'new from those days? It hadn't come up recently?'

'What do you mean?'

'I don't know. Been discussed. Threats, that sort of thing.'

'Threats? It was *ages* ago. They did their time. Too much time.'

We arrived in Pratello, a quarter which was famously packed with pubs and bars and tended to be the area students "graduated" to once they had grown out of the scene around the university area. Some, of course, never went any further, and stayed put, like Paolo Solitudine.

At first I had thought it hypocritical for Solitudine not to bed down in the old hospital along with the young anarchists, but then I decided, fair enough: making do without basic utilities might be a bit of an adventure when you're in your twenties, but for someone in his late middle age it would be taking revolutionary sacrifice a bit far.

We walked up a dark, featureless staircase to the first floor. In contrast to the apartment across the landing, Paolo Solitudine's place did not have a *porta blindata* – the kind of security door that was increasingly common in the city, set in a sturdy iron frame, nor even a barred gate. It was just an old wooden door that had probably been there for a century or more and it swung open as Dolores was about to insert the key into the ageing Yale lock.

We looked at each other. I placed a finger to my lips and bade her step back. I pushed the door the rest of the way. It opened onto a small corridor painted aquamarine. A mirror, framed by starfish, was lying shattered upon the white painted floorboards in front of us. I stepped gingerly around the broken glass.

The apartment had been turned over good and proper. It had been lived in a long time, I could tell – a melange of old furniture, abstract *arte povera* paintings and sculptures, and books, lots of books – but the books, sculptures, even paintings, were now carpeting the floor. The cushions on the old leather sofa had been slashed and even some of the sculptures appeared to have been pulled apart, their pieces now littered among the books, shards of glass and pottery and clumps of upholstery.

'You swine! Come out, you swine!' Dolores raised her fists as I furiously signalled her to keep quiet.

We stood waiting for the onslaught, or escape attempt, but none came. We made our way further into the apartment.

'You've been here before?' I asked. Solitudine's apartment was not what I had been expecting, although what I *had* expected I couldn't say for sure: something more down at heel, perhaps, less evidently cared for, less lovingly crafted – the den of a sad bachelor who had devoted his life to a deluded cause – while this . . . once you looked past the upheaval, this place had a . . . *good* feeling. It was bright, by Bolognese standards, and there was an unselfconscious style to it. I could well imagine Paolo and Marta here, in each other's arms upon the cast iron bed, albeit that its linen was now piled on the floor and the mattress was hanging half off; making a home together in this little oasis of seventies hippy-dom, like its owner a little frayed around the edges perhaps, but no more so than his lover with those streaks of grey in her hair.

'All the time,' said Dolores, looking forlorn. 'Even when he wasn't here – he said I could use it to study. Others, too – he was like that.'

I tried to get my head around what we were looking at here – a bog-standard burglary, or something else?

'I used to be one, you know,' Dolores was saying. 'Like them in the basement. A druggy. But Paolo wouldn't have it – he straightened me out.'

I looked around. She was standing there with her fists clenched by her sides, her jaw jutting out.

'You're clean now,' I said.

'Thanks to him. You should know that – despite everything, him going to gaol – he was a good man.'

There were steps outside. Someone was coming up the stairs. We stood in silence, staring at each other as the footsteps echoed up the stairwell. They arrived upon the landing outside Paolo's front door but didn't even pause, despite it being wide open, and continued to ascend.

'And the last time you came here?' I said.

'With Beppe and Mario. When we were sorting stuff out for the funeral. But it wasn't like this, obviously.' She shook her head. 'Bastards.'

'That's what I'm wondering,' I said. 'Which bastards.'

'Don't you get it? The police, of course.'

'It could be anyone, Dolores. There was no security gate on his door, anyone could have broken in, and once they knew he was dead—'

'No one would have done that. People around here loved Paolo.'

'Did he have anything of value?' I asked. 'Computer . . . jewellery . . .' I looked at the white patches on the walls where the pictures had been removed and tossed upon the floor. 'Art?'

Dolores shook her head. 'I don't know . . . don't think so. He used the computer at the collective.' She smiled. 'He was always asking for my help . . .'

She blinked, once, twice. A tear escaped from the corner of her eye. She wiped it away with a twitch of her bony shoulder. 'I don't know. I never saw him with jewellery, rings or things. I don't know what any of this art is worth . . .'

'There's no TV.'

'Never was, he didn't believe in it.'

I went back into the living room. There was an old valve radio in a teak case, and sitting on top of it, perhaps the sole thing I could see that post-dated 1980: a digital radio. I switched it on. It was tuned to Radio Radicale, naturally.

'He loved his radio, Paolo,' said Dolores.

'It's worth money, too,' I said. Perhaps Dolores was right – the old man was so respected that even the local crooks would refrain from breaking in when he had kicked the bucket.

I followed her into a small office that was even more of a mess than the rest of the apartment: hundreds, if not thousands, of typed papers adding to the chaos, so we were literally up to our ankles in it. All the drawers had been pulled out of a cabinet, their files, held in brown folders, piled up on top of the desk. I picked one up at random. It was dated 1997. Twelve closely typed A4 pages of minutes from the Santo Stefano Anarcho-Syndicalist Chapter. *Item Four: Cleaning Rota. It was claimed that although cleaning and maintenance of the social centre was allocated without prejudice, female comrades were much more likely to undertake the required activities. Female comrades stated they had no confidence in the males to attend, and to actually do the work required when they did. Comrade Antonini argued that the notion of a rota contradicted the founding articles of the Chapter, while Comrade Lima said that without a rota it would be impossible to maintain the facility. Comrade Antonini said this was not the point and requested the matter be referred for arbitration to the Bologna Forum. Comrade Ponzi accused Comrade Antonini of using this request as a tactic to avoid participating in maintenance activities, but Comrade Antonini said, on the contrary, he would be happy to participate, but refused to do so in principle* . . . and so it went, on and on, for pages. There were flyers from various events, copies of anarchist news sheets, folded up posters, leaflets. 1997 was a busy year, but so was 1996, 1995, the files all bursting with old papers, going back to 1988. I opened it up and it was full of much the same stuff, even the flyers printed on the same paper by the same machines using the same images. The same typewriter typing the same minutes, the same obscure arguments, but there, at the very back of the final, or first, file – a black and white photograph. I turned my back to Dolores and slipped it into my pocket.

'The keys would probably have been in one of the desk drawers,' she said, crouching down and plucking out an emptied drawer from the depths. She began clearing the papers aside. I picked up an *arte povera* statuette and tried to work out what it was trying to say – if anything. It was a piece of driftwood supported by two glued-solid balls of newspaper from the 1960s, resting upon a plinth created from an old street sign. The point of the movement had been to attack the commodification of art by creating works out of garbage. Some of it could go for a bomb, these days, I understood. The rest, according to the arbitrary rules of good taste, might as well return to its prior state: trash.

'Look!' Dolores held up a chain of keys as if she had just hooked a fish. She went through them until she came upon a large, old-style key. 'It's got to be this one . . . what do you think? Well, you could try to look pleased.'

'Bravo,' I said. 'What do you think they were looking for, Dolores?'

'Looking?' said Dolores.

'They must have been looking for something ... and if they weren't after valuables, what was it? Was there anything Paolo was doing, that he was involved in, that might have led to this break in? Documents he might have possessed, that sort of thing?'

'The police have always been interested in our activities,' said Dolores. 'Maybe they were searching for a membership list ...' She was looking up at me, cross-legged among the mess like an over-grown child. 'Or maybe they just wanted to send us a message. Paolo was always fighting. He was always trying to find a way ...' she looked around the wrecked office, 'to beat them.' She rubbed her eyes with the back of her hand.

I warily handed her a tissue. She blew her nose, looked up at me, unembarrassed. 'Have you ever wondered why, Englishman, there's so much graffiti here in Bologna?'

'Graffiti?' I shrugged. 'Italy ...'

'It's all we can do,' she said, 'they've got it all sewn up. Business, the universities, the media, state, police, they're all in it together – the same people, same families, keeping the wealth, the opportunities, *la dolce vita*, to themselves, keeping the rest of us shut out. That's why we scribble on the walls of their *palazzi*: because they won't let us in.' She shook her head. 'Come on,' she began to get up, 'let's see what's behind that locked door.'

Only this time Mario came down to the basement along with us. He didn't seem very surprised that Paolo's apartment had been ransacked. 'What did you expect?' he said. 'I would be surprised if they hadn't – they want to remind us who's boss.'

We were back at the door, shining our lights onto the lock while Dolores went through the keys. 'I realised why you didn't look so pleased when I found them, by the way,' she said as she inserted the old key. She tried to turn it but it stuck. Tried again but it was no good.

'Here,' I said, 'let me have a go.' I twisted it hard and, finally, it gave. With a shudder, the door yawned open into darkness and the sound of rushing water.

We shone our lights onto slimy red brickwork, beneath it: the water from the Reno – water that would, incidentally, carry a body out toward the suburbs. A narrow stone bank was visible on both sides, just wide enough to walk single file.

'Hold on,' I said. I stretched out my arm, barring Dolores from barging through while I ran my light up and down the floor. If this was a crime scene, then we were about to contaminate it, although as the police were among the prime suspects, I had to assume I was on my own, at least for the time being.

'It's because,' said Dolores in my ear, 'if the keys *were* at Paolo's, and Paolo had used this entrance to get into the canals, then how come the keys were still in Paolo's apartment?'

'We'll make a detective out of you yet,' I said, treading warily onto the stone bank and taking care not to slip.

'You've got to be kidding,' said Dolores, following on behind, 'who'd want to be a bourgeois parasite?' Mario chuckled approvingly.

From what I could make out, although the bank stretched in both directions, only the left side led to the bridge, or whatever it was, indicated upon the plans. I headed in that direction, trying not to rub against the wall and get covered in dirt, while Dolores and Mario fell in behind me.

There, up ahead: some kind of structure traversing the canal but, when we reached it, it was not a bridge at all but an old pipe, barely seventy centimetres in diameter. Hanging behind and below it, a rusting, chain-metal fence. The kind, I supposed, Paolo had ended up hanging on. I tested the pipe with my foot. It seemed sturdy enough, although I wasn't sure about the fence. I gave it a tug. It appeared to hold. 'No more than one at a time,' I said, stepping onto the pipe. I grabbed the fence and the rust flaked into my hands, but it otherwise seemed firm enough. I began to walk across while the water gushed below, Dolores' light flickering upon me.

I stepped down, took out my phone and shone it toward Dolores and Mario over on the other side. They were talking, Mario shaking his head. He stepped onto the pipe and grabbed hold of the fence. It bowed alarmingly toward him. He adjusted his not inconsiderable bulk and it billowed forward. He wobbled precariously back and forth. 'Wait!' I shouted. 'It's too dangerous. I'll go on alone.'

They both shouted back at me, but I couldn't hear them over the sound of the water. Then I saw Mario step back. Dolores handed her phone to Mario and clambered onto the pipe. Under both our lights, she darted across.

'I told him he was too fat,' she said, jumping down. She looked back. 'Wait there,' she shouted, 'and don't drop my phone!'

I checked the plan then shone my light further along the bank. 'I think there should be some kind of connecting tunnel along here.'

We made our way into the darkness, the light from Mario

growing dimmer. It felt lonely down here, accompanied only by the rush of the water, rats darting ahead. Could Paolo Solitudine really have come this way? Dolores was right about the keys, but how else could he have got down here if he had disappeared during the police raid? Maybe the door had been left unlocked (but how, then, did it become locked?) and, even if he had managed, could he have made it this far? Possibly. He seemed a nimble older guy, given to cycling around the city, romancing radical ladies of a certain age, and younger ones too, no doubt. So, yes, I could see that. But it would only have taken a misstep, a slip upon one of these pipes or along the canal side, and he would have been pitched into the water. The official scenario wasn't looking so outlandish after all, except Solitudine hadn't been found here but in another canal altogether.

The blueprint, I began to realise, was worse than a map of the London Underground – the distances made no sense. We could continue for another mile, or the tunnel could be around the corner, if it was there at all. Then, just beyond the reach of my phone's light, I noticed a flickering. I stopped, and Dolores walked straight into me. She grabbed hold of my waist to stop herself toppling over the edge and into the water. 'Watch it!' she said.

'Have you seen that?' I whispered.

'What?'

I killed my light. 'That.'

A beam, far stronger than ours, was bouncing across the water, projecting onto the opposite wall. I crouched down and felt Dolores do the same. I tried to work out if the light was moving toward us or further away. I realised it was doing neither – that it must be coming out of the connecting tunnel we were searching for.

'You stay here,' I said, moving into the dark.

'No way,' said Dolores.

'Okay, but don't get too close . . .' Keeping my own light switched off, and careful to keep my hand tracking against the cold, slithery wall, I got closer. I soon came to see that the light wasn't shining directly across the canal, but bouncing around the walls of the tunnel as it moved. And, as I approached, it was growing weaker – it was moving away.

By the time I'd reached the opening, I had to distinguish it by touch, the light had grown so faint. 'Are you still with me?' I whispered.

'Too right I am.'

I stepped into the tunnel, and into a channel of water that went up to my ankles. '*Shit,*' I said in English, then tried to suck it back as it resounded around me. I looked up to see a silhouette pause at the exit. Suddenly, I was bathed in a spotlight. I barely had time to cover my eyes before the light died and I was seeing stars.

'What the hell . . .' Dolores had jumped into the tunnel behind me. 'Are you all right?'

'Fine,' I said, trying to get my vision back and fumbling for my phone. 'Wait!' I called down the tunnel. I handed my phone to Dolores. 'You get it working,' I said, 'I can't see a thing.'

LED light surrounded us. 'Stop!' I shouted, but there was no response. 'Come on,' I said. We began moving forward.

It was some kind of overflow channel, designed to carry water running from street level straight into the canals, which meant there had to be a storm breaking above. I pressed ahead, my urgency driven as much by a creeping sense of anxiety as pursuit. I noticed the flow of water was growing stronger and I had no idea about the science of sewers. At any moment I was afraid a jet of water could come gushing down and knock us back into the canal.

We reached the other end and climbed the steps. I had Dolores kill the light as we came out and we were plunged into pitch black. I took the phone and shone it carefully up and down both the sides of the canal.

'Hello?' I called, but there was no response. 'To have disappeared so quickly,' I said, 'there must be some kind of exit close by.'

I checked the blueprint. Attempted to match our journey against its obscure markings.

'Let's try this way,' I said. Sure enough, we soon came upon a dark set of steps, seemingly embedded into the wall. I shone my light – they led to a door hanging partially open. It was as black and age-marked as the door at the hospital.

I looked at the map again. 'Hold on,' I said. I directed the light into the darkness, began to make my way past the door.

'Where are you going?' said Dolores.

There, up ahead, was another pipeline, and beneath it, trailing into the water, a fence.

I ran the light along it. Like the one we had crossed earlier, it was a trap for trash. A ribbon of refuse was waving in the current – a couple of cans, plastic wrappers, and lots of leaves. A used condom was draped just above the waterline, and alongside it, something black, sinuous, snaking through the litter. I got onto my knees, reached out for it.

'*Che schifo,*' said Dolores, then took a short intake of breath.

'That's where they found him, didn't they, that's where they found Paolo.'

I managed to pinch the thing between my fingers and draw it out of the water.

'What are you doing? What is it?'

'Probably nothing,' I said. I held it up. It was black with muck and water but slippery between my fingers. Silk? I sealed it in a plastic bag.

'Evidence?' said Dolores.

'Unlikely,' I said, 'but you never know.'

We went back to the door. I gave it a hesitant push, then, when it stuck, a harder one. It scraped all the way open and I peered into the darkness. It had that same dank, musty atmosphere as the hospital: old stone steps chiselled out by some medieval men, as narrow as they had been. I was about to go in when Dolores barged in front of me. There was another door up ahead and my heart sank – this one was sure to be locked – but without missing a beat Dolores gave it a shove and it swung open.

I followed her into the basement. Machinery hummed under an amber light. The floors were shiny smooth concrete, the dials on the boilers and ventilation systems sparkled.

'Dolores . . .' I said, but she was marching ahead. She went up another set of stairs to an emergency door then halted me with a raised hand.

'Better brush yourself down,' she said. She batted the grime from the front of my jacket.

'Dolores, do you know—'

'And the knees,' she said. I did as I was told.

'Okay,' she said, 'now, act normal.'

I looked at her standing there with her piercings and

half-shaved hair, but she seemed dead serious. She pushed the bar across the door and stepped daintily forward.

We were standing in a broad *palazzo* corridor with high, frescoed ceilings. Beyond it was a courtyard featuring the life-sized sculpture of a rearing white horse. Around us, sharp-suited men and women were sitting in marble-clad alcoves bent over their laptops and smartphones while a small mob was approaching with a man in a black cape at the centre. It could have been a vignette of the busy Italian lawyer and his hangers-on, from blue-suited advocates waving papers in his face, to the litigants and their families tagging after him, looking variously worried, bored and defeated. I realised, shabby and somewhat shifty though we may have appeared, Dolores and I would not look too out of place in the corridors of a court.

'Waste of space,' said Dolores softly.

'What do you mean?'

'This was one of the first places I stayed. Civil Action were using it for the homeless before they turned it into this sausage factory.'

'That's how you knew your way about downstairs,' I said.

'Come on,' she said. I followed her down the corridor in the wake of the legal mob. The rooms were lined with doors, some open to small courtrooms, others to large, plush offices. 'I don't think it's a criminal court, actually,' Dolores said. 'It's for divorces, suing, and so on ... did you know,' she said, 'that Bologna has more lawyers than the whole of France?'

'I find that hard to believe,' I said.

Dolores shrugged. 'Just look around you.' We crossed the courtyard. 'I liked it here,' she said, 'even though there wasn't any heating or running water and it was winter, snow and everything. God, it was *so* cold.' She looked up at the frescoes. 'But nice pictures.' She slapped her forehead. 'Damn it.'

'What?'

'Mario's still down there.'

Dolores, of course, had left her phone with him, so tried to call it from mine, but it just went through to voicemail. 'He probably wouldn't know how to use it, anyway,' she said. She sighed. 'Shall we go back the normal way? It's longer but at least we avoid that water.'

'Once is enough for one day,' I said. We headed for the automatic doors at the main entrance and stepped into the street, walking in the direction of the old hospital.

'I read them, you know,' said Dolores.

'Read what?'

'Your articles, the ones online. I mean, sometimes I had to use Google Translate.'

'Probably improved them.'

She shook her head. 'You're a good writer. But I know, you know.'

I looked at her. '*Among the middle-class drug dealers*?' She nodded.

'It was my first conviction,' I said. 'I was lucky – handed community service instead of a jail term. I mean, it wasn't like it was heroin.' She glanced at me, she understood what I was talking about. 'I was about your age, a runner for a tech company in east London. A *gofer* – go for sandwiches, go for sushi, go for tea, beer, you name it, and then it was go for cocaine. I was paid a pittance and it helped cover my rent – I didn't have the bank of mum and dad.'

'What?'

'My parents, helping me out. Anyway, one day I was picked up, and that was that. Only I got lucky. I had a sympathetic judge who sent me to some charity where they encouraged me to write about my experiences – how the tech boom, the long working days, the crazy deadlines, were basically fuelled by Charlie . . . I mean, coke, and it was picked up by a paper called the *Post*, when it had *been* a paper . . .' She looked at me. 'It's just online now. And it somehow became my job.'

'That would never happen here,' she said.

'What?'

'Getting a job like that – becoming a journalist like that. You'd have to have qualifications. You'd have to *know people*.'

'It's really not so different in England,' I said, then I smiled. 'I suppose you could say I was the exception.'

'So, was I right?' she said.

'Right?'

'About the keys, about it meaning that Paolo didn't go down the canal that way.'

'It was an interesting journey, though,' I said, 'and who would have thought it would have ended there, at the court house?'

'And who was the guy with the light,' she said, 'and why did they run away?'

'It could have been anything,' I said. 'Maybe he was simply spooked to find other people down there.'

'Who's to say it was a "he". It could have been a "she".'

'You said "guy", *il tizio*.'

'*Tizio* can refer to woman or man.' She smiled. 'Maybe *you're* the one that needs language lessons.'

'Thanks,' I said.

'Actually, your Italian's all right.'

'*Thanks*,' I said. She looked at me out of the corner of her eye.

'Don't think that means I want to fuck you.' She spotted Mario standing at the entrance of the old hospital beneath the banner, prodding confusedly at her phone. 'Leave it alone!' she called, and ran toward him.

Chapter 10

One thing you won't read about on the Bologna Welcome website is the bag snatching. Bologna is the second most likely place to get robbed in Italy, after Rimini. There are many opinions about this, the most popular from defensive Bolognese is that the statistic somehow reflects their inherent Northern sobriety: that it was garnered from the *denuncia* reporting these thefts to the *carabinieri* filed by the victims, whereas in Naples or Palermo, well, those Southerners, they just don't bother. But that doesn't add up: these days almost everyone carries some kind of cash card, and certainly a driving licence or identity card, all of which require the official documents as proof of theft in order to be replaced.

No, I think there are just more thieves in Bologna. They swarm to the city like bees to honey, just as they travel to the resorts during the summer for the rich pickings. The north of Italy also favours the independent thief, whereas the south is largely monopolised by the multinationals: organised crime has bigger fish to fry than having the cops poking around, whereas the north provides a more hospitable environment for your 'ordinary decent criminal', the kind that was dying out in England even in the days of the Sweeney, but in Italy appears to persevere, alongside independent pharmacists and newsagents.

Like so many others, they are often a family business. Nonna Miranda had started as a prostitute back in the days when brothels lined Via Mirasole and had continued as a madam after they were made illegal in the late fifties. Nonno Salvatore was an ex-bank robber you could imagine creeping around sixties Bologna with a facemask and sack marked SWAG slung over his shoulder. I had been introduced to them by the Comandante on a trip out to Casalecchio where they were now living, as were most of their brood, the suburban dream. They embraced like old friends, despite the Comandante having accounted for more than a dozen of Salvatore's years in gaol, and Miranda insisted we left with some of her famous *parmigiana*, although the *parmigiana* of every Italian grandmother is, with some justification, 'famous'.

Jacopo and I had arranged to meet them in the corner of a pub in the university zone. The Nonnies were wrapped up as if for the Arctic, although it was actually quite mild outside, and suspiciously eyeing a pair of half pint glasses of artisanal beer, which would remain untouched throughout our meeting.

'That's why I never come to the centre these days,' said Salvatore. 'All this mess, the graffiti. It's like a zoo.'

'Have you seen the blacks?' said Miranda. 'We may as well be in Africa.'

'I remember when,' said Salvatore, leaning forward, 'if you weren't wearing your best clothes in Via Zamboni, you felt underdressed.'

'Everyone says Bologna's changed,' I said.

'Not just Bologna,' said Miranda, 'Italy.'

'So you're Lega voters, then?' I meant the anti-immigrant party.

They looked at each other. Miranda cackled: 'Vote? For any of those crooks?'

Their nephew, Diego, joined us. While their kids had mostly gone straight – into the law or medicine – the family firm still provided an income for other members. Diego did not look much like a thief: more an estate agent or salesman or the generic 'manager', which in a sense he was. They contracted much of the sharp end out these days to Romanians or Bulgarians, like any other small business. 'But no blacks, that's my rule,' Miranda cheerfully explained, 'even when I was on the game, I wouldn't have blacks on the books.'

'Why's that?' said Jacopo, who I could feel trembling with anger beside me, 'Isn't a whore a whore, whatever her colour?'

'Just like his daddy,' said Miranda, her watery eyes sparkling with malice, 'so very passionate.'

'Hold on,' said Jacopo, 'are you suggesting—' I took his arm and got us both to our feet.

'Diego, let me get you a drink.' I pushed Jacopo out of the booth and steered him toward the bar.

'What are we doing working with these racists?' hissed Jacopo.

'Look, Jacopo, we're not Save the Children. They're criminals – what do you expect?'

'Not all criminals are racists.'

'No, we wouldn't want to tar all criminals with the same brush,' I said. 'But these criminals, sadly, are. Can't you see she was winding you up? They're not good people, Jacopo, they've grown fat on other people's misery.'

'Then what are we . . .' But his voice trailed off. He knew precisely what we were doing with them. We returned to the alcove, which was now fully occupied, a pair of young women having slid in beside Diego. They were gum chewing, dull-eyed girls of the sort you would usually see standing along the Viale, the ring road that encircled the old city, in thigh-high white Polyurethane boots and boob tubes, waiting for passing trade, but tonight they were a little more expensively, if not modestly, dressed. We pulled up a pair of chairs and completed the circle.

I smiled at the girls. They looked at Diego as if to ask permission to smile back. 'They know what to do?' I said.

'They go with your boy here,' said Diego, 'identify the girl and get her phone, right?'

I nodded. 'We don't want her hurt, or even to know, if possible.'

'Don't worry.' Diego grinned and squeezed the knee of the one next to him. 'These girls are lovers, not fighters, right?' Now the girls smiled, although I doubt they understood a word he was saying. One of them could have only been about sixteen, or looked young enough to pretend. I felt like punching Diego in the face, and at the same time sensed Nonna Miranda's all-seeing eyes upon me. She gave me a wink. The wicked old bat had got my number, sure enough.

I stood up. 'Let's get going,' I said. On our way out, I held Jacopo back. 'If anything happens, and they get caught, don't do a thing,' I said, 'don't react, try to help them, panic, run. Act dumb. You have nothing to do with them and they have nothing to do with you. We're a world apart from these people.'

'I thought you just implied this *was* our world,' said Jacopo.

'Maybe it is,' I said, 'but we're in their jungle now, and if you forget that you'll get eaten alive.'

We split up as we left the pub and headed toward La Stanza, a pricey bar at the rear of the former palace of the Bentivoglio family, a huge stone monolith from the Renaissance projecting the wealth and menace of the city's former ruling clan. The palace was now divided into apartments occupied by local grandees, home grown popstars, and – who knew – secret societies. La Stanza was one of a number of bars, theatres and restaurants now occupying the palace's ground floor and oozed refined decadence, the walls and ceilings still boasting their original *trompe l'oeil* landscapes while customers sipped twelve-euro cocktails.

Chiara Delfiori's social media had indicated she 'would be attending' a graduation party at this typically *fighetti* venue, and we had sent Jacopo for a makeover accordingly. Under Alba's supervision, gone were the piercings and the tangled black mop, the black t-shirt, raggy, baggy jeans and trainers. Now he had a sharp, razored haircut that made him look like a soccer player for Napoli, tight, pressed jeans and a pale blue shirt with a cream jersey hanging around his shoulders. Okay, it may have been a bit over the top, but no one was going to collar this kid for pickpocketing.

Of course, we could have just passed the details to the Nonnies, but I decided against that: I didn't want anything linking us electronically with them, and I didn't want them to have anything permanent on the girl. Better to minimise their contact with her as much as possible – they were a necessary evil, but they *were* evil. So Jacopo would go in, spot Chiara Delfiori, and the girls would do their job.

I meanwhile went to sit at the bar of a nearby *piadeneria* where I could keep an eye on the entrance.

The *piadina* is an unsung local delicacy. Consisting of flatbread fashioned from flour, lard and olive oil upon a terracotta plate, it's said to come from the days when the area was under the control of the Byzantines, and has the look and taste more of Greece or the Middle East than what many expect from meaty, pasta-heavy Emilia-Romagna. But the *piadina* occupies a special place in Bolognese life. I knew folk who would travel across the city to eat at a particularly revered *piadineria*, which would usually turn out to be a kiosk on the fringes of an anonymous industrial estate, often close to the *autostrada*, run by a no-nonsense guy with rolled-up sleeves and uncultivated stubble who looked as if he'd just nipped out from one of the nearby auto-repair shops to throw together your favourite combination of local cheese, cold-cuts and salad slammed into the salty-sweet bread. There you'd stand with an assortment of workers from the nearby industrial units and guys (it was usually guys, it had to be said) who had just turned up in a sports car or climbed out of the back of a limo, united in your enjoyment of the best *piadina* in Bologna, washed down with a Sprite, Moretti or mineral water, before returning to the shop floor or board meeting. Whatever its divisions, Italian society invariably met over lunch or, at least in this neck of the woods, *piadine*.

The *piadeneria* on Via Molline was not quite *that* special, catering mainly to students and assorted youth enroute to their night out, but it was hard to go far wrong, and my piping hot satchel of soft *squacquerone* cheese, *prosciutto cotto*, and inevitable *rucola* garnish, certainly cut muster. I took a swig of Coke and watched the cocktail bar entrance.

It began to rain the way it does in Bologna, splashing in great dollops upon the asphalt and blurring the window. I saw the first girl step up to the door and stride right in, with barely a glance from the woman on the door. Then came the other – attaching herself to the back of a group of youngsters, sheltering together beneath an umbrella. Jacopo was already inside. It would be crowded in there while it rained, with few stepping out for a cigarette. The perfect environment for the task at hand, I supposed.

'So, what makes you so interested in this girl?' Diego slid onto the stool beside me.

I smiled. 'Now, that would be my business,' I said.

'You're English, right?' I nodded. 'Nonna was saying. I love London, I try to go at least once a year, especially now it's gotten so cheap . . . Nonna was saying to treat you well. I saw you looking at Roxanna, you like her?'

'Diego,' I said, turning to him, 'I thought your firm's core business was more to do with theft than pimping.'

He shrugged. 'As you'll know, a business has to adapt to survive – this,' he nodded toward the bar, 'is mainly a goodwill gesture on our part, seeing as we have such a long-standing association with your company. These days, theft, like your game, is all about the web, isn't it. From a cost-benefit analysis . . . well, this kind of thing just doesn't add up. We tend to leave it to the Slavs and gypsies. I've got a qualification in digital marketing, you know.'

'And the girls?'

'Ah, the girls . . . well, they were always an aspect of our offer, thanks to Nonna, but then, with the opening of Europe to the east we just couldn't compete. But recently we've identified a niche.'

'How so?'

'The more high-end clients, older . . . they don't use the web, and don't trust foreigners, with good reason! As an Italian-run service they don't have to worry about having their throats cut.'

'Trust is important in any business,' I said.

'Absolutely,' he said. 'You know, you and me, we're the new generation. We should do lunch.'

'Look,' I said, 'I think we're done.' One of the girls – the younger one, Roxanna – was leaving the bar. She turned down the narrow lane and walked toward the main road. A bit of a giveaway, I would have said, since it was still pouring with rain and she didn't have a coat or umbrella. The other one followed shortly thereafter. She was a bit more canny though, picking up an umbrella from the stand as she left, although it was obviously stolen, as she didn't enter the bar with one.

'You go,' I said, as Jacopo arrived at the exit. Confronted by the rain he stood there looking like an idiot. I waited until Diego had left – call me, he mouthed, holding his hand to his ear – then I called Jacopo.

'What are you doing?'

'It's raining!'

'Just get a move on. *Now.*' He dashed across the rain and under a portico.

I left the *piadeneria* and headed after Jacopo. I found him standing outside a bar further along the road, smoking a cigarette.

'I suppose it went all right?' I said. He gave me a wary look. 'What?'

'I, er ... used my ... um, initiative, like you're always telling me.'

It was true, I was always telling him to use his initiative given how discouraging his father was, although I wasn't sure this was exactly the right time.

'Chiara,' he said. 'She was there, but we didn't get her phone.'

'So ...' I felt a surge of panic. What had we just splashed five-hundred euros of our client's cash on?

'There was the other girl. The pregnant one, alongside her. Anna. I recognised her from her social media ... I got the girls to lift *her* phone.'

'Anna Bellidenti?' I said. 'Cabin fever must have finally got to her.' I slapped him on the shoulder and he looked at me anxiously. 'You did well,' I said.

Chapter 11

There wasn't a moment to lose. The compulsion with which people checked their phones these days was such that their owners soon realised they had gone. The challenge was to get into it before Anna had it blocked. Technically she could do so with a simple telephone call, but we were gambling she would be complacent enough to leave it until tomorrow, or at least later tonight. She was out with friends and in any case, didn't her smartphone – and Jacopo had confirmed this as he glanced over her shoulder while at the bar – have fingerprint security? There was no need for troublesome numeric codes that a crafty thief could glimpse and use to gain access to your personal details. Fingerprints were super-safe, right? No one else had your fingerprint, so no one was going to get into your iPhone.

Half right. Actually, numbers are safer. This was why the FBI had such a hassle – and a bust-up with Apple – over breaking into an iPhone belonging to a terrorist set to delete all data after ten unsuccessful attempts. In the end, after a long-running court case, they were able to hack it, but only with the help of the Israeli secret service.

We didn't have Mossad on our side, but we did have Massima. We found her sitting in the Comandante's office where the pair of them were smoking and chatting about national politics. Massima's Staffordshire Bull Terrier, Gertrude, was prudently curled up in the doorway with her snout pointing away from the pollution. She got to her feet and tottered toward us (I had once confused her over-fed belly for pregnancy, and silently thanked God I had referred to the dog and not her owner) wagging her tail, her broad tongue lolling out of the side of her mouth.

'Ah,' I heard Massima comment dryly, 'it's Laurel and Hardy. Hello, boys!' She filled the doorway, side-to-side at any rate, a bulldyke, as she liked to call herself, who had much the same temperament as her beloved Gertrude: a big softy, but with the potential to deliver a fatal bite. 'What the fuck, Jacopo! What have they done to my handsome boy?' She held his head in her hands. 'Mother of Mary.' She turned to the Comandante. 'You know who he reminds me of? Mika! You know, the one who's always on *X Factor*.'

'You watch *X Factor*?' I said. 'I thought Vasco Rossi was more your type. *The Rocker from Zocca*.'

Massima shrugged. 'It's more Barbara's thing,' she said, meaning her partner, 'you know how it is.'

I nodded. 'Rose is a big fan.'

'Ah! Your beautiful flower! Giovanni showed me a photo, but she must have grown . . .'

'Are you two going to stand around chatting or are we going to do this thing?' said Jacopo, still smarting from the Mika comparison.

'Mika's . . . sorry Jaco's got a point,' said Massima, 'sooner the better. It could be a long night.'

Massima already had her kit set out in our office, and I was daunted to see it spread along the cleared desks. Heavy-duty, portable black electronic equipment stamped PROPERTY OF FORENSIC SCIENCE POLICE SERVICE – Massima's daytime employer – along with various semi-transparent plastic tubs of chemicals and other obscure materials.

'First,' she said, 'for the easy part.' She snapped on a pair of blue surgical gloves and tossed a pair to Jacopo. He put them on and handed the phone over. She sat down and placed it under the table-mounted magnifying glass. She switched on the arc light. 'Very well, very well . . .' She opened a beaker of black powder and sprinkled it liberally over both sides of the phone, then began to lightly remove it with what looked like a make-up brush. 'Of course,' said Massima, 'this would be even easier if you had told your bitches to wear gloves.'

'It hadn't occurred to me,' I confessed. 'Maybe if you'd mentioned it?'

'Fortunately,' she said, 'I'm an expert. I can see that these digits here – well, they're a different size and shape. Pattern. Straight off. These are our girl's. Anna *Bellidenti*, you say? "Beautiful teeth"! What wonderful names we Italians have! As well as having a fine pair of gnashers, you can see, also, that she even applies a different degree of pressure when she holds her phone. People don't think about that – that our grip can also be a signature . . . anyway. Now it's simply a question of elimination . . . of finding the correct digit . . . we could be unlucky, you know . . . our night could be over before it begins . . .'

'Is that a promise?' said Jacopo.

'If you're not careful, Mika, darling, I'll have Gertrude bite you . . . It's a question, you see, of identifying the digit in question, which will typically be fractured by the fingerprint sensor – most probably the thumb – and then seeing if we can match it with a full print elsewhere on the phone. How much time do you have?'

'Not enough,' I said.

'I ask because, strictly speaking, I would want to remove a number of likely candidates and give them a once over before I could be sure about which one she uses. Or reasonably sure.'

'In percentage terms,' I said, 'if you cut corners, how sure do you think you could be about identifying the print?'

'Percentage terms? Judging from my experience . . . seventy-five, eighty per cent, I would say. But we only have the time to conduct the process once, otherwise we really will be here all night.'

I looked at the Comandante. He nodded. 'Okay,' I said.

Massima got to work, bent over an island of light in the otherwise dark office, the three of us crowding around her, half hidden in the shadows as if we were in a painting by Caravaggio.

'You're in luck . . . I think . . . yes . . . fingers crossed, ha, ha . . .' this running commentary as she swung the lens aside, 'can you turn on the lights, please?' She switched on a desk lamp and directed it toward the phone. She took out a high-powered digital camera and focused in on, I presumed, the print in question. She then swung around and opened up the heavy-duty laptop she had brought with her, police property, of course.

'Now comes the tricky part, like on the TV . . .' Massima

took the memory stick from the camera and plugged it into the computer's USB.

'Couldn't you use Bluetooth?' Jacopo asked.

'Tell that to my boss, sweetie. He's suspicious of any technology he doesn't understand, and considering he went to school with your papa, well, you can imagine . . .

'In fact, most of this I've just done myself, bought it thanks to the fees from private clients, like you. I worked it out – the great thing is, he only understands hardware, he doesn't understand what software is: because he can't see it!'

'And this is the head of forensics?' I asked.

'It's merely an administrative role,' said the Comandante defensively. 'Gabriele is a good man.'

'Tell us what software is then, Dad,' said Jacopo.

'So what are you doing now?' I asked Massima.

'Now.' She pulled up a screen with the enlarged print. 'We give it a flip . . .' The mirror image of the print came up, with the raised parts in white and the background in black. 'And print it out.' I noticed she had already hooked the laptop to our printer, which spurted out a sheet of tracing paper. Massima scooped it up and opened a black, rubber edged, metal case.

'Fritzer,' said Jacopo. 'I've been wanting one of these.'

'They don't come cheap,' said Massima.

'They use them for making circuit boards,' Jacopo explained with the obsessive's relish, 'it's the same principle as photography . . .'

'If you say so,' I said.

'The UV light,' he said, 'cuts into solid state objects, just like a laser.'

'I see,' I said. 'Practical application?'

He gave me a look as if I was another Gabriele. 'Well,' he said, 'this is one.'

'I've already loaded up a piece of board,' said Massima. She laid the paper flat onto the screen of the glass, which looked pretty much like a bulky scanner, and locked the lid down. She went back to the computer and clicked start. The machine began with a buzz, then started to chug, light seeping out from its sides. 'This may take a while,' said Massima. She looked up at Jacopo. 'Coffee?'

While the pair of them went out in search of a coffee at midnight, the Comandante invited me into his office.

'You don't need to stay, Giovanni,' I said, although admittedly he didn't appear any more weary than usual. The Comandante looked at me as if it hadn't even occurred to him to leave. He may have increasingly been a constitutional monarch, but he took his duties seriously.

'I'm fine,' he said, and for the first time ever, I think I may have offended him. 'But thank you for asking, Daniel.' He lit a cigarette.

We discussed my earlier underground excursion. 'So, it is not inconceivable, then,' said the Comandante, 'that Solitudine could have found his way down there and managed to wind up being flushed into one of the canals.'

'Flushed?' I said.

'All right,' said the Comandante, '"washed".'

'I've already checked the weather report for that day,' I said. 'It was dry, there hadn't been any rain for a week. Although it is dangerous down there, it's certainly possible he could have slipped and fallen.'

'Of course it is, my boy,' said the Comandante, 'which is presumably why my former colleagues arrived at that very conclusion.'

'But will Signora Finzi be happy with that answer?'

'Signora Finzi will be happy if we can establish Signor Manzi did not give Signor Solitudine a sharp shove over the edge. Or get someone else to do so.'

My phone buzzed. A message. I was expecting it to be from Rose or Jacopo. Instead it was from Dolores.

'Problem?' said the Comandante – he, presumably, had thought the same thing. I shook my head.

'It's from that anarchist girl I mentioned. She wants to meet me tomorrow – apparently she's come across something she wants to show me.'

The chime of the lift, the sound of Massima and Jacopo coming back in, along with their usual jokey banter, interrupted us. I realised they had probably had something stronger than a coffee.

'Alrighty!' Massima lifted up the lid of the fritzer and began delving about inside. 'There we have it.' She extracted the strip and held it up to the light. It looked precisely like what it was – a piece of circuit board – only with the clear pattern of a fingerprint slightly raised in black against its green background. 'Now comes the fun part,' she said. She laid it onto a plastic chopping board and reached for those tubs I had seen earlier. Out of the first one she took a pinch of black powder and began to carefully cover the impression of the print. Then she dipped a brush into a creamy liquid and smoothed it over the powder. When she was satisfied she turned to Jacopo. 'So, did you remember your hairdryer, good-looking?' He looked nonplussed. 'No? Fortunately, I did.' She reached into a bag and plugged it in, switching it to the weakest setting. She began to dry the white blob that ended up looking like a strip of flattened, masticated chewing gum sitting upon the circuit board. She then laid her thumb upon it, and crudely cut out an outline with a craft knife. She unpeeled the remaining strip, still attached to her thumb.

'Et . . . voila!'

I couldn't see much of a pattern, but then I supposed that was the point: it was supposed to be a fingerprint, after all. Massima gave me a sly smile. She pulled out a make-up mirror and placed it on the table. 'Technically, that should be it, but I like to add a little – a touch, in fact – of grease, to give it that human feel, and leave a residue . . .' Using a cotton bud she smeared a clear ointment over the surface. She then pressed her thumb a couple of times onto a white sheet of paper, before placing it against the mirror. Using her other hand, she quickly sprinkled some black powder, brushing it off to reveal a clear finger – or thumb – print.

'Bravo!' said Jacopo.

'Impressive, Massima, dear,' said the Comandante.

'I'm just glad this technology is in the right hands,' I said. 'It could be difficult to explain a stray fingerprint at the wrong crime scene.'

'Oh, anybody can buy this stuff off the internet,' said Massima, 'but why would they? In any case –' she winked '– DNA is harder to fake.' She reached for the phone. 'Now for the moment of truth.' She switched it on. 'We have three goes to get this right. You're okay –' she looked up at us '– if the fake thumb is mine? I've had a bit more experience.'

'Hold on,' I said. 'You've got everything ready, Jacopo?' He nodded. 'Okay, go on then.'

'The trick is,' she said, the tip of her tongue sliding back and forth across her front teeth, 'to do it like . . .' She rested her thumb lightly over the phone's sensor '. . . you mean it.'

Massima pressed. The phone buzzed, flashed: NO MATCH.

She sighed, tried again.

NO MATCH.

'Didn't you say you had three—'

'*Santa Maria, Madre di Dio* . . .' Massima intoned the Hail Mary while Jacopo and I exchanged a worried look.

'Maybe you should . . .' Massima crossed herself with her free hand and pressed again.

The phone lit up to reveal a photo of a woman in sunglasses – Anna Bellidenti – with a cocktail held up to the camera and her studded tongue sticking out.

Massima handed the phone to Jacopo, who plugged it into his laptop and began to skim through the apps and download content. 'Looking good,' he said, 'she doesn't appear to have touched it.'

'Thank you, Massima,' I said, 'for a moment there I really thought we weren't going to make it.'

'Thank Maria,' said Massima and I waited for the knowing smile, but there came none.

Chapter 12

'Wot you looking at?'

'Christ, Rose,' I said in English, breaking my own rule, 'if you're going to speak in English, you could at least do it properly.'

'I don't know wot you're talking about.'

I switched back to Italian: 'Anyway,' I refused to rise to her bait. 'I've never seen those before, what you're wearing . . .'

'Yes, you have,' said Rose gleefully, tugging at the dungarees.

There were three of us around the breakfast table. Alba and the Comandante had their own apartments and usually only appeared for dinner. Jacopo had a place in the complex too, except that he had happened to 'drop in to say hello to his favourite niece' just as we were sitting down, which actually meant he still hadn't got around to buying a fresh jar of Nutella.

'I have?' I said.

'You have.' Jacopo stopped eating to watch the stand off between father and daughter.

'They're not from H&M?' She shook her head. 'The trip to London? Top Shop? Zara?'

'I don't know . . . they could have been . . . *a long time ago* . . .'

My heart, literally, skipped a beat. Jacopo must have realised at the same time, because he looked down and continued with his meal.

'They're Lucia's, your mum's,' I said.

'What do you think?' Rose stood up. They swallowed her – baggy around the hips and she had rolled up the legs – but she gave me an utterly unselfconscious smile and I was instantly reminded of her mother. I closed my eyes to stop the tears. Just in time. I rubbed them in apparent tiredness.

'They almost fit,' I managed to say. I was glad her grandfather wasn't here to see it.

'What do you mean, "almost"? They're perfect! It's the style now to have the legs rolled up,' she said.

'So you've been rifling through your mum's stuff.'

'Not "rifling", but I needed to wear something a bit rough for the trip today and I remembered these . . .' How could she remember? Of course she would remember. 'There's tons up there, some of it's really cool, *vintage*.'

I took a sip of orange juice, watched Jacopo conscientiously covering every last millimetre of toast with chocolate spread. 'Your mum,' I said, measuring my words, 'would be happy to see you putting them to good use. But look, darling, they have sentimental value to us all, especially, probably, your grandfather, so I'd appreciate it if you would ask me before you use a particular item, because you'll want to take care of them, so you can also wear them when you're older, too, okay?'

'Have I done something wrong?' Rose looked genuinely concerned.

'No, it's fine, it's just . . . it was just a bit of a shock, that's all. And I want you to take care of them, for yourself as much as everyone else.'

Rose gave me her sensible nod, the one she reserved when she sensed she had dodged a bullet. But, hey – she had been the strongest of us all. Apart from that initial explosion of grief – her hysteria articulating the sheer horror we all felt – her resilience thereafter had, put simply, saved me. She had been both my example, and my reason to keep going, and I would tell her that one day.

Although not today.

'May I?' Rose picked up her empty dish. 'There's Paola from *X Factor* on *Morning!*'

'Okay,' I said, 'just don't be late.'

'We're meeting late,' she called back, the TV already on, 'it's a trip!' Jacopo was smiling.

'Kids, huh?' he said.

'Just you wait.'

'Oh,' he said, sitting back and resting his hands across his full belly, 'I'm not sure I'll want to go down that road.'

'You may not, but what about her?'

'There are plenty of women who don't want to have kids.'

'What, you mean like the type you hang out with? What are they? Twenty, twenty-five?'

'What's that got to do with it?'

I shrugged. 'People change,' I said.

Jacopo gave me the condescending look I received all too often from my daughter. 'But what do I know,' I said.

'Take this girl,' said Jacopo.

'What girl?'

'This Anna Bellidenti,' said Jacopo, 'I've begun trawling through her stuff. Facebook, Instagram, etcetera. Now, this girl is twenty-two years old, and *she's* definitely straight as a die.' He shook his head. 'Not my type at all.'

'What makes you think she's so "straight", exactly?' I refrained from pointing out his supposedly 'alternative' look was precisely the same as everybody else's.

'Take a look,' said Jacopo. He went and got his laptop, came to sit next to me. 'It's all catwalks and kittens . . .' It was true: Anna Bellidenti's Facebook account was very girly-girl, choc-a-bloc with popstars, tattooed hunks, clothes, sunglasses, fashion shows, and yes, furry animals of the 'aw, cute' variety, along with photos of herself at various social gatherings, mainly at night in bars and clubs, although these had petered out over the last few months. She had more than a thousand friends.

Fair enough, this wasn't the kind of girl Jacopo would hang out with – Dolores, the *punkabbestia*, was more his type – but then a girl like Anna probably wouldn't give him a second glance, either. I imagined her with sharp-suited types who wore expensive loafers without socks. Or there, dressed in a revealing red dress, arm-in-arm with Chiara Delfiori at an event, the pair of them raising a glass of Prosecco to the camera. 'Hold on,' I said, peering closer.

'Yeah, it's her – Chiara,' said Jacopo.

'And isn't that . . . in the background . . .' It was Mayor Manzi, that wolfish grin smeared across his face as someone spoke in his ear. But he wasn't looking toward the speaker or the camera, he was looking at the rear of Anna Bellidenti.

'Have you got anywhere with her messaging apps?' I said.

'Come on, Dan, we got in late last night. It's all down-loaded – ready to go. I'll start going through them when I get in the office.'

'As long as that's the truth,' I said, 'and you're not develop-ing a crush on Anna and her glamorous lifestyle, because I'm sorry, mate, but I think she's already taken.'

'You're so funny,' said Jacopo, getting to his feet.

'Are you going to wash your plate?' I said. 'I don't think your favourite niece is going to do it for you.'

'Like I said,' Jacopo picked up the crockery and took it over to the sink, 'so funny.'

Chapter 13

There was no one at the front entrance to the old hospital and the doors were chained shut, although the banner still hung outside, so I presumed the anarchists hadn't been swept away by another raid.

I went around the back, where the large gates to the farm were, and sure enough, these were open.

I heard a bellow from a makeshift cowshed, then a squeal, a ripple of childish laughter. I made my way toward it, stepping between muddy puddles. The doors were wide open and Desdemona was stood facing me, her dumb eyes rolling in my direction. She was standing above a milking stool as Dolores pulled at her udders, weak threads of milk ringing into a steel bucket. A group of youngsters was standing in an arc around her, variously fascinated, disgusted and bored. Rose was among them, seemingly enrapt.

Dolores noticed me and paused. Everyone else turned to look.

'Dad!' said Rose.

'*Rose.*' I nodded.

'Signor Lie-chest-er.' A woman, little taller than the

youngsters, stepped out from behind them. Their teacher. She had always struck me as a bit of a hippy. I should have guessed she would take them to a place like this. Permaculture, my arse.

'Signora Manfredi,' I said.

'Is everything all right?'

'Fine, thank you, *signora*.'

'You signed the form,' she said rapidly, 'for her to visit the city farm.'

'I certainly did,' I said, looking at Rose, although had I actually known where the so-called farm was, I would have thought twice about allowing her to come. I didn't want her here when the police next came crashing in. But at least this explained the dungarees.

'Who wants to have a go?' Dolores got to her feet. Half the group drew back, half shot up their hands.

'How about you?' said Dolores. 'Rose, is it? Show your dad how it's done.'

Rose stepped bashfully forward. Dolores brought her around the side and sat her upon the stool. She crouched down beside her. 'Now, get a hold of the udders . . . don't be afraid.'

Rose reached tentatively out, then flinched. 'They're warm!' she said, 'and hairy!' One of the boys in the group whispered to another and they sniggered.

'Go on,' said Dolores. She took Rose's hands and closed them around the udders. 'That's it,' she said. 'Now, we pull. Don't worry, it won't hurt her.'

Milk squirted out. There was a round of applause. 'Well done,' said Dolores, 'now, we do one, after the other, after the other, a rhythm . . .' She let her hands go and Rose continued milking the cow. A memory, not so long ago: running behind Rose in the park, having a hold of the rear of her bicycle, letting go . . . watching her ride away, giving me a commentary as if I was still there, still holding on . . . *'Don't let go! Don't let go! You let go!'*

'You see, Dad? You see?'

I focused on my daughter in the present. 'Well done,' I said. Dolores stood up, her hands on her hips.

'I wasn't expecting you here so soon,' she said. The kids and their teacher looked at me again. All except Rose, who was still working away at Desdemona.

'If we could step outside . . .'

'Un attimo,' said Dolores. 'Rose.' She crouched down by her side. 'Now you show your classmates. Come on,' she called, 'who's next?' There was a rush as the kids crowded around them.

'They'll be all right?' I asked as we went outside.

'Why shouldn't they be?'

'With the cow,' I said.

'Oh, she's used to it,' she said. 'Cows . . . but you're the expert, after all. That was a neat trick you pulled off with the pigs . . .'

'The police aren't farmyard animals, you know, Dolores.'

Dolores looked as if she was seriously considering this. 'Maybe you're right,' she said. 'I'd trust Desdemona over them, any day.'

We went to sit on an old bench. Across the cultivated land I could see the kids bunched together around Desdemona, who was, as Dolores had predicted, stoically bearing their pokes and prods.

'What are you doing here?' said Dolores. 'In Italy, I mean.'

'I . . .' I raised my face to feel the sun breaking through the clouds.

'And don't say you should be the one asking the questions.'

'My wife was Italian. We came here shortly before Rose was born and then . . . well, Lucia, my wife, that is, died.' I watched Rose talking excitedly to Stefania. 'But my daughter had her friends . . . a whole family here. I mean, I've got family in the UK, too, but . . . it's different. Here . . . family means something.'

Dolores took out a cigarette paper and a pouch of tobacco. 'Smoke?' I shook my head, watched as she expertly constructed a roll-up. 'That explains it. About your wife, I mean. Why you seem sad, despite that smile, the jokes.'

'Haven't you heard of our famous English sense of humour?'

She shook her head. 'You don't fool me. But why did you give journalism up?'

'I think it's more a case of it giving up on me,' I said. 'You remember that newspaper I mentioned? The *Post*? When it went online it cut back on paying for articles, among them, mine. People are no longer interested in the truth, or rather, paying for it. It's far cheaper to carry opinions – there's no shortage of them.'

'Fake news.' Dolores nodded sagely.

'Certainly no one believes anything any more, or rather, everyone seems to believe everything, with much the same result – the bad guys are free to get on with it, without worrying about prying eyes.'

'Like the ones that killed Paolo?'

I shrugged. 'Who knows.'

'See,' said Dolores. 'I was right, You *are* a cynic.' Just then, Rose emerged from the cowshed, waving proudly.

'Where there's youth –' I waved back '– there's hope.'

'Which reminds me,' said Dolores. 'A clue!'

She went back into the cowshed and returned with a back-pack. 'I found it when I was putting Paolo's apartment back together. Do you want to know where?'

'Tell me.'

'I'd put his radio on while I was doing the cleaning up, and when I'd finished, I went to turn it off and I wondered if that old one worked. It's got things on it like Radio Moscow, Paris, Berlin, Cairo, right? All this stuff from around the world. I thought: how cool would that be? So I tried it, and of course it didn't work, so then I started messing with it, and you'll never believe it.'

'I'll never believe what?'

'I opened it up and half the insides were missing. There was this kind of gap at the bottom, and in it, I found this.' She produced a black covered book that looked like a battered Bible.

'What is it?' I said.

'It's some kind of journal. It's Paolo's writing, from the 1970s, best I can tell. Anyway, it was hidden, so it's got to be important . . .' She grinned and I noticed her teeth, although strong looking, were coffee- and tobacco-stained. Vegan toothpaste, probably. 'This *must* be what they were looking for. It's probably what got him killed.' I looked at her. 'Well,' she said, 'maybe . . .'

I reached out to take it, but she kept hold of it. 'Can I trust you?' she said, suddenly serious.

'You mean you can't tell?' I said. I shook my head. 'Of course you can't trust me, Dolores. But you can believe me when I tell you I'm not one of the bad guys.'

Dolores thought about it, then let go. 'An Italian would never tell me I *couldn't* trust him. He'd say "*of course* you can trust me, *cara*" then screw me over just for being so naïve. But maybe you English are different.' There was laughter from the cowshed. 'Anyway,' she said, 'your girl, Rose, seems like a nice kid.' That serious look again. 'Be careful, though.' She looked at the book. 'I don't want her to become an orphan.'

'Don't worry,' I said. 'Neither do I.'

Chapter 14

3 February 1979. I love her, if this is what love is. Is this what love is? The violence, the anger, the urgency? Jesus said, 'I come not to bring peace but with a sword.' Is this what he meant? Is this what real love is? Violence? She likes to bite when we make love, she likes to scratch. She doesn't say 'make love', she says 'fuck'. She says 'fuck me'. She likes me to 'fuck' her hard, it sometimes feels like I am stabbing her, but me – I'm not permitted to leave marks, of course. Of course! She may mark me, she may brand me, under the collar line, but she must remain pristine. I want to slap her. I want to show her who's boss. Just once, to leave a bruise beneath her eye, leave _my_ mark. She could say she walked into a door, she could even whisper to her female comrades that _he_ had hit her. They would like that, they would probably get a buzz . . . but who am I kidding? _She_ is the boss of me. Power relations. La deuxieme sex . . . *I wonder how many of them _he_ is fucking? We replace ownership, but with what? Rage? And we call it passion. Love through the lens of dialectical materialism. It is almost funny – I am studying Hegel during the day, Marx at night, and putting it into practice in the afternoons between classes. I am part of a process, a creative conflict, the pair of us*

— Marta and I. Carlo, him too, of course. I do not hate him. On the contrary, perhaps I want to be like him. And Marta, what is she looking for? Does she even know? Or is she, as de Beauvoir would have it, the embodiment of spirit, crafted by Man and her own biological destiny? Oh, so mysterious, Marta. I am burned by the intensity of your love as I am by the sun, but is this your love for me, or does this furnace simply rage regardless? In short: Marta, Marta, Marta Finzi, what on earth do you see in me?

Marta, Marta, Marta Finzi . . . at least that explained what the Mayor's wife was doing with one of her husband's sworn enemies – their fling had nothing to do with current politics but was the renewal of an old flame.

It was pretty hot stuff, not least Paolo's violent fantasies, unrestrained by the etiquette of our age. I looked at the young people sitting around me in the bar, absorbed in their personal dramas. *Hot stuff.* The sex, or sexual intensity, at least – the act of deriving meaning through sheer physicality, I knew that well enough – but the feelings that linger, that develop with age? Neither should their potency be underestimated. They were plainly strong enough to renew a relationship between Paolo and Marta. And powerful enough for it to end in violence – *real violence* – too, on the part of Carlo Manzi?

Journal was the right word for it – as well as more traditional diary-style entries there were random thoughts, sketches, lists . . . *June 7, 1979. Eggs. Wine. Cigs. Nose trimmers. Either/ Or to Giuseppe (borrow Mant. discourses on K). Bologna-Nap tickets . . .* that, presumably, the young Paolo Solitudine had carried around with him through 1979. In fact, there appeared to be two journals squeezed into one: an additional set of pages were glued into the inside back cover, even though there were plenty of blank pages at the end of the book, all written by a fastidious hand in light-blue fountain pen ink or an almost charcoal-dark pencil.

I took out the photo I had pocketed at Solitudine's apartment and rested it against my cappuccino cup. *There* was the earnest, intense-looking student with the unruly mop of dark hair and Che Guevara-style beard who was still discernible in the photo of the old man I had downloaded onto my phone, sitting alongside a hearty, barrel-chested Mario Cento, stunning Marta Finzi, and an amused-looking, clean cut Carlo Manzi, the four of them in the countryside in the black and white snap. Look at the body language: Manzi standing behind the three of them perched along a log, his proprietary hand upon Marta's shoulder, her head inclined toward it and partly covering it with her dark, frizzy hair. Next to her, but a palm's width apart (the palm in question resting flat between them upon the bark, his little finger touching the fringe of her dress) Paolo, looking directly into the camera as if willing it to reveal his secret; and finally (always last? always least?), with a comradely arm around Paolo's shoulders, his shirt open mid-way down that broad chest of his, Mario Cento, his joyous face the only one looking entirely without guile. I could find no immediate reference to this outing in the journal, but there were plenty of others. To Trento with Carlo, who was an assistant professor in the sociology department at Bologna, for a series of talks (his carefully annotated list of seminars: *Marx and Unlocking the Revolutionary Potential of the Proletariat. The Fundamental of Continuous Revolution:*

Mao Zedong. What Che Guevara's Liberation Struggle Means To Us), to Turin and Milan for more of the same. Then the rallies in support of the workers, the pickets of banks, corporate headquarters. The sit-ins at the University of Bologna itself. The sense, shot-through – of momentum. *Carlo reports considerable success in his seminars with the Fiat workers, despite the best efforts of the management to interfere. They are organising, and not only organising but, with our help, coming to realise that the official parties will offer them no real progress – never mind the CD or Socialists, the Communists will never achieve their objectives by <u>definition.</u> They call themselves Communists, but the ballot box will always be weighed against them – and 'winning the ballot of democracy' is a cynical misreading of Marx. This, the workers are beginning to grasp – in Turin, in Milan, even here in Bologna, I have spoken to them, <u>they</u> have told <u>me</u>, that this is a dead end. Go to la Luna and ask any group of men with dirt beneath their fingernails – they will say the same thing. The system is stacked against them, they are <u>becoming aware</u> (CF: Kierkegaard, Infinite Resig.? La Nausée?) that even the 'Communists' are no help and yet . . . awareness is the first step, the second is <u>always</u> <u>action</u>!*

Because, of course, they had it all to play for. It was easy to dismiss these ramblings in retrospect, but these were not only the juvenile fantasies of a young man, they also constituted serious, settled opinion: with the Soviet Union only a few hundred miles to the east, every Western politician and commentator believed it was all to play for, and people like Paolo, and Carlo, had good reason to believe that they would end up on the winning side. And everyone likes a winner – Marta Finzi, naturally she would go to the leader of the group, she was his by *right* as, it appeared from Paolo's writings, were most of the women in their circle, but perhaps that was simply his jealousy speaking. They were still young, *so young* – even Carlo must have only been in his mid-twenties, Marta and Paolo and Mario younger still, mid-way through their studies. And yet, examining these words like the ruins of an old city, can I see it already? The future? The fracture? The foreshadowing of a world to come?

Carlo says Cremoni is a fool, but not as foolish as he appears. He says the Communists who run this city think they are being canny, that by demonstrating their municipal competence, they can garner support. In fact, they simply line their own pockets, build their own careers – they are <u>part of the problem</u>. M ignored me all night, just as she said she would. It was hard, but not as hard as I thought – in a sense it helped me engage with the dialectic. I almost forgot, for one evening! But then, as I was coming out of the toilet, she was coming back from the kitchen. She pushed herself against me, back into the coats, and snap! She had bit my earlobe! When I went back in, Carlo noticed it – your ear is burning, Paolo, he said, and we weren't even talking about you!

Flicking back and forth, a green and white slip the size of a medical prescription fell from the journal. My first thought was that Dolores had been using it as a bookmark. My second got me on the phone to the Comandante.

'Your contact at the Records Office,' I said.

'Giuseppe.'

'Could you give him a call? I may have something.'

'What is it?' It was a docket with a list of serial numbers representing documents Paolo Solitudine had accessed a week before his disappearance.

'Something that was hidden,' I said, 'something that mattered.'

As so often occurred in Italy, what could have been a laborious process that took days of coming and going had been swiftly facilitated by a simple phone call to a trusted friend – in this case from the Comandante to Giuseppe, who had had copies of the documents waiting for me by the time I had walked across the city to the Records Office. 'Convince the old scoundrel,' he said, every bit as aged as the Comandante, 'to come in with us on that beach house in Cesenatico.'

'Sounds like a good idea to me,' I said, having no idea what he was talking about. I went to a nearby bar and took the documents out of the manila envelope. From what I could tell, they were receipts of property sales, registered with the Comune and going back five years. There was only one that rang any immediate bells, typewritten in a box at the top of a page of officialese: *Ospedale Santa Maria Maddalena, Via Mazzini, Bologna.* The old hospital where the anarchists had their squat. My first instinct was to call Dolores, but I thought better of it. No, I decided it was time I caught up with Signora Finzi.

Her office was in the heart of the university area. The porticoes were thick with students moving between classes in the buildings that lined Via Zamboni. I glimpsed courtyards enlivened by *trompe l'oeil* landscapes, blotted by drinks dispensers and rubbish bins; frescoed lecture halls jammed with tatty tables and chairs. Political graffiti covered long stretches of wall, while in Piazza Verdi red and black banners proclaimed the coming revolution. Clumps of youths were standing behind fold-up tables piled with political books and handing out electoral leaflets, although none of the main political parties appeared to be represented and few of these kids were likely to vote in any case.

It felt like not much had changed here in twenty, thirty, forty years. As I weaved through the crowds of young Italians, dark and skinny and beautiful, I imagined Lucia among the throng, Lucia before she met me, when she was a student at the university, chatting excitedly along the portico, all her hopes and plans and dreams. To escape, make it to a place where they didn't have to spray-paint their frustration upon the doors and walls. In Lucia's time it had been London, although how we'd met – as baristas for a high street coffee chain – hadn't exactly been top drawer career-wise, at least for her. I was actually undercover for the *Post* on a story aimed at exposing the working conditions, while she was simply happy to have found a job, along with the chance to practise her English. When she discovered the truth, she wasn't best pleased.

'You say me now? After we have sex?'

'I wanted to be honest with you.'

'And you couldn't have been honest before we fucked me? What's so funny? You think it's funny?'

I shook my head. 'I'm sorry,' I said. 'It's just what you said. I mean, an error . . . I mean . . .' Her nostrils flared. She looked ready to strike.

We were both naked, in bed, in *my* bed, thankfully, otherwise I expect she would have thrown me out. I held up my hands. 'Look, I'm really sorry. I should have. Of course I should have but . . . I like you. I didn't want to lose you.'

'But now we fucked me is okay?'

'Of course it's not. It just made me realise, even more, how I *didn't* want to lose you. How I want to be honest with you.'

'Anyway.' She pulled on her t-shirt. 'There's nothing wrong with how we work. It's normal!'

'It's not normal, Lucia,' I said. 'Zero hour contracts, no breaks. It's exploitation.'

'How can I be exploited if I'm happy?'

'I . . . *look*, the point is, the company brands itself as upmarket, ethically sourced, organic, you name it, but it treats its own people terribly. That's what my story will be about.'

'You British,' she said. 'If you think that's terrible, you should try Italy.'

Miraculously forgiven, miraculously married – a few years later we're on a one-way flight to Bologna, my commissions dried up and her salary at a charity hardly enough to pay the bills, never mind the rent. But I would write my book and make our fortune. We had it all worked out, didn't we, *amore mio*.

Hopes and plans and dreams.

Professoressa Finzi's office took some finding. Few of the buildings had been custom built for the university, even though it was almost a thousand years old. Over the years the institution had hopped from one old *palazzo* to another as noble families had risen and fallen and their homes had been squatted in, sold off or swallowed up. Welcome to Italian academia: at once itinerant and rooted, some might say stuck, in the past.

The *professoressa*'s office was a variation on this theme: sited along a corridor constructed under the frescoed ceiling of what had obviously once been a ballroom, judging from the stone seats built into the alcoves and the ancient, corroded mirrors studded between them. The wall of the offices, which ran from one end of the corridor to the other, stopped about half a metre beneath the ceiling as if it was only a temporary measure and in due course the dance would begin again.

'Come.'

Marta Finzi was sat behind a huge desk piled with books and papers, a pair of spectacles balanced imperiously upon her nose. She seemed startled to see me.

She pushed her chair back, plucked off the glasses, and straightened herself up. 'Please.' She indicated the chair on the other side of her desk.

'I apologise for the intrusion.'

She shook her head, surveying me intently. 'Not at all.' The *professoressa* cleared her throat. Over her shoulder I could see a courtyard littered with smoking students. I was partly reflected by the speckled mirrors on either side of her disappearing behind walls that didn't quite reach the end of the room. 'I was wondering, *signora*,' I said, 'what is your area of expertise?'

She looked surprised. 'Marx,' she said, 'Theory of Value.'

'I'm sorry,' I said, 'I'm not familiar with it.'

'Oh.' She shook her head. 'Don't worry. Few people are these days.'

'I'm sorry to hear that,' I said.

'Don't be,' she said, 'after all, it *is* Marx, and this is the twenty-first century.'

'There still seems to be a fair amount of revolution on the streets,' I said, 'at least here, in Bologna.'

'Not in England, though.' She crossed her arms. 'Germany, or France. Not *our kind* of revolution anyway. Bologna is like a time capsule. History has passed us by.'

'So, you lecture in Marx,' I said, 'and your husband has plainly been involved in politics for a long time. Was that how you came to know Signor Solitudine?'

Marta Finzi gazed toward a bookshelf full of tomes earnest young activists would once have pored over, or at least pretended to, then back at me. 'What's that got to do with the present, Daniel?'

'I'm just trying to build a picture, that's all. Did your husband know him then? I realise, as you say, that you have no reason to believe he was aware of your relationship now, but did he actually know Signor Solitudine in the past?'

She raised her hands before her mouth to make a steeple, viewing me above it as if from an infinite distance. Clearly, she was deciding what – how much – she wanted to tell me, which of course made me wonder, before she had even spoken, how much she was not going to tell me.

'We all knew each other when we were young,' she said, 'everyone knew each other. It was Bologna, it's a small city. Then . . . Carlo and I got married, we settled down. The others, well, we all went our different ways, like everyone else.'

'Forgive my impertinence, Signora Finzi, but did you have a relationship with Signor Solitudine back then?'

'I . . .' She shook her head. 'I mean, like I said, we were young, it was the seventies. There was a certain culture, in our circle . . . of free love.'

'So you did sleep with him?' She seemed lost in thought. 'Signora Finzi?'

'What?' She blinked. 'No.'

I waited to see if she would blurt out the truth, but she looked almost defiantly back at me. 'And Paolo,' I said. 'Signor Solitudine, I mean, he ended up in prison, didn't he?'

She nodded. 'I believe so, yes.'

'But you all remained in the same city. You must have bumped into each other, presumably that's how you got to know Signor Solitudine again.'

'Yes,' she said, 'obviously. Like I said, we knew *of* each other. Paolo and Mario continued down one road, everyone else took another.'

'Mario,' I said, 'you mean Mario Cento?'

Signora Finzi nodded. 'Of course, he and Paolo are famous in Bologna, *the 79ers*.' She sounded almost bitter. 'I see Mario has now taken Paolo's mantle . . . poor Mario, he must feel lonely.'

'Why lonely?'

'Well, they, the pair of them, sacrificed everything. Now there's only one left.'

'I met him,' I said, 'Mario Cento.'

'Oh?'

'Yes, he's claiming it was the police, but you know that. I also saw your husband speak,' I said, 'at Palazzo d'Accursio. About the future of the city.'

'You've been busy,' she said. She placed her still-laced hands upon her lap.

'On your behalf, Signora Finzi. I have been careful to itemise my hours.'

'Please,' she said, 'call me Marta.'

'Marta. I should have asked you this before, but considering his behaviour, and your affair with Signor Solitudine . . . I presume you have no reason to believe Signor Manzi might have been involved with anyone himself, now or in the past?'

Marta Finzi did not react. 'Have you?'

'At this point we are simply looking at the various scenarios,' I said. 'Given your suspicion is based principally on his recent behaviour, you can understand why it would be remiss of us not to consider this possibility.'

'Do you think this could have motivated him to kill Paolo?' she said. 'Why? If it was about divorce, then surely he would have wanted to get rid of me.' She spoke with the fluency of someone who had already thought this through. Did she already know about Manzi's affair? And, if so, why not tell us in advance? That much was simple – even if she knew, perhaps she was ashamed to admit that she had been allowing him to carry on. Better for us to discover and for her to play wounded . . . well, 'innocence' might be a bit of a stretch. I heard the Comandante in my ear: *Human emotions don't abide by the rules.*

'When you embarked upon your affair with Signor Solitudine,' I said, 'it was not something you undertook lightly – you told me you were very careful to keep things under wraps . . .'

Marta looked away again, and it may have been my imagination, but her profile against the window seemed fleetingly to crack, as if the truth was finally about to break through.

'What were you worried about, specifically?' I asked.

'The consequences,' she said, still in profile. 'I suppose. I mean, obviously.'

'His anger?'

Now she turned toward me, but her expression remained as inscrutable as before. 'It depends what you mean by "anger". I've never seen . . . What I mean is, I have never seen Carlo lose control . . . but that doesn't mean he wouldn't have shot us both.'

'Forgive me, but I'm not sure if you're joking.'

She shook her head. 'Neither am I, and that's the problem, no?'

I smiled as if that was, indeed, the problem, although it was not my only one.

'Anyway,' she said, 'have you found anything out?'

'We are beginning to build a picture of what happened that day,' I said, relieved to at last be on solid ground. 'And the most likely scenario.'

'Which is?'

I shifted in my seat. 'It's too early to say anything definitive, but I've taken a look in the canals and it is easy to see why the police believe he may have stumbled into the water, although only if he was in a hurry, for example with the police in pursuit, in which case then they probably know more than they are letting on.'

'But what about my husband?'

I thought about it, shook my head. 'I can't say that we have found anything that points directly to him at the moment.'

She nodded solemnly. 'And how long until you are able to give me a definitive answer?'

'Not long, I hope.' I took the envelope out of my case. 'I

was wondering, did Signor Solitudine ever mention property sales to you?'

Marta Finzi shook her head as I took the documents out.

'He accessed these from the Records Office a week before he went missing. You see one of them is for the sale of the hospital the anarchists are currently occupying, to this company – Omega Holdings.' Marta flicked through the pages.

'I've no idea,' she said.

'He never mentioned anything, about any research he was doing?'

'Nothing.'

I put the documents back.

'Do you think this could have had something to do with it?' she said. 'Why he was killed?'

I shrugged. 'I really can't say.'

We sat in silence. *Why did you lie to me about the past,* I was wondering, *and what else could you be lying about?*

She glanced at the clock behind me. 'Is that all? I mean –' she shook her head '– I have this marking.'

I stood up. 'I will keep you informed.'

'Thank you.' Marta Finzi gave me a tight smile. I went to open the door. When I glanced back, her head was already bent over the papers.

Chapter 15

I went to stand in a bar and take a coffee, casually glancing at the guy in a leather jacket who appeared to be inspecting watches in the jeweller's window across the street, and I wondered for how long I had been followed.

All I knew was that after I had left the university area, Leather Jacket – reflected in a shop window – had crouched down, apparently to do up the laces of his tan Caterpillar boots, while I dawdled at a crossing, only to get to his feet when I had moved off, shadowing me along two minor streets then onto Via San Vitale, where he had now, conspicuously, paused.

I had to assume he had seen me going into the university building, although once I passed under the threshold, I had been a bit twitchy about being spotted visiting a client in public, and I hadn't noticed anything, or anyone, out of the ordinary. But considering the halls were packed with students that's not to say there hadn't been.

How long? Panic prickled my skin. Could the Nonnies have ratted us out? It seemed unlikely – that was one of the reasons we hadn't shared any details with them. Massima? The

Comandante's contact at the Record Office? Giovanni trusted them. No, the most likely place was the squat. It was probably under observation and I'd picked the tail up from there.

I paid for my coffee and headed toward the two towers, stopping by the *gelateria* at the crossroads, ostensibly to hand a migrant stationed at the doorway fifty cents, but actually to see where Leather Jacket had got to, and, sure enough, there he was across the street, walking stiffly ahead as if he had a gun barrel poking in the back of his neck. I turned in the opposite direction, down Via Zamboni, then ducked into a trendy Scandinavian knick-knack store. I pretended to examine a pair of shark-themed rubber oven gloves while keeping an eye on the door and beyond. I didn't spot anything, but then I didn't expect to. Either the young woman or the couple who came in after me could be part of the team, or not. They certainly didn't appear to pay much attention to me, but that was kind of the point. Still, I took extra care to remember the woman – good looking, in her twenties, brushed back black hair, apparently interested in party packs of paper plates – not least because I had never encountered an unattractive Italian policewoman.

That was a question – was this private or public? An individual or team, even? I presumed a team, but perhaps I was flattering myself.

I left the store and continued along Zamboni at a stroll. I then turned sharply around, as if I had forgotten something, and headed back toward the store. I passed the young woman, apparently in deep conversation on her mobile telephone. I went back into the store, picked up the oven gloves and went to the cashier. When I emerged, the young woman was nowhere to be seen but, as I passed the open-air bar in Piazza Achille Ardigó, there was a man standing at the entrance, also apparently glued to his mobile, wearing a Bologna FC beanie hat and dark-blue Puffa jacket. His face was obscured, but his tan Caterpillars were not.

I headed further down Zamboni, under the porticoes and into the dimly lit Irish pub the Cluricaune, empty except for a table of becalmed foreigners – well, English tourists – already stacking up the empty pint glasses. I headed down to the toilets and locked myself in a cubicle.

The transformation of Leather Jacket into Puffa had told me I had a team on my trail, and one with back-up that could supply a change of costume. This wasn't some ad hoc thing, like Jacopo and I, it was co-ordinated, which indicated public rather than private – only the public sector had the time and resources to spare. The police, then, most likely.

I took out the envelope and laid it on the lid of the toilet. I removed the papers and took a photo of each page.

I attached the PDFs to an email, which I addressed to Alba. I wrote: *See attached docs for safe-keeping. Will explain later.*

I tried to send it but couldn't get a signal.

I put the papers back in the envelope, and the envelope in my case. I looked at the journal. I could hardly start photographing that. Anyway, it would take all day and they would guess something was amiss. I took out a plastic shopping bag and wrapped it up, tying it tight. It was the best I could do. I lifted the toilet cistern and laid it inside.

I opened the cubicle door half expecting to find a reception committee of *carabinieri*, but there was only a mountainous Brit swaying in front of the urinals.

I washed my hands and headed back upstairs.

I could see neither Puffa nor the woman, but I was sure I was not alone.

I ordered a pint of Guinness and sat on a stool at the bar, phone in hand, searching for a signal. I kept tapping send and it kept saying my attempt had failed. But I didn't want to wave it around in case someone realised what I was up to.

'Don't suppose you have wireless here?' I asked the barman in Italian.

'Sorry, mite,' he responded in heavily accented English.

In the bar mirror I spotted the woman from the Scandinavian store enter. Her hair was hanging down now and she was wearing a silver Puffa, but the same high-laced black boots.

Leather/Puffa, came in, only without the beanie, his gelled jet-black hair gleaming in the amber light. He went to stand beneath the flat screen TV so he was half-facing me.

Manchester United scored in a repeat of the weekend game and there was a muted cheer from the Brits. I didn't miss England much, I thought, even at times like this.

Someone came to sit beside me, resting their elbows upon the sticky wood surface of the bar. I felt the man turn to look at me.

I took a gulp of Guinness. 'This stuff,' I said in English, 'is the only thing worth drinking here.' I turned to face him and raised my glass.

It was the security guard who had been at the Mayor's speech, the one with the goatee, which struck me as oddly impermanent up close, as if it had been grown expressly to disguise him in the present, or to be shorn off in the future.

'I'm sorry,' I said in English, 'can I help you?'

'We can do this easy,' he said in Bolognese-accented Italian, 'or hard.' I felt someone step behind me. In the bar mirror, I saw Leather/Puffa jacket.

'Is this mayoral . . . or police business,' I asked in Italian. Goatee gave me a thin-lipped smile.

'Police,' he said.

'Ah,' I said. 'Then may I at least finish my pint?'

He shook his head.

I took out my wallet and waved to the barman. I gave him a ten – twice the price – and told him to keep the change. 'Just remember, my name is Daniel Leicester and I'm leaving with these police officers,' I said.

'Oh, he'll remember,' said Goatee, 'whatever we tell him, won't you, Giorgio.' The barman grinned.

'Certainly, Sergeant Romano.'

I noticed a dark-blue limo with tinted windows – the classic car of Italian officialdom – pull up outside the entrance.

'Let's go,' said Romano.

'Sergeant Romano,' I said, 'of the famous raid on the old hospital?'

'Get a move on,' he said.

I pocketed my phone and got up from the stool. The pair of them flanked me as I began to make my way out of the bar. Romano grabbed the case out of my hand, twisting my wrist as I tried to hold onto the handle and forcing me to let go.

The rear car door opened and I felt my phone vibrate four times.

A signal, at least, had finally been located.

I felt a hand on the crown of my head and was pushed into the car.

'Daniel Leicester.' He leaned across the seat to offer me a rough but manicured hand. He was one of the few Italians to have ever pronounced my name properly first time. 'Ispettore Umberto Alessandro.' Smartly turned out in a dark-blue suit and tie, with combed back, bountiful grey hair, and a Cartier Tank watch on his wrist, he was quite the contrast to Romano in his bomber jacket and jeans getting in the front and opening my case, a black plastic Casio visible beneath his sleeve.

The car pulled smoothly away. 'A pleasure to finally meet you,' he said. 'I am a former colleague of your father-in-law's.'

'Am I under arrest?'

Alessandro looked startled. 'Of course not, Daniel.'

'Then why's he going through my bag?'

'Police work,' he said.

The porticoes glided by. We turned onto the Viale. As long as the car didn't head away from the centre, I thought, I would be all right. 'Are you going to tell me then, what this is all about?'

'You know, I am seeing your father-in-law shortly.'

'And it couldn't have waited until then?'

'I didn't want there to be any ... misunderstandings. We're one big happy family, aren't we?'

Technically, I couldn't disagree – these days the main thrust of Giovanni's detective work seemed to centre around the *osterie* near the Questura, and at least half of our jobs came as referrals from his old cronies. On the other hand, like many a seemingly happy family, there were the ones that held the purse strings, and the ones that eyed the purse.

'And yet, you were you having me followed.'

'We placed you under surveillance,' Alessandro spoke as if he was reporting to a magistrate, which he may have done, 'as part of our investigation into the death of Paolo Solitudine.'

'I didn't think you *were* investigating it.' I said. 'Maybe you should tell . . .' I was going to say our contact at the Questura. 'The press. It might quieten the anarchists down.'

'You were a journalist, weren't you, Daniel?' said Alessandro. 'You know not to believe everything you read in the newspapers, and the reds certainly don't need any encouragement. An investigation was opened as soon as the body was discovered, although that does not mean,' he smiled, 'the death is necessarily being treated as suspicious.'

'You mentioned "misunderstandings", Ispettore.'

'Well, since you mention the elections, we were wondering why you were asking about the Mayor's movements on the same day that Signor Solitudine disappeared.'

'You mean the day –' I glanced at Romano '– the police attacked the hospital? Did no one see our missing anarchist? Not even the gentleman in the front there, while he was directing operations under a blue helmet?'

Romano turned around. 'Neither sight,' he said, 'nor sound.'

'We don't need this, Daniel,' said Alessandro, 'you're right – with the elections, it's the last thing we need. But what has the Mayor got to do with it?'

'How do you know my questions had anything to do with Paolo Solitudine?'

'Give us some credit. One: you go around town announcing you are investigating the death of Paolo Solitudine. Two: you appear at a mayoral event asking questions that pertain to the Mayor's movements on that day.'

I thought about the anarchists . . . the circle at the Osteria della Luna . . . I wondered which one of them was on the police books. Or how many. I began to feel a little bit sick.

'It's . . . confidential,' I said. Alessandro looked amused.

'That's not how things work here, Daniel,' he said. 'You're in Italy now – confidentiality . . . well, it has its degrees.'

'Maybe you're right,' I said, 'I'm a foreigner. I'm not familiar with your ways, so you'll forgive me if I defer that question to your meeting with the Comandante.'

'And exiting the university building, where the Mayor's wife works . . .'

I noticed Romano had pulled the envelope out of the bag and begun going through the papers.

'That's enough,' I leaned forward and also spotted my phone on his lap. How had he got hold of that? 'Tell him to give it back,' I said.

'*Basta*, Sergeant.' Romano begrudgingly returned the phone. The briefcase, I noted, he did not. 'Tell me,' said Alessandro. 'Really, what does the Mayor's wife have to do with your investigation?'

'Who's to say she has any connection?'

Alessandro sighed. 'We Italians, Daniel, we love to gossip. We are not discreet like you English. That's why information has a tendency to worm its way into public here in a fashion that would, I believe, be unthinkable in England. And once it becomes news, no matter how inaccurate –' he shook his head

'– it somehow transforms itself, as if by magic, into *fact*. And facts have consequences.'

The car had stopped in the traffic by the railway station. We watched the travellers flow across the traffic lights. 'A private investigator asking around town about a dead anarchist, about the Mayor, about his wife . . . well, frankly I'm surprised it's not already on the front page of the *Carlino di Bologna*.' He shrugged. 'Who knows,' he said, 'someone might even be writing a play.'

I felt my throat tighten. 'Ispettore Alessandro,' I said slowly. 'If anything should happen to Signora Finzi, I will not forget we had this conversation.'

The lights turned green, our car moved forward. I could see the driver hesitating as we approached the junction with the bridge out to Bolognina.

Alessandro gave an almost imperceptible shake of his head. 'Marconi,' he said. We turned into the centre and drove in silence along the first part of the road. At the roundabout Alessandro said, 'Why on earth should anything happen to Marta Finzi, Daniel?'

The car pulled up outside our office. I waited until my case had been given back. I opened the door.

'I won't forget,' I said.

Chapter 16

I stepped out of the lift. 'Bastards,' I said.

'What's that?' Alba looked up from behind her computer.

'Bastards, *bastards*.'

'What wrong, Daniel?'

'He took my SIM card,' I said. 'Hold on.' I checked my bag. The envelope was still there, but when I opened it, it was empty. I shook my head. 'Idiots,' I said.

'Who?'

'The police.'

'The police stole your SIM card?'

'Never mind,' I said. 'Look, Alba, could you check some documents for me. I've already emailed them over. Or at least I should have, if everything went according to plan.' She nodded without comment or complaint. I didn't feel great about shoving the paperwork in her direction, but there was no doubt her grasp of officialese went well beyond mine: the impenetrability of Italian bureaucracy was the nation's last line of defence.

'Jacopo,' I said, coming into the office where he had on a pair of headphones and was playing a video game, 'good to see you're hard at work.' He looked around.

'What?' he mouthed. I took off the headphones.

'You're not busy,' I said, 'good. I've got an important job for you: I need you to go to the pub.' I told him what happened and to watch his back. I didn't know whether to believe Alessandro about ending the tail, but I doubted even the cops would have the resources or interest to go after Jacopo, particularly if he left by the rear and took his Vespa. 'But first, I guess that since you're exterminating the undead you've finished cataloguing Anna Bellidenti's life?'

'Just finished, actually,' he said. 'I sent you a report.'

'Highlights?'

'Her phone,' he said, 'was full of it. Two-way, three-way messages between her and Manzi and Chiara. Two-way it's mostly her complaining to him . . .' He clicked to another tab on his computer screen and the raw text came up. '"I'm bored and I'm fat. I hate being fat! I should never have listened to you. I'm so lonely here. When are you coming to see me? You don't care!!!" Now him: "Darling, of course I care! You know your wellbeing is the most important thing. Is there anything you need? Anything I can get you? Anything at all?" Her: "I saw a juicer on PWC. It's by Alessi. It could come in handy, for the nutrition of the baby. Your son." It goes on and on like this,' said Jacopo. 'She complaining that she's fat and lonely then asking him to cough up for something.'

'Not a very warm relationship, then,' I said.

'Transactional,' he said. I gave him a curious look. 'I minored in psychology, remember?'

'Nothing discussing problems with his wife?' I said. 'Or wanting to get rid of her? Or anyone else? Anyone threatening to expose them? Promises along the "soon all our troubles will be over" lines, and so on?'

'Nothing like that . . . just she moans, she asks, she gets. Except, on the afternoon Solitudine went missing.' He scrolled down. 'From her: "I'm here, inside."'

'From him?' I said.

'No answer,' said Jacopo.

'What time was that?'

'Two fifteen, in the afternoon,' he said.

'And the raid took place around twelve,' I said. 'Good work. Off you go then, but don't have anything more than a pint for appearances sake – I want you to bring the journal back here in one piece. And yourself too.'

I switched on my computer and checked that my email to Alba had gone through, then that my SIM contacts were where they should be, and was grateful to Jacopo for constantly nagging me to back up everything on the Cloud.

I opened an email from Massima. It was about the scarf I had found. As she feared, the river water had eliminated the possibility of extracting viable DNA, but in her opinion the stains were consistent with blood. 'That would certainly be my bet,' she wrote.

I thought of Marta Finzi in her kitchen, running her hands through her hair. The scarf hanging between her fingertips with its dancing dragon; the one I had sent to Massima from the area where Paolo Solitudine had been fished out of the water – another oriental design, circles like coins bearing intricate markings. The kind of keepsake a lover would carry, and the provenance of which could be confirmed by a simple question to Signora Finzi. But I wasn't going to ask her just yet. There was something that was not right. Why would she have lied about her earlier relationship with Paolo? What was she trying to conceal? If Manzi had found out all those years ago, for example, it could provide us with a semblance of motive, if a very slow-burning one. Surely she wouldn't have been embarrassed about revealing those details when she had not hesitated to confess her most recent tryst.

Something didn't add up, so I would hold off on revealing too much to the client before I could see where this was heading.

I opened another tab on my browser and clicked through to the PD website where Carlo Manzi was scheduled to give a hustings speech in front of the main post office, a handsome *fin de siècle* edifice that had been obscured by trees until the Comune had pulled them down to show off the building, prompting some controversy. The trees had provided shade during the summer and from June to September the benches were now bare, save for hardy tourists wondering where all the people had gone.

But today, beneath the mild autumnal blue sky, the square was crowded with party loyalists waiting to hear from their leader. The view switched to an empty plinth, with the post office as its backdrop. A political functionary stepped up and fiddled with the microphone, another – the Star Girl, Chiara Delfiori – stepped up with a sheaf of papers. Finally the sound came on and there was a smattering of applause. The screen switched back to the gathering of apparatchiks then to Manzi stepping up to the platform and waving down the applause with an embarrassed smile.

'You are too kind, too kind . . .' He adjusted the microphone. 'Friends,' he said, nodding. 'Friends. What a beautiful
day to spend in a beautiful piazza with,' he grinned, 'such
beautiful people.' Laughter. 'Does it get much better than
this?' He nodded. 'Does it? Of course! Of course it does. Over
the past five years we have seen Bologna transform from a
city considered as something of a . . .' He shrugged. 'Let's
face it, an *afterthought* by Rome, by the regions. Overseas?
Would they have even known we existed were it not for our
famous – although never dare request it, at your peril, here! –
Bolognese sauce? I swear, to much of the world we were known
best for an American sausage or the name on the side of a jar!
And now? Just four years later we have cleaned up the old
buildings, we have cleaned up –' he opened his arms '– the
piazzas. Bologna, the city of enterprise, has reinvented itself,
yet again, and we are *all* the richer for it.' Applause. 'But,' he
said, looking suddenly quizzical, 'friends, comrades, is this
enough?' He shook his head. 'Is it? Of course it's not! Alas,
I am old enough to remember when we held higher ideals.
The spirit of sixty-eight. Really – is this what we manned the
barricades for?'

'When he says sixty-eight,' said Alba, who had wandered
in to stand behind me, 'does he mean how old they all are?'

I turned around, expecting to find her smiling, but she was
straight-faced. I shook my head. 'The year,' I said, '1968, the
year of revolution, although when they were actually man-
ning the barricades, even Carlo Manzi must have still been
at school . . .'

'What revolution?' said Alba.

I turned back to the computer, increased the volume.

' . . . a fairer Bologna, a Bologna in which everyone, man and woman, straight and gay, rich and poor, native-born or tossed onto our shores from the Mediterranean, has an equal say, an equal stake . . .'

'And equal pay!' Although the camera remained on Manzi, it was clearly a heckler in the audience. The Mayor grinned.

'Magari,' he said. *I wish.* There was laughter. Then more shouting. Manzi, his eyes darting from side to side, managed to keep the grin plastered across his face. 'You see,' he said, 'that is the difference between who we were then and who we are now. We have learned that, despite our best wishes, it is not so simple. It is about more than slogans, it is about rolling up our sleeves and making the kind of choices that won't go down well in the Osteria della Luna . . .' He frowned as there was more shouting, met by boos, presumably from his supporters. Then a boom, so loud it cut out the sound of the broadcast and was audible in our office more than a kilometre away. Manzi had flinched, ducking briefly behind the lectern, but now began to straighten up, shaking his head. He continued speaking into the microphone, but the sound was still out and smoke had begun to waft across the screen.

'Bomb?' said Alba.

I shook my head. 'Banger,' I said. I shrugged. 'Big one.' The screen went blank.

Jacopo returned with the journal and Guinness breath. I left him to his video game and slipped out of the building by the back exit.

I walked down Via Riva di Reno where, I noted, work had stopped for the day. They were opening the street up – quite literally. Fifty years ago, a canal had flowed along this thoroughfare before being paved over to make way for the march of the automobile. Now it was being returned to its former glory, regardless of the disruption to traffic, as part of Manzi's plan to evoke 'a new Venice'. Before, I had hardly noticed it, but now everything bore fresh significance. I stopped by a letterbox-size opening in the boarding and looked into the building site. I couldn't see much in the dimming light, just some rubble and the sound, if one really strained, of running water. Beside the opening was a sign that read: THE OMEGA GROUP, REBUILDING BOLOGNA BRICK BY BRICK.

I turned down Via Galliera, which had been one of the most sought after addresses in the city when palaces had been all the rage. While retaining its beauty, it had now become a sort of Bolognese Sunset Boulevard. Despite the 'rush hour' traffic of pedestrians along the grand porticoes, the *palazzi* were, on the whole, uninhabitable. The rooms were too large, too expensive to heat, too dark . . . and their status as historic monuments made them more or less untouchable. So it was mostly offices now, on short leases – until they could afford somewhere more convenient to move to.

I stopped at a bar, ordered a Montenegro. Sat on one of the stools placed outside for smokers and watched the world go by. But this was no *passeggiata*. The dark-clad Bolognese could match Londoners stride for stride. It was not so much a parade, as in the South – of display, and judgement – more a high-speed catwalk, with the models focused solely upon themselves, and the end of the runway.

Rebuilding Bologna, I thought, *brick by brick*. No, this was certainly not the South, where the State comported itself, and was largely treated, as a kind of colonial power. Those tropes did not, on the whole, apply here. Emilia-Romagna was a veritable industrial powerhouse, the home of Ferrari and Lamborghini, and on its own as rich as Luxembourg. And yet . . . this *was* Italy. Everything was connected, as surely as the south was connected to the north.

A coincidence that Omega was buying the hospital and was behind this other piece of public work? For sure, a proper process would have taken place to award the contracts, and it was unlikely anything so crude as cash had changed hands. But . . . there was something under every stone, as Paolo Solitudine may have found out.

I thought of Anna Bellidenti, hidden away in that apartment. Marta Finzi, with a secret lover of her own, and of the secrets she had chosen not to share.

Sergeant Romano – a nasty piece of work, but not stupid. *'Neither sight, nor sound.'*

Alessandro, that almost imperceptible shake of his head. *'Marconi.'*

You're investigating the death of Paolo Solitudine, Ispettore, but what is it, precisely, you want to find out?

I thought of Manzi, at the pinnacle. I looked at his picture on the leaflet I carried around with me. What did you have to do, what kind of person would you have to be, to get there?

'A transactional relationship.'

And what made Marta Finzi so afraid of you?

I paid for my drink and continued on toward the two towers. Police were everywhere, the taint of tear gas still in the air. The spirit of sixty-eight, I thought. Or seventy-nine?

Chapter 17

I want to set this down now, so I never forget: Carlo was in Trento for the weekend. M was supposed to be in Milan with friends. Nobody cared about me — I could disappear for days and no one would notice. Well, Mario, yes, but I told him I was visiting my parents.

It was her late grandmother's place in Monte San Pietro. It used to be a farm — the old buildings around the main house are all tumbled down, there's a hayloft and everything. There are still stakes lined up along a field with their withered vines, an orange grove heavy with fruit.

Lying with you, Marta, in your grandmother's bed. Let now be forever, I thought, let us never leave this island. Naked across each other, sticky with sweat. The bee trapped inside the window. The wildflower still tangled in your hair. Tracing the path around your nipples with my tongue.

Dawn. Walking barefoot through the pasture. You shrug off your dress, step naked into the lake, and I hesitate, looking around, but of course, there is no one. I try not to flinch at the cold! Your playful smile: 'Come on . . . come on . . .' I have never felt so cold, but you drew me in, you drew me deeper and wrapped your legs around me, raised your arms and cast yourself backwards. I began to levitate, resting back myself, the pair of us joined, conjoined in the lake. Theophrastus on the hermaphrodite: the joining, conjoining, the masculine, feminine – the symbol of marriage, made sacred by our sacrament of the lake. I would have loved to have told you what I was thinking – I didn't dare tell you.

11 March 1979. *When I call Mum she says, did you hear about that boy who was shot in Turin? You're not getting involved in any of that 'nonsense' are you? I try to explain – it was Prima Linea who had claimed responsibility, apparently an off-shoot of La Lotta Continua. They were after some policeman and he was caught in the crossfire, an accident, poor guy. 'So, Mum,' I said, 'I'm not planning on joining the police, I assure you.' She didn't get it.*

28 April 1979. *There's only a month to go before the end of the season and Bologna are still in the running for the UEFA cup. We had Fiorentina at home, and they were only three points ahead. 'If you had to choose,' I asked Mario as we watched from the stands, 'would you rather we qualified for the Cup or ended the season ahead of Fiorentina?' 'What kind of fan do you think I am?' he replied. 'Above Fiorentina of course!' We were holding on 1–0 at the end, and Mario was quite a wonder to behold, his eyes squeezed shut, grasping his baptism medal close to his lips while praying to all the saints – including San Petronio – for victory. When we had managed to make it, he gave a special thanks to the Holy Mother. 'Some kind of Marxist you are,' I said.*

3 May 1979. *A dozen Brigate Rosse attack the Christian Democrat HQ in Rome. Two cops dead, one wounded.*

3 June 1979. Carlo eyes me coolly, as if he knows everything. Then he says, like a priest, 'Tell me, Paolo, how are things?' What, like I'm fucking Marta, I want to say? Did he even see me thinking that? – 'Your studies, and so on.' I felt like I was having a meeting with my supervisor, which I suppose he could be if I was part of the sociology faculty. 'All right,' I said. 'You should keep them up,' he said, 'it is easy to get distracted by our political activity, but look around you, what do you see?' I looked around. We were in a bar on Zamboni. 'Students?' I said. 'That's right,' he said. 'They are studying, but they are not <u>acting</u>. You don't want to become, through missing your exams, a permanent student. There are already too many of them here. Useless idlers. The revolution will need qualified people, engineers, doctors, what is it you are studying again? Philosophy, is it?' He smirked. I wanted to say fuck you – and you think the world needs more sociologists? And I am fucking your girlfriend! Then he said: 'And certainly philosophers, to make sense of our world.' And in his eyes I detected a certain warmth, a compassion, I hadn't seen before. It sounds crazy, but I suddenly wanted to <u>weep</u> for this compassion, I suddenly wanted to take his hand, to bow down and kiss it! I suddenly understood the depths that stood behind this individual who, true, had always been impressive, but for the first time, I glimpsed what I really thought was special about him, what he keeps hidden behind that sardonic veil, what he must share in his private moments, here, with me, for example, with <u>Marta</u> – finally I understood what it is that he keeps concealed, as one must if one is to prosecute the revolution, if one is to lead, to take the necessary measures for future generations: it is his <u>love</u>. This is what ties Marta to him, what binds me, all of us, perhaps, what is needed from a leader. I felt so loved *in that moment, and at the same time I felt so terribly, terribly unworthy. I felt like a Judas.*

I looked up. La Luna was full, heaving. I imagined Carlo's group gathered around one of these tables in their denim and flares, excited, beautiful as only youth can be, plotting the revolution that was just around the corner. More of a fug of cigarette smoke back then, of course, but apart from that, little else would have changed. The same bad art on the walls, the same drunks, simply grown young. That one, already slumped, face-forward in front of a wall featuring yellowed newspaper clippings and dusty old photos of communist gatherings, resting his forehead upon his arms, what was his sad story? But as I passed him, I realised I already part knew it – it was the old boy, Franco, the foul-mouthed sea dog.

I was sliding past him when he toppled off his chair and onto the floor.

I crouched down beside him, others crowding around us. He was lying on the floor much as he had on the table, his head cushioned by his forearms, his old body heaving, still asleep.

'For Christ sake, Franco.' It was one of the barmen, leaning over us. He helped me lift him back onto the chair.

'Via Gerusalemme 15,' Franco mumbled, his head slumping forward like a newborn's.

'I'm not carrying you home,' said the barman. 'Not again. I've got work to do.' He looked at us. 'Anyone going that way?'

The kids all looked at their feet or each other. It wasn't on my way, but Via Gerusalemme was only around the corner.

I was about to volunteer when two loud popping sounds

came from the front of the bar. White smoke began to billow towards us. The crowd let out a collective gasp and started to scramble out of the way.

Within moments the entire *osteria* was filled with smoke. Ahead of me, transformed into shadows by the fog, I could see there was a rush to get out of the front door, people pressing forward, coughing, shouting. Shrieks pierced the air as people stumbled, panicked in the crush.

Space opened around me but I held back. Experience had taught me to keep apart from the crowd at times like this. I noticed Franco was on the floor again and bent to pull him up. Only this time he wasn't unconscious, he was on all fours. He looked up at me with bleary eyes. 'There's air down here,' he croaked. I got down. He was right.

'It'll get worse,' he said.

'What do you mean?'

'They'll be waiting,' he said. He nodded toward the front door then looked in the direction of the toilets. 'Come on,' he said, and began crawling towards them. I hesitated, but I didn't like the look of the bottleneck at the front – I would take my chances with the old drunk.

We had almost made it to the battered, graffiti-covered entrance to the toilets. The smoke was thinning and I was helping Franco onto his feet when I heard more screams, realised whatever it was Franco had been saying was true. The crowd at the door was surging backwards into the bar, crashing into scattered chairs and tables, smashing bottles and glasses and stumbling over each other as they rushed in our direction. Through the front door I could see the silhouettes of the police, their batons striking downwards.

I followed Franco through the entrance to the toilets. He passed them and headed for a door marked private. 'There,' he said, lifting up the handle and giving it a push. 'Installed it myself when Barrio was in charge. Saves having to lock and unlock it, you see, but still keeps out nosey parkers.'

It was a narrow room with barrels and bottles lined on either side, along with all the usual detritus associated with running a bar. I followed him to the end where there was another door, bolted from the inside. Behind us I could hear the incoherent noise of terror. Franco unbolted the door. 'Course,' he said, 'they could be waiting here too. Still, eh?' He unbolted the door and it opened out onto an empty lane. We stepped into it just as the crowd found their way into the room behind us. They stumbled outside, yelling, coughing and making a hell of a row.

'No point hanging around,' Franco said brightly. He looked ready to set off but then his eyelids came down like store shutters, his legs gave way. I managed to catch him just in time. His eyes opened again, seeing but unseeing, his previously vivid face blunted as if back in a dream. He gave me a woozy smile.

'Franco,' I said.

'Via Gerusalemme 15.'

Chapter 18

4 July 1979. Antonio, who is a quiet sort, picked me up in his car. He's always struck me as one of those on the fringes and does not play much of a part in our discussions. Yet Carlo appears to trust him – it is always Antonio who is doing the legwork, who has got the leaflets ready, the banners, sets up the projector, looks after the logistics. Each according to their ability, says Mario, and he's probably got a point – Antonio seems happy in his own quietly industrious way. 'Nice car,' I said, although it wasn't anything special, just a Fiat 128, but still as fastidiously clean and tidy as I would somehow expect from Antonio. 'I bought it from my earnings,' he said. There was a southern lilt to his voice. 'From the packaging factory.' 'You were working, then?' I said. 'It took me a while to cotton on,' he said, looking straight ahead, 'education is power.' That all added up, why he focused on getting things done, why he preferred to keep his mouth shut. 'If you ever have any questions,' I said, 'about theory, I mean, Marxist theory, or anything else, you can always ask me, in confidence, I mean.' Now he looked at me, seemingly amused. 'Thanks,' he said, and returned his eyes to the road.

Where was that music coming from? Over and over it played – a piano riff . . . what was it? *The opening of an old Paolo Conte track* . . . Then I realised. I scrambled for my phone.

'Dad?'

'Rose?'

'Where are you?'

'Via Gerusalemme . . .' I thought about it, 'fifteen.' I was propped up on a sofa, fully dressed, while sun forced a dusty haze into the shuttered room. 'That song,' I said. 'I didn't realise it was my phone. I told you not to play with it.'

'It's your favourite song! I thought you would like it!'

'Is everything all right?'

'That's what I was going to ask you! Why aren't you here?'

I looked at the table, the bottle of Montenegro, the empty glass. The old-style TV, the battered armchair, the mantelpiece crowded with knick-knacks, walls covered with photographs of family, line-ups at political and social gatherings, drawings and photos of building projects. A portrait of Stalin. 'I had to follow up a lead,' I said, 'got stuck at a contact's.'

'*You're with a woman!*'

'Sadly, no.' I sat up. 'I'm sorry I'm not there, sweetheart. Really, I got distracted—'

'I hope you used condoms!' The phone went dead.

'Good read, is it?' Franco was standing in the doorway in a filthy white t-shirt, baggy sweatpants and slippers.

'I fell asleep,' I said, 'having delivered you here.'

'And drinking my booze, I see,' he said.

'Just a sip,' I said.

'I suppose you'll be wanting some of my coffee too.' He shuffled past and went into the kitchen. I checked my watch

– Rose would be out before I could make it home. Feeling like a suitably terrible father, I followed him through.

'You were in quite a state last night,' I said. 'Is that how you usually get home?' I nodded to a wheelchair folded up against the wall.

'It's from the social centre,' he said. 'I volunteer, take the cripples for a spin.'

'They must love the conversation.'

'Coffee?' He placed the *moka* on the ancient hob. Everything was spick and span, although worn within an inch of its life.

'An impressive collection of certificates,' I said, 'you were an educated man.'

'*Were*?'

'I mean,' I said, 'I had you down as some kind of ex-navy, a fisherman—'

'*Were*. I'm not dead yet, you know. I'm an engineer,' he said. 'A chief engineer, since you're interested, which you're not, of course. It's just your way – to dig. I found out what you are – a private detective, a leech for the ruling class in other words. Couldn't you do something useful?'

'Do you know a girl called Dolores?' I said.

'Who?'

'Never mind,' I said. 'Wife not about, then?'

'Dead,' he said.

'Well, that's something we have in common.'

'About the only thing,' he said.

'You're a laugh a minute in the mornings,' I said. He gave me a toothless smile. 'You used to be a dedicated Communist, Franco. Tell me more about those times.'

'Is this to do with that book you're reading? Looks like someone's diary, as if you're poking your nose into someone else's business.'

'You may be grumpy in the mornings, but you're sharp,' I said.

'We lost,' he said, 'that's the "narrative", isn't it. We lost, we were "wrong" . . . but, tell me, is the world we live in today as good as it's going to get?'

'Is that a rhetorical question, Franco?'

'Do you give a shit about anything? Or is everything a joke to you?'

'If I didn't laugh,' I said, 'I'd cry.'

'I don't know what you're complaining about,' he said, 'you've got the little girl, that's not nothing.'

'Well,' I said, 'I must be the gossip of the Osteria della Luna. No wonder the police appear to know my every move. It's not you that's been having a word in their lughole, is it?'

Franco didn't even look offended – I realised the notion of him being an informer was so self-evidently inconceivable. 'That's what they never understood – they thought they were so clever, those so-called "revolutionaries" of Brigate Rosse, La Prima Linea, all the rest,' he said, 'but by working, as they saw it, outside the system, they were in the world of the criminals, and that is also the world of the police. In the legitimate movement, we could sniff the odd turncoat out, not least because it was tough to fake an enthusiasm for *Das Kapital*. I mean, have you tried reading the thing?

'But there – in the world of robberies, riots, kidnaps, murders, they required a different sort of person. The kind who didn't care much about the cost, wasn't much interested in the cause. The type that was looking for any excuse to make a bit of trouble, get their kicks, grab what they could for themselves. But the police knew how to deal with that sort, could manipulate them, use them,' he shrugged, 'for their own purposes.'

'Did you have much to do with Paolo Solitudine and Mario Cento back then, Franco?'

He shook his head: 'What do you think?'

Chapter 19

Mario emerged from the house, lumbering toward us with his belly full of Mama's cooking. Antonio, who had sat there most of the time looking ahead in a kind of trance while Radio Radicale droned on, brightened up and got out of the car to greet him. The pair clasped hands, embracing like old friends.

Mario and Antonio seem cut from the same cloth, even though Mario is the son and grandson of pharmacists. Despite emerging from lunch at this upmarket address, he seemed to have no sense of embarrassment, no problem, in fact, affecting proletarian airs while I, the son of factory workers, struggle: I'm the one that sounds bourgeois, patronising. I wear my identities like ill-fitting suits – perhaps that is what it really means to be born into privilege: the suit always fits.

We drove out to Monte San Pietro, the windows wound down, the warm air blowing in. Today I truly wished I was at the beach instead of here, I wished I was anywhere, in fact, but here, not because I had lost faith in the cause but because we were going to Marta's farm, and it would not be just the two of us, it would be invaded, overrun.

'Marco' and 'Patricia', the new arrivals call themselves, but

Carlo has made it clear that these are code names. They are a little older than us, about Carlo's age, and it is clear they all go some way back from the quiet appreciation they show for each other, compared to their chilly attitude towards the rest of us. Both are from Trento and have that almost-German look: large boned, blue eyed, pale skinned, oh how we've seen a lot of that, given the way they like parading around naked as if it is the most natural thing . . . and the others act as if it is, except, that is, Antonio and me, the true proles.

Carlo briefed us before we departed: they are on the run (for what? The actions in Turin? Rome? Something else?) and on their way to France to lie low. Our role is simply to 'normalise' their presence there – everyone in the village knows everyone else's business (or thinks that they do) and that this is Marta's place, etc., so our job is simply to act as if we are holding some kind of workshop here, so these two – 'Marco' and 'Patricia' – are considered simply a part of that. Innocent students doing heaven knows what crazy stuff, but presumably harmless. Everyone in the village loves and admires (like good peasants) Marta's family, and particularly 'La Principessa' as one old crone called her, so once it is gilded by her presence, no questions will be asked. As for 'the Germans', as I tend to think of them, Carlo told us: 'Don't speak to them', and that's all right as they don't seem inclined to speak to us!

I'm sharing a tent with Antonio and Mario (who goes to sleep as soon as he lays his head down and snores like a contented baby, while Antonio turns away and is silent and deathly still) and through the flaps I watch Marta and Carlo enter their own. I stay awake half the night straining to hear the noise of their love making, but there's only Mario's high-pitched squeaks and the steady buzz of the cicadas, which could muffle an army. And I wonder about that: I wonder whether we are being watched in the night, if our tents will be shredded by the gunfire of machine-gun-wielding carabinieri, then I think about lazing on the beach, sipping lemonade; the buzz of the cicadas, the hush of the waves, and . . . it is the morning.

I crawl out of the tent on my knees, the baked ground already warm to the touch. I watch Marta leaving her tent, walk bare-foot down to the lake. She pulls off her t-shirt, steps out of her panties, enters the water. She raises her hands above her head and arches her back, precisely one half of our hermaphrodite, before reclining into the water and floating there, the tops of her breasts and the thickness of her pubic hair visible above the still, green water. Then I realise, Carlo is standing in his trunks at the opening of their tent, a towel over his arm, watching me.

I look down at the ground, then across to the smouldering remains of the fire, which I prod with a stick. I look up only when I hear the sound of splashing water – Carlo has dived in, Marta is laughing.

The kids began to stream out of the school. I put the journal in my pocket and made my way over.

'What are you doing here?'

'Is she still angry with me, do you think, Stefania?' Stefania guffawed and hid behind her smartphone. 'Would you like to join us for lunch?' I asked.

Stefania guffawed again.

'Dad, you're embarrassing her. You're embarrassing me!'

'Isn't that what dads are for?'

'Does Alba know?' Alba would usually be cooking for Rose, if not us all.

'I gave Alba the day off,' I said. 'Is that a "no" then, Stefania?' I spotted Stefania's mum emerge from her white SUV, double-parked, naturally, and completely blocking the roundabout.

'Daniel!' She gave me a dramatic embrace, fitting to her station as *One of the Poor Englishman's Daughter's Friend's Mothers*. 'I just wanted to say how much we love having your darling Rose over at ours, she's such a sweetie, and –' she straightened up and I could see what was coming next '– she has teach us such *wormerful* English!'

'You are very kind,' I said, in Italian. Cars began to back up behind her SUV and horns sounded, but she appeared oblivious.

'I hear you are investigating the death of this anarchist. Do you know who did it? I simply presumed it was the police . . .'

'Word gets around,' I said. I glanced at Rose who was suddenly fascinated with the messages on her smartphone. 'Well,' I said, 'the jury's out, I suppose you could say. But, Cristina, I wouldn't necessarily conclude that simply because we have been engaged to look into a certain matter there is any more to it than there appears to be, so to speak. A client's a client . . .'

'Oh, I know exactly what you mean,' she said. 'Money talks!'

'Something like that . . .' Having tired of hooting, a couple of drivers had got out of their automobiles and were now peering into the SUV. 'I think,' I said, 'perhaps—'

'Oh! Hey! Don't touch my car!' She grabbed Stefania and tottered toward them, waving her free arm and batting back their insults. I wondered how much time she had expended on preparing for the school run – well, she might as well make the most of it.

We went to American Graffiti, a faux-sixties diner at the end of Via Ugo Bassi. 'There's no need to look so glum, Rose,' I said as she examined the menu, 'now you're here you may as well enjoy yourself. You know I only take you on birthdays and when I have to apologise.' Rose looked up immediately.

'You're forgiven,' she said, then looked down again.

'Look,' I said, 'I even took a video to prove I was not with some fancy lady this morning.' I waved my smartphone beneath her nose.

'*Dad.*'

I could hear Franco saying: 'Your father asked me to explain where he was last night . . .'

'*Dad.*' She batted it away as I heard Franco say: '. . . drunk.'

'Well, it's there if you don't believe me. I'll have a bacon cheeseburger,' I told the waitress, 'and she will have a Tuscany burger.'

'How do you know that?' said Rose.

'It's what you always have.'

'Let me look at that.' I played her the video again.

'Who's he?'

'Like he says, a worthless old drunk. I bumped into him in the Osteria della Luna and took him home because he couldn't look after himself, and then I fell asleep. I'm sorry, Rose, it was wrong of me not to be there this morning.'

'That's all right.'

'No,' I said, 'it's not really. Even if I was with a fancy woman, I should have let you know, at the very least.'

'It's all right.'

'Surely, you mean, it's "wormerful".' Rose began to blush. I shook my head. 'I get it, Rose, but Stefania's a real friend of yours, and all girls need friends. You piss her mother off by teaching her the wrong words and embarrassing her when she speaks to someone sometime in the future and she's going to tell her friends and they're going to say that you're a girl that can't be trusted. Despite your complaints she does do a lot for you, and that'll mean no more invitations to parties, outings, the ballet . . . I know they can be a pain, some of them, but they mean well, these women. If you embarrass them, though . . . then I imagine they could act just like little girls.'

Rose sighed but said nothing.

'I don't want to see you unhappy, that's all,' I said, 'because I love you. As for,' I said, 'this other thing . . .'

Now Rose looked at me. 'I only said to Stefania . . .'

'And Stefania told her mother.'

'I told her not to tell anyone! After I'd said it . . .' Rose knew that she was forbidden to talk about work. In fact, we made an effort not to say too much in front of her, but it was easy to forget she had such sensitive antennae – maybe that detective gene ran in the family after all.

'We have to take responsibility too,' I said, 'we should be careful about what we say, but look – we don't want word to get around that we make public what we're working on, because people come to us on a confidential basis.'

'It was only Stefania!'

'Who told her mother, who doubtless told her friends.

These people are our potential clients. Think of it like this – it's because of the money I make from *keeping secrets* that I can buy us lunch today. It's our secrets that pay for your subscription to *X Factor*. Got it?' She nodded. She'd got it. She furrowed her brow.

'What did you want from Dolores, at the farm?' she said. 'She's so *cool*, isn't she?'

Great, I thought, now my daughter was treating a pierced *punkabbestia* as a role model. Still, better that than dreaming of getting stars tattooed up your neck and pimping for people in high places.

Chapter 20

7 July 1979. *The heat bludgeons you, now even the cicadas sound drunk, play at half-time, out of tune. We crawl upon all fours, seeking shelter beneath the canvas – the house is reserved for the Germans, and Carlo and Marta, naturally. Apart from an open air 'lecture' on the first day about 'engaging the elements of civil society', held in the shade of a half-fallen tree for appearances' sake, we are otherwise left to our own devices. Carlo encourages us to brush up on our Gramsci, but I've barely enough strength to flick through the latest issue of* Kriminal . . . *Antonio isn't much company, frankly, while Mario seems happy just lying on his back, hands behind his head, eyes either open or closed.*

I needed some air, I pulled back the flap and tumbled into the open. It was around three o'clock in the afternoon, the time of the monsters, as Mama used to tell us kids to keep us out of the afternoon heat.

I stumbled, dazed, toward the bathing block – the only part of the house we were permitted to enter, and which was basically a cowshed that Marta's grandfather had converted into bathing facilities for the workers when the landowners had been worried about uprisings. There were three old baths, a set of toilet cubicles and washbasins. I began to run one of the baths. There was only cold water, but for once that was a plus. Even the lake would feel like soup this time of day. I stripped off and lowered myself in. Felt myself cool down, stared up at the ceiling and thought about . . . nothing. Then I began to think about Marta, me and her, here, in this tub together.

A noise. I opened my eyes. There she was! Leaning against the wall in a tight t-shirt and cut-off jeans. I instinctively covered myself and she laughed. 'It's a little late for that,' she said.

'Where's Carlo?' I asked.

'Sleeping,' she said, 'snoring.' She came to sit on the side of the bath, dipping her hand into the cold water. She began to run her fingers up and down the inside of my thigh. 'There's no need to be shy,' she said. I removed my hands and lay back. Marta began to excite me. I closed my eyes, lifted my feet out of the water, stretched out . . . this, I thought, is the life. But then she stopped. I opened my eyes to beg her to continue, but realised: Carlo was standing by the door.

'What do you think you're doing,' he said quietly.

'I . . .' Marta took her hands out of the water, 'nothing.'

'Nothing?' he said. 'It doesn't look like nothing.'

'Nothing, Carlo. Just . . . messing . . . around.'

'Messing around.' He nodded. He reached behind his back and produced something black. Metal. A gun, I realised. He was holding a gun. I suddenly felt the cold of the bath water, the cold of the grave.

'What's that?' It was Marta's voice, from the land of the living.

Carlo looked down at the gun as if it had just materialised in his hand. 'What, this?' He pointed it directly at me. I drew back.

'Carlo, no,' said Marta, 'no.' He turned the gun on her. 'No, please, Carlo, think about what you're doing.' He turned the gun on himself, pushing its barrel underneath his chin.

'Carlo, <u>no</u>.'

He kept it there, looking her coldly in the eyes. Then he let it drop. 'Just "messing around",' he said. He stuck the gun back in his belt. 'Do you want to stay and play your games here, Marta, or do you have time for the revolution?'

Marta got up and followed him out. I lay there for I don't know how long before pulling myself out of the tub. I sat on the edge, dripping, trying to make sense of what had happened, and what the hell was going to happen next. By the time I was ready to head back to the tent I didn't need the towel – I was bone dry.

Chapter 21

The Comandante called me into his office. Of course, we had both been having working lunches – me with Rose, and Giovanni with Ispettore Alessandro.

'He was very complimentary about your Italian.'

'That was nice of him.'

'However, I had the impression that you two may not have got off on the best foot.'

'His flunky, the bald guy with the goatee, certainly rubbed me up the wrong way. Did you get to meet him?'

The Comandante shook his head. 'We had a very pleasant lunch in Leonida, although we were lucky to get a table. The *padróne* actually suggested I book in the future.'

'Tourists are prepared to pay more for the authentic experience. Soon the Bolognese will have to travel to Modena to get a decent meal.'

'Perish the thought! In any case, the Ispettore did ask me to extend his apologies if there was any perception that they had been heavy handed.'

'I don't suppose his apology went as far as returning the SIM card and the papers.'

The Comandante smiled. 'I didn't press him, given the circumstances.' He shook his head. 'I realise I may have been remiss – we have a very close relationship with the forces of law and order, as you know. But I believe I may have had a tendency to keep my contacts to myself. I will have to include you more in that circle in the future, Daniel.'

'The police have a relationship to us,' I said, 'like we have to the Nonnies. That's the truth.'

'Perhaps,' he said, 'except, I hope, somewhat more legitimate. We all lean on each other, to some extent.'

'In more ways than one, Comandante? What is it they want from us?'

'They want what they always want, to be kept informed of anything that might threaten to unbalance the status quo.'

'So, they're not actually interested in what happened to Solitudine?'

'If that might cause problems, affect the equilibrium.'

'Which our investigation might.'

'It *could*. Umberto wanted to emphasise that we have to tread carefully . . .'

'But aren't we compromised? How can we investigate a killing that might involve the police if they know our every step, or one that involves the Mayor, for that matter?'

'I think you are presuming, Daniel,' said the Comandante, 'that we have conflicting priorities.'

'How don't we?'

'Our priorities might *compete* with Umberto's,' he said, 'but conflict? Not necessarily. Perhaps it serves Umberto's purpose for us to dig into this death – we can reach places he would struggle to, undertake activities he would have difficulty explaining. Our "unofficial" investigation avoids official scrutiny . . .'

'You mean that Umberto is happy for us to investigate the Mayor?'

'Better us than them,' said the Comandante, 'providing we don't make too many waves.'

'But you said their priority was to preserve the equilibrium.'

'It is,' said the Comandante, 'which is why he is content for us to perform this function. A formal investigation would soon leak and could create a scandal, whether Signor Manzi was involved or not. It is far better for them that we do it.'

'And if we uncover something to do with the police?'

'Better to be forewarned, no? Information is always power, even if it leads in unexpected directions.'

'And he can cover his back. Do you really think he wants to nail the Mayor?'

The Comandante frowned. 'We are not a law enforcement agency,' he said, 'we are an intelligence-gathering one. It is not for us to consider what use our intelligence is put to, whether it is by our client, Marta Finzi, or by our collaborators . . .'

I wanted to say that we always considered the impact of the information we supplied, not least because it could make us legally culpable if a vengeful wife shot her cheating husband, or a stalker used it to harass their victim. I knew that, the Comandante knew that: information was anything but neutral. Still, I wasn't going to argue. This wasn't a debating society.

'You discussed Marta Finzi, then?' I asked.

'At this point, Daniel, it was inevitable.'

'And you're certain you can trust Alessandro?'

The Comandante sat back in his chair. His glance fell on

a postcard of a painting by Artemisia Gentileschi, of Judith – actually a self-portrait of the painter – cutting the throat of Holofernes, who stood in for her rapist, that was modestly framed among family photos upon his desk. 'Yes,' he said, 'I believe I can.' He pushed a file across the desk. I opened it up. It was full of numbers and coordinates. 'Umberto provided me with Signor Manzi's location according to his mobile phone records for the time in question.'

'Just like that?'

'Just like that.'

'But it says here,' I checked the movement of Manzi across the city again to be sure, 'that at the same time Solitudine disappeared, the Mayor was at the courthouse.' I looked up. 'Do you think the Ispettore also knows what I've discovered?'

'I don't think he would be surprised.'

'So he does want to nail the Mayor.'

'That might be going a bit far,' said the Comandante. 'I think it would be more accurate to say he would like to have as full a picture as possible.'

'To maintain the equilibrium.'

'Umberto's role,' said the Comandante, 'involves quite a balancing act.'

Alba was ready to report back on the documents. The Comandante took a seat at the end of the long table with me and Jacopo on one side and her on the other. The rest of the ancient, polished, English oak, complete with upturned, dusty water glasses and green blotters, stretched emptily along the remainder of the room where once had sat the rest of the Comandante's employees and associates.

'They're bills of sale, copied from the Comune, as far as I can tell,' she said. She had been her usual industrious self and prepared a PowerPoint presentation, projecting the enlarged PDFs onto the blank wall. 'There's nothing especially irregular about them that I can see. They cover a number of public sites that have been sold off over the past few years, although I have to say, the prices seem rather low.'

'I'd say,' said Jacopo. 'Two hundred thousand for the old barracks on Viale Aldini? Hasn't that been turned into luxury flats now?'

'A nominal value,' said the Comandante. 'Who else was going to buy it? And then there is the cost of developing the site.'

Alba clicked through a couple of other slides.

'Hold on,' I said, 'that's the one being developed by Omega, the old hospital, where the anarchists are. Three hundred thousand? That's what you'd pay for a two-bedroom apartment. The place is ancient, enormous. It's going to be a hotel. Signed for by . . . *Marco Venerdi*, on behalf of Omega Group.'

'Venerdi?' The Comandante leaned closer to the Power-Point, squinted at the name. 'Can you go back, Alba, dear?'

Alba went back to the previous slide on the sale of an army barracks. 'Favola,' said the Comandante, 'Luigi Favola, on behalf of Atlante Development SPA.'

'Someone you know?' I said.

'This Omega company, what do we know about them?'

'Alba?' I said.

'Hold on.' She minimised the PowerPoint and went online, bringing up their webpage. It was a slick, animated design making bountiful use of the Greek Ω. BUILDING A BETTER BOLOGNA flashed up in cool grey.

'About?' I said. Alba clicked through. There was just a 'contact us' page with an online form to fill in. 'Projects?' The hospital and the canal came up, alongside snazzy artist's impressions of how both would look when they were finished. 'Hit me with it, then,' I said. 'Vision.'

Omega Group is helping make Bologna beautiful again. From large-scale infrastructure projects to reconditioning some of the city's most treasured landmarks, Omega is at the heart of the rebirth of Bologna as one of Italy's premier global destinations. Our team of dedicated professionals is committed to ensuring Bologna recaptures its past glory in high quality, high value projects. The city of UNESCO-nominated World Heritage porticoes, the cuisine capital of Italy, the first seat of Europe's learning, deserves the very best, and at Omega we believe we can deliver it.

'Well, that tells us a whole lot of nothing,' I said. 'I suppose we could go around the corner where they're working on the canal and simply ask to speak to the person in charge. But why does it interest you, Giovanni?'

'Can we see the information about Atlante, dear?' he said. Alba brought the page up. It featured the same slick design as the Omega site, as well as the same kind of animation, only this time in sea blue.

'Contacts,' I said. It had the same kind of form as the Omega site. 'Vision?'

From reconditioning some of the city's most treasured landmarks to large-scale infrastructure projects, Atlante Development is making Bologna beautiful again. Our team of dedicated professionals is committed to delivering high quality, high value projects to help Bologna become one of Italy's premier global destinations. The cuisine capital of Italy, with its UNESCO-nominated World Heritage porticoes and world-class university, deserves the very best, and at Atlante we can deliver it.

'That's quite a coincidence,' I said. 'I wonder if the dedicated professionals at Omega know the dedicated professionals at Atlante share the same vision.'

'Can we go back to the presentation, please, my dear,' said the Comandante. Alba brought the slides back up again and the Comandante peered more closely, asking her to click from one to the other.

He sat back. Lit a cigarette, silently contemplated a slide of a bill of sale.

'So,' I said, 'are you going to let us in on the secret?'

'These individuals,' he said, 'when they signed the documents on behalf of their respective companies, you will see they were also required to provide their home addresses. I would like to pay these gentlemen a visit.'

Chapter 22

Mario Venerdi gave his address as an apartment in a tidy suburb out towards San Lazzaro. It was quiet, middle class, leafy – tall trees and expanses of closely cropped grass, along with neat basketball courts and five-a-side football pitches, divided smart-looking, low-rise tower blocks clad in smooth, baked red Bologna stone. There was a new church, a line of retail units, including an abundant-looking *pasticceria*-cum-bar, some surprisingly upmarket furniture brands, and, set back from the main drag, a sizeable Esselunga supermarket. In a sense, these suburbs were as 'authentic' a slice of Bologna as the city inside the walls: a major part of the population had migrated here in the decades after the war, happy to be shot of dark, chilly homes built to satisfy the needs of sixteenth-century Bolognese and enjoy the bright, modern, centrally-heated accommodation to be found on the periphery, although that didn't stop them flocking back to enjoy the delights of the old city at the weekends.

We were spared having to trick our way into the building's pristine lobby by coinciding with a young mother and her pushchair. She thanked me for holding the heavy glass door open for her, and we were in. Only there was no Mario Venerdi inscribed upon the shiny post boxes. 'Check the bells, will you?' said the Comandante. I went outside, holding the door ajar. No Venerdi there, either. I watched the Comandante step back and examine the names on the boxes. One in particular seemed to excite his interest. He frowned.

'Would you mind waiting down here?' he said, and called the lift.

'What is it?' I said.

The Comandante shrugged. 'Probably a coincidence.' He stepped into the lift. I watched the numbers ascend to the fourth floor. Read the names on the letterboxes: Varesi-Feltrinelli, Sciascia-Lucarelli, Boschi, Fois-Machiavelli.

After a couple of minutes the lift began to descend. The Comandante stepped out, looking grim. He brushed past me and headed toward the car. I followed him outside, swivelling back to look up at the fourth floor where I spotted a set of grey blinds shiver, as if someone was standing behind them and watching us leave.

I got in and started the engine. 'Where are we heading?' I said. 'Comandante?'

'Just drive,' he said, 'for the time being.'

I steered us back toward the centre. I could see the Comandante needed some time to process whatever had happened and I knew enough not to press him. I brought us onto the Viale. This way we could simply loop around the city, much as I had with Ispettore Alessandro. The second time around the ring road he said suddenly, 'Turn here.' We came off the Viale and under the old brick gate at Via Saragozza, the car rumbling along the cobbled street. 'Park here,' he indicated a small island where the road divided around the imposing battlements of the Spanish College, an urban castle that was actually the fifteenth-century equivalent of a student hostel.

'Over there,' I said, indicating a door between two restaurants, 'that's the address of Luigi Favola, right?'

The Comandante sighed. 'Luigi Favola, correct.'

'So,' I said, 'are you going to tell me what all this is about?'

Another long exhalation, then a string of words: 'Luigi Favola, and indeed Mario Venerdi, were aliases created for operatives during Operation Resilience, which I was involved in during the seventies and early eighties. The objective of Operation Resilience was to penetrate far left and far right groups during the Years of Lead in order to gather evidence against the activists and avert serious acts of terrorism.' He searched for his cigarettes, lit one, and unwound the window a couple of centimetres. 'Obviously, I recognised them during the presentation. I presume authentic addresses were given in the event there was any post generated by the sales, which would then inevitably be left by the post boxes when no name could be found. This could then be collected by the operative.'

'Operative . . .' I said. 'But these sales can't have anything to do with infiltrating terrorist groups, can they?'

'However,' said the Comandante, 'I recognised a name on one of the boxes, from a long time ago in the force. Boschi. I thought it was worth checking out – as I said, it could have simply been a coincidence – but, as it turns out, it was not.'

'And this Boschi, when you turned up at his door, what did he have to say for himself?'

'Not much, as soon as he saw me, in fact, he slammed the door shut. He used to be a sergeant in the squad.'

'Strange,' I said, 'almost as if he had been warned.'

'Indeed,' said the Comandante.

'And now we have arrived at the address of "Luigi Favola".'
I looked around. 'I can't see anyone.'

'When you filmed that girl . . .'

'You mean Anna Bellidenti?'

'That's right. How did you manage it again?'

I took out my phone, switched on the video, and slipped
it into the top pocket of his suit jacket. 'It doesn't look quite
as inconspicuous as when I did it,' I said, 'you're hardly the
smartphone type, but I doubt "Luigi Favola" will notice.'

'Luigi Favola,' said the Comandante, getting out of the
car, 'whoever he is.'

The Comandante crossed the road and stepped under the
portico. I watched him examine the doorbells, tracing the
names with the tip of his finger before pausing at one and
pressing the buzzer beneath it. When they, presumably, failed
to respond, he tried the one below that. He spoke into the
grill and the door opened.

He went inside. As the door closed, it was only then that
I thought to myself: I should have gone with him. Even if he
had said no, I should at least have offered. Presuming they
are on to us, if they're not outside, they could be waiting
inside, and then what? I didn't doubt that Giovanni could
have looked after himself in his prime, but now?

I switched on the radio. I switched it off. I pulled the
door handle, then let it go. I watched people pass under the
portico, lost in their own lives. I checked the rear mirrors,
the side mirrors, swivelled around – saw nothing suspicious.
Turned back.

I waited. And watched. And waited.

The Comandante was leaving the building with that same grim look on his face. He crossed the portico and was about to cross the road. And that was when I saw it, the black Toyota SUV hurtling toward him.

I was halfway out of the door and shouting *'Watch out!'* as the Comandante began to step onto the street. He snapped out of his trance and paused, one foot floating in the air just above the road, looking questioningly at me as the SUV thundered past. It rumbled off before rounding the corner, tyres screeching.

The Comandante was nowhere to be seen. In the gloom beneath the portico, a woman stopped, then a man coming the other way. As I ran toward them, a shopkeeper emerged. I heard him say: 'Call an ambulance!'

The Comandante was lying on his back on the paving, his legs outstretched, his head in a pool of blood. His hands were describing shapes in the air, as if he was still falling; his eyes were darting about, frightened, confused. Then they seemed to find a focus, to find me. He clasped my hands tightly in his. He passed out.

Chapter 23

8 July. 5a.m. *I want to write this down while the details are still clear in my mind. I know that by doing so I am incriminating myself, but I don't count on this journal being found (no one knows I keep one, and if they don't know that, why should they look very hard for it?) and I think it is more important for me to remember, so whatever happens, I have a faithful and true account.*

It was night. I woke up, alone. When I'd returned from the bathing block Mario had been sleeping, Antonio was buried in a book. I had lain down, my mind buzzing . . . and then? Maybe it was the adrenaline – the effect of being found out, having a gun pointed at me – but the next thing I knew, there I was in the dark.

I pulled back the tent flap, crawled out. Up above there was this dazzling night sky – the whole of the universe seemed to be laid out, as if I had opened a book on the stars. For a few moments I scanned it with the wonder of a child. Then I heard a noise – the scrape of a chair. A light was on in the kitchen. I picked my way toward it.

I found the others sitting around the table, smoking. Jesus. I thought, this was it, my time had come – they had gathered here to discuss what had happened in the bathing block. God knew what story Carlo had been spinning. I thought of his gun and felt like throwing up. Yet when I came in, no one – not Marta, not even Carlo – seemed troubled by my presence. They barely even registered me, except Mario, who smiled and made a space.

'It's like this,' said Carlo. 'There has been a significant increase in checks on routes into France and we have had a number of safe houses uncovered by the authorities. As a result, our couriers at the border are asking for more money . . .'

'Parasites,' said 'Marco'.

'Trento is unable to provide us with any additional funds,' he said, 'and has instructed us to raise them ourselves.'

There was silence around the table. Then, to my surprise, Mario, who rarely contributed, said, 'It won't be easy – university's closed. Most of our supporters are away, but if you like, comrade, I can head down to the coast, see what I can collect.'

Marco snorted. 'That's not what he's talking about,' he said. 'We need real money and we need it now. We're going to carry out an action.'

'Action?' Mario said dumbly.

'A robbery, you numbskull,' said Marco. He looked at Carlo. 'Is this the best you can do?'

'We've always known it might come to this,' said Carlo, looking at each of us – even me – in turn.

'Count me in,' said Marta. She looked intensely at Carlo and squeezed his hand.

Then I realised Carlo was staring directly at me. 'Me too,' I said.

It sounded simple enough: it was the close of the Festa dell'Unità *at the Parco Nord. Tonight there would be a big dance, and at the end they would count the money – along with what was donated in the big glass jars as people had come into the event over the weeks. That's when we would swoop. There was a certain poetry about it – stealing from the fake revolutionaries to fund the real revolution – and Carlo said they wouldn't have security, not real security, anyway. They wouldn't want the police about. And what if they recognised us? I didn't ask this, I didn't say a word – I suppose I was still reeling from the events of the afternoon – no, it was Mario who asked. I've got friends who go to the Festa, he said, we both have, haven't we, Paolo? He nudged me. I shrugged, yes.*

Marco said not to worry about any of this, all they will be looking at will be your guns, that's all they'll remember, and I thought – guns? Of course guns. Guns like Carlo's, and it was true: it was all I could look at as I felt my mortality flash before me. 'But I don't know how to fire a gun,' said Mario. 'Of course you do,' said Marco, 'you've seen the cowboys, haven't you? You just pull the fucking trigger!' Then he laughed. 'Anyway, don't any of you kids worry,' he said, 'no one's going to be shooting anyone.' 'Or at least,' said 'Patricia', looking at the three of us with undisguised contempt, 'if anyone does any shooting, it's going to be us – me and Marco here – you just do as you're told.' And we bobbed our heads up and down like schoolboys.

A couple of hours later we were setting out in two cars from Marta's – me and Mario with Antonio, the Germans in the other (Marta had not been selected to come, she and Carlo were supposed to wait for us at the house). It was just before midnight and the starlight cast everything in monochrome like in an old movie, yes, that was how it felt, with the Luger sitting heavy on my lap, an old gangster movie with James Cagney. I flicked the safety catch back and forth, then stopped myself. It might go off, after all. But that light – it added to the sense of unreality. I turned around – Mario was sitting passively in the back, watching the world go by as if it was some kind of routine trip into town, while Antonio, he was wearing a look of grim determination. There would be no backing out from Antonio. Antonio was James Cagney, and I?

We met a line of traffic coming the other way – the dance was ending, the communists were going home. I looked at them in their cars, joyful, tired, relaxed, not a few quite drunk. Their open, happy faces. Tomorrow they would be back at the factory, doing the boss's bidding, but still, they had danced for the revolution! They had danced away the downfall of capitalism, for another year . . .

The car park was almost empty by the time we arrived. In fact I was worried we might have missed them, but the Germans seemed relaxed, totally at ease. They were standing by their car smoking. We got out of ours, jackets draped over the guns in our hands. Patricia handed us the balaclavas. 'But wait until we are across the road,' she said, 'outside the tent, before putting them on.'

Then suddenly it was happening, something clicked and I was no longer in that movie – this was taking place for real. I, Paolo Solitudine, had a gun in my right hand and a balaclava in my left. A voice in my head began shouting: what do you think you're doing? Run! Run you fool! Get away from there! But my legs were carrying me forward like a soldier to the front. It began to dawn on me – too late, far too late – this wasn't me. I was in the wrong place, the wrong time, the wrong fucking life, but at the same time the urge not to mess up was somehow greater. Now I wished I had spoken to Mario – perhaps there had been the possibility, when he had raised the issue of fundraising and Marco had slapped him down, perhaps he had realised how deep we had gotten, we could have stolen away – but I had said nothing, tangled up in my thoughts, my worries about Marta, who had not even glanced at me since it happened, since we were caught. Meanwhile the world around me had been moving furiously forward.

Patricia was peering through a slit in the tent. She turned around. 'It's just as they said it would be,' she said. 'Right, cover up.' We put our balaclavas on. 'Okay,' she said, 'remember what we said – we'll do the talking, you three –' she meant Mario, Antonio and me '– just keep the rest back. Got it?'

Then she was gone, into the tent, just like that, a machine gun nestled in the crook of her elbow. Marco followed right behind, then Antonio, then Mario, then me.

A harsh, post-dance light, a quiet conversational buzz, condensation and stale beer in the air. No one had yet reacted to these five darkly clad, armed figures in balaclavas, no one had noticed. Or seemed to. Or processed it. Then it happened, or began to, the buzz dropped off, the people – there must have been about a dozen gathered around the long table where the cash was spread out, smoking, drinking – stopped, looked. A woman shrieked. The man at the centre of it all, his thumb halfway between a wad of notes, looked up. 'No,' he shook his head, 'this can't be.'

Patricia waved her machine gun and yelled at them to get back. The crowd gave way but the man, and a young woman standing next to him, stayed put. Patricia screamed at them again to move away.

'Listen,' said the man, getting to his feet and holding out his hands, 'you don't want to do this. This is money ordinary people have given, for the struggle.'

'Fuck your struggle,' said Marco, moving forward to scrape up the notes into a tennis bag while the rest of us just stood dumbly behind him, pointing our guns in their general direction.

But the young woman shouted 'No!' and lunged across the table, grasping hold of his arms.

Marco tried to detach her — 'Get off me!' — but she clung on. 'Bitch!' As he tried to pull the woman off him, the table upended, scattering the money onto the floor. The pair of them fell to the ground.

The man stumbled toward us, as much in surprise, I think, as intent, and there was a huge bang. Patricia had fired her machine gun. Or, rather, she had tried to and it had blown up in her hands. She let out a cry. Metal fragments were embedded in her chest, glowing like coals. The smouldering, useless gun fell to the floor as she began to tear at her melting bomber jacket. She pulled her balaclava back to expose a neck and chin transformed into a mess of flesh and smoke.

'Get them!' someone yelled, and the crowd pushed away the remaining tables and came at us. I looked around — Antonio was already on his way out the back, Mario was looking at me as if to say, what should we do? Marco had managed to get to his feet, but the woman was still clinging to his ankles. He brought the butt of his revolver down on her head with an audible crack. She flopped onto the ground.

Marco grabbed Patricia, who was now sitting on the floor, gibbering and burned, and began to drag her out. I was turning to run for it when I saw Mario being set upon by two men, *propelling his pistol upwards. A group were approaching me and I levelled my gun. 'I'll fire!' I shouted, 'I swear!' and they fell back.*

'Leave him!' I screamed at the men still grappling with Mario. They cringed away and Mario staggered backwards. 'Come on!' I grabbed him by the shoulder and, still training my pistol on the crowd, pulled us toward the exit. When we got outside, we turned and ran.

Antonio was already pulling out of the car park when we arrived (I could see Marco bundling Patricia into the back seat of their car) and had I not thrown myself in front of it, I'm sure Antonio would have just left us there. As it was, we dragged the doors open with the car still moving and jumped in. Mario was in the front, I was lying across the back, as we sped away. We went under a bridge and, driving one-handed, Antonio tore off his balaclava. 'Take them off, you fools,' he said. We did as we were told. When Mario removed his, he looked over the seat at me and that broad, round face of his was wet with tears.

Chapter 24

The Comandante had not actually been hit by the SUV but had stumbled backwards and fallen. Still, because he had suffered a nasty bang on the head, the doctors decided to admit him to hospital for observation.

He had been given a two-bed room with a view toward the two towers. The other bed was unoccupied, so Jacopo perched upon it, while Alba claimed the chair. Rose and I stood by his bedside.

The Comandante was uncharacteristically subdued – I had expected him to complain when the doctor had insisted we admit him – but of course this place had history for all the family. It was where he had said goodbye to his wife, and his child. Perhaps he felt a kind of closeness to them, or a grief, or perhaps he simply did not have the strength: he looked exhausted.

Alba settled herself into the chair. I could feel Rose rigid by my side – I realised she must be in a kind of shock, seeing her grandfather like this, who was usually so smartly dressed and . . . *self-contained*, looking dishevelled in a hospital-regulation smock, with a tube sticking out of his arm, and . . . very old. I rested my hand on her shoulder and she leaned into me.

'Alba, dear,' the Comandante said weakly, his voice little more than a smoker's rasp, 'can you take Rose for a Coca Cola?'

'But I don't want a Coca Cola,' said Rose.

'He means he wants to talk business, darling,' I said. Alba got up.

'Come on, love,' she said, ushering her out, 'I think I saw some magazines in the shop downstairs . . .'

'Your phone,' said the Comandante. I had forgotten all about it. I went to his jacket – fortunately it was still there, though signalling low battery. The video camera had kept running, but quit after thirty minutes. I tapped on the video, skipping the part where I set him up with it and he had headed across the road. Pressed play as he arrived at the front door. The view tilted up and down as he checked the names.

'Benassi,' he said from his bed, and it was repeated on audio: 'Of course, *Benassi*.'

He rang the bells, announced he was the postman, and was buzzed in. He laboured up two flights of stairs, pausing at the first landing for breath, before arriving outside a dark wooden door with the security gate closed in front of it. He paused to get his breath back, then adjusted the phone in his pocket, aligning himself with the door. He pressed the buzzer twice in quick succession. And waited.

And waited.

'I know you're in there, Enrico,' he said loudly. 'There's no point pretending you're not. I've got all day.'

The door finally opened: it was an old man, grey, hollow-cheeked, slightly hunched, but there was still a certain vigour about him – like the Comandante, he had probably been looking this way since he was forty. He stood behind the gate, holding onto the bars.

'I've been told not to speak to you, Comandante,' he said. 'I've been told not to even answer the door.'

'But you did, Enrico, you did.'

'Out of respect for you, Comandante.'

'Then perhaps you can tell me what you are doing buying this property, an entire army barracks, no less.'

Enrico Benassi shook his head. 'I'm not telling you anything, Comandante.'

'Are you scared, Enrico, is that it?'

Benassi gave a slow smile. 'No,' he said, 'I'm not afraid.'

'Then what is it?'

'Look, it's all right for you, Comandante, you've always been well off, what with your family palace and so on, but did you ever wonder how we ordinary soldiers would survive when it was all over?'

'A *carabinieri* pension is very generous—'

'Well, that depends on how you define "generous", Comandante.'

'Still, to become involved in something . . . well, I'm sure it cannot be legal . . .'

'Legal? Illegal? Oh, Comandante, how can it be either, if it doesn't even exist?'

'I'm sorry, Enrico . . .'

'I preferred it when you called me Benassi, Comandante,' he said, and closed the door.

The Comandante let out a long sigh and began walking back down the corridor. I stopped the film and the phone died almost instantaneously.

'This Benassi is . . .'

'He was on our squad, a corporal.'

'So where did he get this money from, then?' I shook my head. 'Silly question. The cash to buy these properties, set up these companies – it's from your pal, Alessandro, isn't it.'

'He runs the department now, he would have access to the funds.'

'But what did he mean by it "not existing"?'

'It was a black squad, it was black money . . . it officially did not exist . . . the minister at the time, Andreotti, made the arrangements because he didn't know who he could trust. It was the middle of the Cold War and our country was a battleground. Political assassinations, bombings. A struggle for power between the two great blocs. *Le Brigate Rosse* were backed by the Soviet Union, the fascists by elements within our own security apparatus, themselves controlled by the Americans. And in the centre of it, Italy, poor Italy . . .'

'And this black money,' I said. 'How much of it was there?'

'It was a one-off payment,' he said, 'given its high degree of sensitivity. It was meant to make our operations sustainable for many years to come.'

'How much?'

'Even in the 1970s, it amounted to several million US dollars.' The Comandante let out a long sigh and his eyes began to close.

'What would that be worth now?' said Jacopo.

'Invested wisely . . .' I said. 'A lot more.'

The Comandante was still awake, but only just. That was enough for today. We left him to get some rest.

He hadn't mentioned the car. I suspect he preferred not

to dwell upon the possibility that it was more than just an everyday example of reckless driving. Certainly, since I had had the run-in with Alessandro, I hadn't spotted any further tails, but it didn't take much of a leap to presume Boschi would have got straight on the blower to Alessandro after we visited him, and Alessandro would have tipped off the other aliases, and maybe decided to turn up the heat on us for good measure. Enough to consider killing the Comandante? If it comes to a choice between you and the other guy, why not? When you've dealt with death your whole career who's to say it can't become like any other currency: the question only, can you afford to spend it?

Chapter 25

The rain – *Bologna rain* – drilled down, washing across the cobbled street and choking the gutters. Humidity fogged up the bar window and I wiped it with my sleeve. Every autumn was the same: the rain hosed the city down, before winter and the big chill. The Bolognese kept to the porticoes – they knew better than to stick their necks out.

I took another look at the video Jacopo had just sent through. He was sitting in my car opposite Benassi's place and had a camera trained on the doorway. It zoomed in on Sergeant Romano waiting by the intercom. He spoke into the grill and was buzzed in.

I wasn't surprised to see the sergeant there, but my satisfaction was tempered by an edge of dread, a sense of skating on thin ice. Italian might be a culture that judged a lot by appearances, but it was what was beneath the surface that was worrying me.

Giovanni could have been killed. Presuming it hadn't been an accident, and I was, they would expect us to have got the message, run for cover, back off. That would be the Italian way. People here responded to threats. To do otherwise would be considered foolish, and often for good reason – whether they were unions taking on employers or small businesses being threatened by gangsters, the understanding was that they would carry out their menaces, be it strike action, broken windows, or worse. In Italy extortion is the continuation of negotiation by other means, but I wasn't about to back down, for all my qualms. This may be Italy, but I wasn't Italian.

Another video was coming through: Romano was leaving. I paid for my coffee. The rain had ceased as suddenly as it had begun. I went around the corner to the Fiat, where Jacopo was sitting in the passenger seat, his knees propped against the dash, his chin resting on his palm.

'Oh,' he said, straightening up, 'hi.'

'Good work,' I said. 'We're beginning to join the dots. You can consider yourself relieved.'

'Is this really necessary?' he said. 'Isn't there another way?'

'You tell me,' I said, 'you're the technical genius. But I want to nail this, and until you come up with a better idea, a bit of old style legwork seems the best solution. Hello, what do we have here?'

There was movement under the portico. Luigi Favola – AKA Enrico Benassi – had opened the front door wearing a brimmed hat and dark green overcoat. He began to head toward the centre. I got back out of the car and waved my phone at Jacopo, switching on the tracking app. Just then I received a message and stopped in my tracks.

We need to speak urgently.

It was from Marta Finzi.

Chapter 26

I told Jacopo to keep an eye, and a distance, on Benassi and got back in my car, heading toward the address Marta Finzi had given me – Tower Two in the Fiera district.

The Kenzo Towers were a product of the modern Comune's flirtation with Japanese architecture and constructed in a style you wouldn't expect to encounter outside Tokyo – a clump of utilitarian but emphatically non-European skyscrapers just 'outside the walls' that were meant to pay homage to the famous towers of old Bologna but were somehow more reminiscent of a Godzilla movie set, as if they had been constructed from giant kitchen rolls and industrial quantities of *papier-mâché*.

I parked nearby then crossed an empty square dotted with blackened, apparently dead trees in concrete tubs, and made for the second of the four towers.

Like the others, Tower Two seemed quiet, as if only semi-occupied. Despite the chrome and black leather seating in the reception, the glass tables were dusty and bare, the front desk deserted, only a full ashtray and piece of scrunched-up paper sitting on its smooth marble top.

On a board by the side of the lift was a directory of the building's occupants. The first to fourth floors were apparently occupied by INPS – the government's social security agency – on the seventh floor something connected with the Fiera, and on the eleventh, Omega Group.

Signora Finzi had asked me to meet her on the eleventh.

I messaged Jacopo: *If you don't hear from me in an hour, tell the Comandante.*

The lift arrived. I hesitated, and stepped in.

I'd like to say it all crystallised over that eleven-floor ascent but instead vague outlines loomed in the misty landscape of my mind with apparently momentous, but frustratingly obscure, meaning.

So Signora Finzi was connected to Omega. Omega was connected to this black fund, and, of course, the Special Operations Group. Meanwhile the Comandante was laid up in a hospital bed, and Paolo Solitudine in a black bag.

I was arriving on the eleventh floor. The door opened. In front of me, a pair of glass double doors. I pushed through and stepped into an apparently deserted, L-shaped, open-plan office. There was a small reception desk, but no receptionist; the desks were scattered at angles across the floor. There were a few office chairs, placed seemingly at random, cables where computers would have sat at desks, but no computers, monitors or keyboards. One or two phones, unplugged. An empty mesh wastepaper basket lying on its side.

I walked around the corner and there they were: Signora Finzi sat behind a desk looking bereft. Sergeant Romano at a right angle toward her with his feet up on another swivel chair. And behind the pair of them a figure standing at the window, apparently taking in the view over the city. He turned around.

Carlo Manzi smiled, a politician's smile, pleased to see me despite not having the foggiest idea who I was. But I was wrong.

'Signor Leicester,' he said. 'You made it.'

Chapter 27

The Mayor walked around the desk and held out his hand. His palm was smooth but he had a firm grip, and he added an extra little squeeze as he let go, as if to indicate he really meant it.

'Apologies,' he said, 'for the short notice. And for surprising you like this.' Up close he was an inch or so taller than me, and although he must have been at least thirty years older, he seemed almost pathologically lean. I instantly got why Paolo and his friends had fallen for him all those years ago; how he could have become the boss of Bologna – Carlo Manzi had the air of a man who really believed in something, although I guessed that somewhere along the line (and, presumably in the Mayor's case, that had been quite early on) it had become solely himself. Still, I couldn't help admire how he felt compelled to direct his charisma toward a fresh audience, even if in this case it was his wife's spy. He shook his head. 'You must be wondering what the hell I'm doing here.'

I looked at Romano, who still had his feet up on the desk.

'I wish that were so, Mayor, but seeing the sergeant rather

confirms my suspicions.' There was an involuntary twitch at the corners of Manzi's too-tight mouth.

'I'm sorry Marta has wasted so much of your time.' He shrugged. 'And my money.'

I looked at Marta Finzi. 'Signora,' I said. 'Would you like me to accompany you out of the building?'

She seemed to register me properly for the first time. She had obviously been crying. She shook her head. 'I'm sorry,' she said.

'For what?' She looked down.

I drew a slow, deep breath. This wasn't the first time in my life I'd been found out, backed against a wall – sometimes literally, and by more frightening folk than this. If there was one thing I'd learned, it was to take control. I looked at the Mayor. 'So you deny you were involved in the death of Paolo Solitudine?'

'Oh, Paolo . . .' Manzi gave me an appreciative smile, as if he understood precisely what I was doing. 'As he lived, he died. In futility. But I . . . *we* –' he glanced at Romano '– had nothing, *absolutely nothing*, to do with his death, Signor Leicester. On the contrary – *che palle*. The unrest – the perception of extrajudicial killing, the police are out of control, in the run up to my re-election . . . the suspicion it cast upon me from my wife, that brought us here . . . all of that, I promise you, doesn't help me, doesn't help *us*, at all.'

'You met Paolo Solitudine,' I said, 'in the court building. Shortly thereafter, you killed him. Or –' I looked at Romano '– had him killed.'

'I met him,' said Manzi. 'Then I had another appointment.'

'Then,' Romano piped up, 'or at the same fucking time,

for all I know, I was busy bashing red skulls in at the hospital. Plenty of witnesses to that – a lot of them from the wrong end of my stick. But, you're right about one thing at least: I probably would have bashed his in, too, if I had seen him. But I did not.'

'Paolo confronted you,' I said to Manzi, 'with evidence about . . . all of this. Omega Group. Your involvement in this conspiracy to buy public buildings on the cheap, then flog them off for a massive profit. That's why you had him killed . . . or for other reasons.'

'*Other reasons?*' said Manzi. 'You mean, like sleeping with my wife? I admit, Signor Leicester – may I call you Daniel? – once, it's true, I might have considered such a radical measure . . . But now I'm older, wiser. You see these things, well, in a *broader* context . . .'

I glanced toward Marta Finzi, her head still hanging. This was it, I thought – the moment of truth. Clearly, I wouldn't have another opportunity. And my client was bound to find out anyway.

'Broader like Anna Bellidenti?'

Carlo Manzi's eyes glinted. 'When the Comandante left the service, I wondered how he would get on in the outside world, but you . . . you're quite sharp. I might even consider hiring you myself, one of these days . . .'

You're wondering, I thought, how much I know. I looked at him so he knew I knew everything. That tight smile grew, just a fraction, wider. 'Yes, broader like Anna, Daniel.'

'Like the baby,' I said.

'Yes, like the baby, Daniel.' But the voice was not Carlo Manzi's, it was his wife's. She gave me a sad look. 'I'm sorry.

For all of this. Obviously, he,' she looked at her husband, 'found out I had hired you. This . . . person,' she nodded at Romano, 'told him.'

'I'm . . . '

Marta Finzi shook her head. 'It was a risk. I knew that when I took you on.'

'I blame myself,' said Manzi. He seemed to think about it. 'Although I ask myself, what more could I have done . . .'

'You could have started by not screwing that bitch,' said Marta.

Manzi gave me a 'what can you do' kind of shrug. 'You knew I played around, *amore*. Didn't you yourself tell me – it was better than picking up some tart from the Viale? At least you knew where she came from? And let's not pretend I was the only one.'

'*Once*, Carlo,' she said, 'I told you so many times, it happened just that once, such a long time ago. We were young . . . so young.'

'So you say.' He caught my confused look. 'Yes,' he said, 'even your English detective here is thinking – hold on, isn't this about her recent fling with Paolo? And of course to him it's all about Paolo, the old man, not the young buck. And he'd be right, in a sense.' He turned to Marta. 'Don't tell me your "return match" was entirely a hardship.'

She closed her eyes. When she opened them they seemed hollowed out. She crossed, in fact wrapped, those long arms around her as if holding herself in an embrace. 'For you,' she intoned. 'I did it for you.'

'For us,' he corrected her, 'you did it for *us*. You did it for your nice car and your nice clothes and your nice holidays.

You did it for your status, and yes, you may conceivably have done it for our kids, but, let's not pretend you sacrificed yourself on the cock of Paolo Solitudine out of sheer selflessness.'

Marta looked back down, shaking her head.

I'd had enough: '*What is this?*'

Sergeant Romano nodded appreciatively.

'A fair point. You've got to admit the Englishman's got a fair point. You can see why he might be wondering.'

Manzi looked at Marta. 'Look, Daniel. It's quite simple – my wife *renewed* her acquaintance with Paolo after we discovered he was collating information about certain property dealings and planning to tell all. We'd hoped Marta might be able to find out more or even dissuade him from going ahead. As it turned out, our plan worked brilliantly.'

'What do you mean?'

Manzi shrugged. 'Paolo got in touch, said he wanted to meet. Aware of the sensitivities – of us being seen together – he suggested the location, the courthouse. Very well . . .

'When he arrived I behaved as if he'd come to talk politics. But, it turned out he had other things on his mind – our ageing Casanova declared his love for Marta. Informed me she loved him too and there was nothing I could do about it. *Che suppresso.* Obviously I'm pretty outraged. *You won't get away with this* . . . etcetera.

'Not so fast, says he – if you don't allow us to be together, I'll expose you. I'll tell the world who's behind Omega Holdings. How you have been conspiring to line your pockets with public funds. Well, that certainly placed a different complexion on things . . . After all these years of playing second fiddle, Paolo Solitudine finally had me over a barrel.

I mean – what could I do? I had to give him everything he wanted. Paolo left my office with his head held high, while I was a shell of my former self. And as soon as he'd left, I messaged my wife to tell her the good news.'

I turned to Marta. She had taken out a packet of cigarettes and was trying to light one but her hand was shaking too much. Eventually Romano reached into his own pocket and flicked a Bic, ever the fucking gentleman.

Marta drew in the smoke, let it out. Only when there was a good cloud between us, did she look at me.

'But,' I said to her, 'if this is true, why did you accuse your husband—'

'Apparently it was a question of *trust*,' said Manzi. 'It turns out our arrangement suffered from something of a deficit.'

'Paolo *died*,' said Marta. 'That wasn't . . . part of the plan . . .' She took another drag then looked across the empty office. 'I realised . . . I thought . . .'

'*Erroneously*,' Manzi cut in. 'Absolutely no truth, none at all.'

'I was afraid . . . confused. I didn't know who I could, yes . . .' Now she looked at him. 'Trust.'

'Of course you could have trusted me,' said Manzi.

'You never told me about the *child*, Carlo. *The fucking child*.' She turned to me. 'I saw a *fattura*, can you believe it? A fucking invoice. For treatment of this bitch, just lying on his desk. And then . . . *Paolo*. All of a sudden, it added up.'

'Two and two made five,' said Manzi. 'Like the sums of some of our populist friends.'

'You were afraid it was not only Paolo who had been used,' I said. 'And if that *was* the case, anything could happen.

You, even, could be next. But, Marta,' I said. 'Signora Finzi.' I looked at the two men, then back at her. 'Are you really telling me you manipulated Paolo, this man who loved you?'

'Or is it just for the benefit of this audience? Look.' I held out my hand. 'I repeat my offer – we can walk out, together, now – I guarantee, nobody will hurt you. We will make sure you are safe.'

But Marta Finzi was shaking her head. 'It's difficult, to explain – what he, what Paolo, was planning . . . It would have ruined everything.' She looked at Manzi. 'So I did what I had to.'

'And then what?' I said. 'Once Paolo had told you he had your husband's blessing? *That you were both free?* What the hell were you going to do then, Signora Finzi?'

'*As I wished*, Daniel. I'm no man's whore, whatever you – whatever any of you men – might think.' She looked at Manzi. 'At least Paolo paid me some attention. Perhaps I would have let him down gently.' She shook her head. 'I don't know. The important thing was to stop him. Carlo certainly didn't care.'

'I wouldn't say that . . .'

'Providing it didn't make the papers, and I wouldn't have wanted that, either. Paolo would have listened to me.'

'And this girl, Anna?' I said. 'Her baby?' Marta and Carlo exchanged a look. '*Christ*,' I said. 'You're taking it.'

'She doesn't want it,' said Marta. 'I can get a nanny. The child will have a brilliant future.'

'And perhaps your husband will pay you more attention again.' I had quit smoking when Rose was born but felt like snatching that cigarette from between Marta Finzi's fingers and taking a deep drag. Either that or punching a wall. 'So, why bother? I mean – to call me here. Why not just fire me by What'sApp if you're now so convinced your husband had nothing to do with Paolo's death?'

'If only it was so simple,' said the Mayor. 'But if politics has taught me anything it's that once Pandora's Box has been opened, it takes some effort to close it again. Which is why I wanted to bring us together, "nip it in the bud", don't you English say? A delicate gardening analogy, entirely lacking in Italian. Here it's "strangle at birth". Well, unfortunately this little monster has been born, learned to walk and been scampering around the city asking awkward questions, so I decided it was time to put it to bed. I don't like the idea of actually throttling the thing.' He looked at Romano. 'I'll leave that to you.'

'You have proof, then,' I said, 'an actual alibi?'

'Directly after my meeting with Solitudine, I had an appointment with Anna's gynaecologist. Both she and the doctor, and my assistant, would be able to confirm this. I even have the ultrasound, if that would help?'

I'm here, inside,' Anna had messaged him. She had indeed provided Carlo Manzi with an alibi. The Mayor nodded to Romano, who produced a tablet. There was CCTV footage, quite sharp, high quality: a corridor. The law courts. A man, *Solitudine*, closing a door behind him, surprisingly dapper looking in a suit and tie, still, I suppose, dressed for the stage. He stood there . . . stunned, then a smile spread across his face, even as he was shaking his head. He began walking, and the film followed him from various angles, the timer in the corner of the screen tracing his every step – to the millisecond –

to the door where Dolores and I had made our entrance. He looked left, he looked right, opened it, and disappeared.

'Now *there* was a revelation,' said Romano, 'I had no idea there was direct access. Quite a security oversight. Will have to have a word with the contractors.'

'Weren't *we* the contractors?' said Manzi.

'There is that,' said Romano.

Then, cut back to the office door. Manzi coming through, putting on his overcoat. A woman tottering down the corridor after him, clutching some documents – Chiara Delfiori. The film followed the pair of them out of the building.

I shook my head. 'So you two are accounted for,' I said. 'That doesn't mean there couldn't have been someone else waiting for him in the canals.'

'Forget it, Daniel,' said Marta. 'In any case, if they really wanted to do away with me now, they would have to get rid of you too, no?'

I looked at the three of them and a chill ran through me. *You're a stranger in a strange land*, Mario had said.

'Did you *never* care about Paolo, Signora Finzi?' I said. 'Not even when you were young?'

Marta Finzi glanced at her husband who was observing her with perhaps his first unfiltered expression – *contempt*. 'I suppose I thought I did,' she said. 'But what does anyone really know, Daniel, when they are young?'

Chapter 28

La Dozza, Bologna. June 24, 1980. *This morning they car-*
ried out the guy in the cell next to me, already rigid, having hung
himself during the night. Crushed by the slow passage of time.
That's what you don't think about, when you're considering
being shut up: the weight of the minutes, the hours, the days. The
different dimensions of time. When you think about the pros-
pect of gaol on the outside, you calculate the time based on your
experience outside – living life – where it slips by, barely noticed.
Four months, six months, a year, three years? Five? That's not so
bad! But this is the dimension of the dead, and every moment
lasts a lifetime. Seven years. The maximum sentence afforded by
the law. Seven years.

I have even been adopted as some kind of martyr – for refus-
ing to give evidence, for keeping my mouth shut. I receive a daily
subscription to Il Manifesto *and various other publications.*
Books (I could do with less worthy editions, frankly). Letters –
oh the letters! Half a dozen girls are writing to me, and most,
the good-looking ones anyway, enclose their photos. The guys on
the wing crowd around to see what I've received. There was a
blonde, Astrid, from Germany, who sent me one in a kind of

naturist pose. I wonder if Gramsci was so lucky. I have received invitations from across Europe, and I pass many hours imagining myself travelling across the continent, the political celebrity. But was it worth it? For my fantasies, for the fantasies of political groupies? My mother fainting, my father weeping when the judge handed down the sentence. 'My boy . . .' Dad said. 'My little boy.' Seven years and I – me, and only me – own every one of them.

June 27. *I kept a record, a journal, once, didn't I? A lifetime ago. Presumably still hidden – I won't say where, for obvious reasons – as it was never produced as evidence. At least I did one thing right! And in that journal, I was telling the story, I seem to recall, so I had it straight in my mind. Back then, I felt some kind of imperative: to set it down, to ensure – to myself, at least? – that I was largely without guilt? Not that it would have been relevant to the court! But of course, neither could I escape the logic that, by participating in the crime, I was morally culpable. Would I have opened fire, as Patricia meant to? No. But I should have understood that the Germans were quite capable of that. Would I have received a lighter sentence had I blabbed, as everyone was begging me to? Probably, but Mario still got five years. And in any case, how could I have faced Marta? Even when she was no longer there, she was always there . . . in my heart, I was always under her gaze. I was not a 'revolutionary hero', but I wanted to be, wanted desperately to play the part.*

Antonio dropped us off by the two towers that evening. There was still a crowd hanging around the Roxy Bar. We stood there, our pistols wrapped in our jackets. Mario had stopped his blubbing. We hesitated, unbalanced by what had just transpired, and the normality of our surroundings – 'See you, then,' I said – 'See you' – as if we had just had an ordinary night out. Then we headed in different directions, home.

I sneaked in so as not to wake my flatmates. Sat on the edge of my bed. Placed the gun beneath it. Lay flat on my back. Tried to get some sleep, but of course it was impossible. The events of the night ran around and around in my head until I had to set them down. I got so far . . . then I heard a clatter, a stone at the window. I leaned out.

'Paolo!' It was Mario. I had never felt so happy to see him – to be able to go over the events of the evening, escape from the prison of my thoughts. I went to open the front door. He came in, looking deathly pale. We went through to the kitchen. 'Well,' I said, 'that was some night.' 'Paolo,' he said, 'I've messed up.' 'Don't be so hard on yourself,' I said, 'we all messed up. I always thought it was crazy – we're not robbers!' Mario was shaking his head. 'No,' he said, 'I've <u>really</u> messed up.' 'What do you mean, Mario?' He was shaking his head. 'I realised, when I was going to bed, it was missing.' 'What was missing?' He looked up at me. 'My baptism medal.' 'What do you mean?' 'It wasn't there, when I was getting undressed.' 'Well,' I said, still quite relaxed, pouring some coffee, 'have you looked for it? Maybe it was tangled in your clothes, or under your bed?' 'I've looked <u>everywhere</u>,' he said. 'Look,' I said, 'I know it was important to you, but . . . these things happen. I'm sorry.' 'You don't understand,' said Mario. 'It's not as simple as that.' 'Why not?' 'It was inscribed with my name.' I put my coffee down. 'Your name?' He nodded. 'And you've looked everywhere, you say?' 'That's what I've been doing all this time.' 'Christ,' I said. I thought about it. 'Maybe it's on the floor of Antonio's car, when you took the balaclava off.' Mario shrugged. 'When I think about it,' he said, 'at the time, I mean, of the struggle in the

tent, I felt it go then.' 'And you didn't check?' 'It was all . . . such a mess.' We sat smoking. The sun was already blazing through the window. Finally I got up and went to the phone. I called Antonio. He answered straight away. 'We need to see Carlo,' I said, 'at the farm.' Antonio didn't seem annoyed or bothered by this call, as I'd expected. He just paused, then said, 'All right, I'll pick you up in fifteen minutes.' What was I thinking? Maybe that's where we would find the medal: on the floor, down a back seat, in Antonio's car. That was the first thing. The second: this is just too big for me. Make this someone else's problem.

Antonio arrived in half an hour. When he did he gestured for us to come down, and for me to bring the gun. I was so relieved! Someone else's problem. 'Now,' I said to Mario, 'remember what I told you.' He nodded: to surreptitiously search the car and let me do the talking. He got in the back, me in the front. Antonio seemed supremely uninterested, didn't ask any questions. It was almost as if he was a taxi service. He pulled out in silence, and drove.

We left the city limits. The sun on my face, a luxury I barely noticed – we were drunk on the sun, sick of the sun by then. I put on my sunglasses.

Sick of the sun.

It was before seven, driving through the countryside, the empty, winding roads, the calm fields, the golden bales of hay standing like sentinels. Mario fidgeting about in the back. Still fidgeting, I noted, with a sinking feeling, still searching.

Antonio pulled in. I wondered if he was on to us, but he barely seemed to notice we were there. He stepped out of the car, went to sit against the bonnet, lit a cigarette. I didn't think to ask him why. I was beyond questions. In any case, I had Mario in my

ear, whispering, 'I can't find it. Can you check under your seat?'
I did as he asked, opening my door and checking under the mat
and so on. Even now, as I did so, Antonio didn't think to ask me
why. He came around to my side and took my gun from the seat,
said, 'I'd better have this,' and placed it in the boot. We both got
back in the car and continued on to the farm.

We travelled along the narrow, pine-lined lane that ended
in the dusty courtyard. I could see the Germans' car was already
there, but otherwise it was still, quiet. A chicken was pecking
around the front step of the cottage. The barn door was open,
the bathing block closed. The sun was climbing in the sky. Only
there, in the field to the side of the cottage, I could see that one of
the tents had collapsed.

We got out of the car, began walking toward the cottage, then
Antonio suddenly stopped, raised his thumb in the air. I heard a
muffled scream then Marta burst through the door of the cottage.
'Run!' she shouted. 'It's a trap!' I stood there dumbfounded as
Carlo came out after her together with a carabiniere. *Then all*
around us the world erupted: from the barn, the bathing block,
the cottage, came more police, bearing rifles, machine guns. I
looked around, Mario was running to the rear of the car – was
he trying to get to the boot? I looked back, just in time to see a
rifle butt blackening the sky . . .

I am lying on my back, consciousness has returned, but slowly
enough (or perhaps I am canny enough?) to keep my eyes closed.
How long have I been out? More than a minute, I'd guess, by
the calm that is surrounding me. I might as well be invisible – I
can even hear them stepping over me. For a moment I wonder –
am I a corpse? I am tempted to open my eyes, just to check, but
something stops me, a whisper in the silence: you're a long time

dead, Paolo, mate. There's no hurry, even if you are. Okay, I think. Okay. Concentrate. I can hear, now, Mario. Sobbing. Oh I know those sobs, the big baby! He is sob-sob-sobbing as he is led past me. A truck's doors clunk shut.

Then in the distance I pick out a voice lower than the rest – I recognise that too, it is Carlo, his reassuring words. Or sounds, in any case. I can't tell what he is actually saying, but I know exactly what he is doing – the clarity of the corpse! – he is soothing, calming Marta. Marta. Marta . . . A door closes. And I am still lying there! I am still ignored. Am I really dead? Then I hear someone coming to stand over me. The toe of his shoe taps against my ribs. Again, harder. I continue to play dead. Someone else approaches. The slap of their palms coming together. I can feel them above me, their jocular, familiar embrace. Antonio's voice: 'She's all right?' Carlo's: 'She will be.' I open my eyes. Carlo and Antonio look down at me. Then Antonio looks up. I realise – there's someone standing behind me.

And the next time I wake up, I might as well be dead.

Chapter 29

The farm was much as I had imagined it, although it was now utterly derelict – the cottage roof half-gone, the windows black holes, doors hanging off or missing, the barn a pile of rotten lumber and old bricks. The road we took to it was still serviceable, though, and the land was being cultivated – I guessed it was rented out to locals – and there was the lake where Marta and Paolo had gone skinny dipping; I imagined them tangled together in that water, Paolo's hermaphrodite. A little jetty prodded into the dark water, sparkling with frost.

I walked to the end of it while Jacopo leaned against the car, playing on his phone. I may be a stranger in a strange land, I thought, but not only me – the Comandante had placed his trust in Marta Finzi too. And Anna Bellidenti was being used as little more than a farm animal. I felt sorry, ashamed for us all. But particularly for him, for Paolo, who thought he had finally won – that smile as he emerged from the court-house office – but who had in fact lost everything.

We headed back into Bologna. Jacopo turned on Radio Neptune.

'Mayor Carlo Manzi this morning announced he would

be attending tomorrow's funeral of Civil Action founder and convicted terrorist Paolo Solitudine, whose body was discovered floating in a canal a fortnight ago. The Mayor, who is running for re-election later this month, told Radio Neptune he wanted to be mayor for all the Bolognese, and that included those who didn't agree with him.' Cut to Manzi's voice: 'The time has come for us to pull together, to put our differences aside. We can't carry on like this, at each other's throats.

'Politics has always been a large part of our life here in Bologna, and I hope it long remains that way. Our friends on the extremes are just as much a part of the local colour as our two towers and *tagliatelle al ragu*. We should be embracing, not fighting each other. Let this sad day mark the beginning of a fresh start for us all.'

Jacopo laughed. 'He'll be featuring *punkabbestias* on the tourist posters next. They'll be like those punks in London, you know, with the green hair you have to pay to photo.'

'What do you think he's playing at, attending the funeral?' I said.

'I've no idea,' said Jacopo, 'but I'll give him this – he must have balls of steel.'

The seat by the Comandante's hospital bed was not occupied, as I had expected, by Alba, but Ispettore Alessandro.

He was sitting forward, cross-legged, with his chin resting upon his palm, in quiet conversation with the Comandante, who was propped up in bed, looking battered, certainly as grey as ever, but in whose eyes I could see the spark had begun to return.

'You've got a cheek, haven't you?' I said.

'Daniel . . .' said the Comandante.

Alessandro stood up. 'The accident didn't have anything to do with us, Daniel,' he said. 'Well,' he corrected himself, 'at least, with me.'

'Forgive me for being paranoid,' I said.

'You've every right to be.' Alessandro smiled apologetically.

'Too right,' I said. 'I met one of your employees, or perhaps that should be two.' I explained what had happened at the Kenzo Towers.

Alessandro and the Comandante exchanged a look.

'Comandante,' I said, 'as well as the Omega Group, was Faidate Investigations, your company, *our* company, also bankrolled by this black fund?' There was another unspoken exchange between the pair.

Alessandro was the first to speak. 'The issue is not the fund,' he said, 'it is the *use* of the money. The fund is not static, it has always relied on investments to sustain it. Traditionally, they were always blue chip, for the benefit of the service . . . It appears my subordinate, Sergeant Romano, may have been using . . . unorthodox means to enrich himself, of which I was utterly unaware.'

'That's convenient.'

'*Daniel*,' said the Comandante.

I looked at him. 'I'm supposed to believe this?'

'I have known Ispettore Alessandro for more than thirty years,' said the Comandante, 'I would trust him with my life.'

'Well,' I said, 'I've known him for little more than a week, so you'll excuse my scepticism.'

'He's right, Giovanni,' said Alessandro, 'why should we expect him to understand?'

'Oh, I understand,' I said. 'Carlo Manzi has been your inside man since the 1970s, when he exposed the raid that led to the imprisonment of a pair of wanted Brigate Rosse terrorists, along with Paolo Solitudine and Mario Cento. God knows how long he had been involved before then, but never mind.

'Your fund bankrolled his political career, which has seen him rise to the pinnacle of Bolognese politics where he has control over the city's budget, alongside a huge influence on the forces of law and order. So, basically, a police employee is running the city. And like any employee, he's there to do your bidding and can smooth over, or push through, any business the police are sticking their fingers into. When the anarchists complain it's a police state, they're not far wrong, are they.'

'How do you know all this,' said the Comandante, 'about Carlo Manzi?'

'Detective work, Comandante,' I said, 'although it would have been far simpler if you had just told me in the first place. But never mind, in your own way you were a victim of Marta Finzi's charms as much as Paolo.' I produced the photo of the group in the countryside. 'You took this,' I said. 'You were Antonio.'

The Comandante nodded. 'It was my first assignment, for the undercover squad. I was a "fresh face" – I'd been at military academy since I was twelve, then assigned to the uniform in Bari. Even though I was technically a Bolognese, I felt like a foreigner, which was how you were treated in those days, if you came from the south . . .'

'You made some kind of deal with Manzi, didn't you,' I said. 'To get rid of Paolo, his love rival, to get him out of the way. *Seven years?* You can't have been interested in the kids – it was the *Germans* "Marco" and "Patricia" you were after. Yet you let the raid go ahead, allowed the kids to be sent down – ruined their lives, for what? To keep your man on the inside happy?'

'I . . .' the Comandante was shaking his head.

'Murky times, indeed,' I said.

'It is easy,' said Alessandro, 'to condemn with hindsight. Oh, we are so *pure* now! But back then we were fighting a war, Daniel – for survival. People like us – like myself and the Comandante – risked everything, *precisely* so people like you could perch on their pedestals and judge us from the heights of history.' He shook his head. 'But we never expected to be thanked.'

'This isn't history, Ispettore,' I said, 'it's happening now. You've got a black fund ripping off the city and lining police pockets in the process, you've got the elected head of Bologna, one of the most important politicians in the country, on the police payroll, and you've got the guy who uncovered this – Paolo Solitudine – on his way to the cemetery. Don't you think you should do something about that?'

Alessandro nodded. 'Don't worry, Daniel, I'm not a complete idiot, although,' he smiled sadly at the Comandante, 'I may have been taken for one. I will be getting things back under control to ensure that these kinds of abuses do not occur in the future.

'But I would caution you not to jump to too many conclusions. True, Signor Solitudine apparently uncovered certain irregularities, but I have yet to see any firm evidence he was murdered because of it.'

'So just like the car that almost flattened the Comandante, you're saying you think it was an accident?'

'I am just saying we should be careful about jumping to conclusions.'

'That's convenient,' I said, 'for the police, I mean. I wonder if you would take the same attitude if it was applied to you.'

'What do you mean?'

'Well, Solitudine winds up dead. The Comandante is almost run down. And now, there's you – the sole person with the power to do something about it. I would be careful, Ispettore, to look both ways when you cross the road.'

'I always do, Daniel,' said the *ispettore*. 'Always.'

'I'm sorry,' said the Comandante, after Alessandro had left, 'I'm terribly sorry, my boy. I should have disclosed everything to you at the outset. I suppose . . .' He shook his head. 'I carried a sense of *shame*, from those days. I still felt –' and now he was rubbing his hands together, as if wanting to wash them clean '– soiled . . . by the bargains one had to make, the betrayals.'

'I'm not so annoyed with you,' I said, 'as myself.'

'What do you mean?'

'For having been played by Marta Finzi. Running around town, in my way every bit as guileless as poor Paolo.'

'Don't blame yourself, my boy,' said the Comandante. 'Marta was not always that way, whatever she might tell herself now. I remember, after we had taken the boys into custody. She was backed into a corner of the farmhouse with a kitchen knife. Carlo was pleading with her. Oh, we had it all worked out, of course, and he gave her the story we had agreed: that he had cooperated with the police for her sake, to save her, and I remember her saying, that knife looking so huge in her hands, *what have you done, Carlo, what have you done* . . . Really, she had no inkling of the depth of his betrayal. Her world was turned on its head. Then I said – it is true, Marta, Carlo did it for you, to save you. In any case, finally, she dropped the knife.'

'And she forgave you, "Antonio", for your part in the betrayal?'

'She forgave Carlo. I thought . . . clearly I believed that she had forgiven me, too. But I can see now she was using me with the same cynicism that I had once used her. And I can't find it in myself to blame her for doing so.'

'I noticed,' I said, 'that the *ispettore* evaded my question about where the funds for our company initially came from. Of course, knowing about this black fund, and understanding how we could also be implicated if it came to light, would have also provided Marta with additional assurance of our confidentiality.'

'You don't miss much after all, do you, my boy.' The Comandante said it with a finality that implied I wasn't going to get full disclosure now, either.

'All right,' I said, 'get some rest.' I brushed the grey hair away from his forehead and kissed him.

'You're not angry with me?' he said.

I shook my head. 'How can I be angry, we're family, aren't we?'

Chapter 30

Funeral weather. Dishwater-dirty clouds, a steady drizzle that drained the colour from this most colourful of cities, dampening down even the bronze and gold of the fallen leaves that lined the route to La Certosa, the city cemetery.

Jacopo and I had followed the funeral procession on foot all the way from the centre, where it had gathered at Piazza Maggiore. Usually the police would have outnumbered the protestors at an event of this kind, but not this time. This time it sounded like thousands, and it probably was. At moments, standing with Jacopo on the fringes of the crowd in the main square, I felt the phantom of the young Paolo at my shoulder, thrilled by the imminence of revolution.

I thought about his gaol dreams, that global tour, bedding the revolutionary groupies of the old continent. I watched while a string of old radicals, including, of course, Mario Cento, raved into a microphone atop a makeshift stage, but I preferred to think of the still-young Paolo Solitudine, fresh out of lock-up, lying upon incense-heavy pashmina sheets, muffled by the milk-white bosom of Astrid.

Finally the new generation – Beppe, the Beard – took the

stage to a particularly hearty roar. I couldn't quite catch those Jesus eyes from this distance, but he plainly had a certain bearing to him, a studied humility, that demanded attention, even when he turned his back to the crowd and began making low, repetitive noises into the microphone.

'What's he saying?' I said to Jacopo. 'Is it my hearing?'

Jacopo shook his head. 'Hold on . . .' he said.

'*Lo*,' Beppe was saying, '*Lo. Lo. Paol-LO . . .*'

'It sounds like some kind of—'

'*Paol-LO*,' said Beppe, 'they wanted to use you, they wanted to abuse you, they wanted to shape you, they wanted to make you, but you wouldn't have it, no, you wouldn't take it, Paolo Sol-i-tudin-e, you told them where they could stick it . . . *Paol-LO, Paol-LO, you stayed true . . .*' Behind him, from the two-metre tall amplifiers standing on the stage, a beat began; heavy bass, a throbbing drum. 'You got your blisters, like the Sandinistas, shoulder to shoulder with all the resistors, you did your time, you gave your time, YO, we can still hear you, through the years, all your efforts, all those tears . . . *Paol-LO, Paol-LO, you stayed true . . .*'

Above the crowd, I realised the stage had begun to move, slowly, in the direction of the road. Beppe continued to pace up and down, seemingly floating above the crowd. Despite its lyrical absurdity, his valedictory rap made a kind of grim sense against the muffled, ugly, angry beat, the weeping sky, the washed-out city.

Jacopo and I fell in beside the crowd decked out almost exclusively in black, hoodies covering their heads like cowls against the rain, though they would probably have had them up anyway. Beppe continued to rap as the cortège headed up Via Ugo Bassi, his voice growing into a kind of growl, his homage to Paolo transforming into a litany of Italy's ills: 'The police they beat us, but they can't defeat us, parliament ain't nothing but a barge, upon a lake of cash, of bullshit, and they'd have you swallow it, but we won't swallow it! We won't swallow it! We won't swallow all that shit!'

My heart sunk at the prospect of trudging the next three kilometres in the rain to this soundtrack. I wondered about going back and getting the car. I gave Jacopo a nudge. 'No need to look like you're enjoying it,' I said.

'He's not so bad, this guy.'

The Mayor had not shown up and I wondered if he was planning to attend at all. Had this been a rare misstep? He was hardly likely to receive a warm welcome from this lot.

The question that still troubled me was: why? Why did he want to come to the funeral? To see an old rival finally under the earth? To reminisce about old times with Mario? To symbolise 'reconciliation', as billed on the front page of the *Carlino*? Of all the reasons, the latter seemed the least likely. Maybe it really was one of the others: he simply wanted to look Mario Cento in the eye as he tramped the dirt down on Paolo's grave.

Beppe gave way to a professionally recorded, but not so very different, rap as the procession passed under the gate of the old city and began to make its way toward the outskirts. I kept an eye out for Dolores but couldn't see her. She was no doubt hanging around at the front with her rapper beau. At least she hadn't brought Desdemona with her – this was definitely no place for a cow.

What a strange procession we must make, I thought, as

onlookers stopped to take in the spectacle, among them, I noticed, Franco from the Osteria della Luna, stationed behind a wheelchair occupied by a rake-thin woman covered by a plastic cape. Beneath Franco's umbrella, I noted a look of quiet satisfaction.

If you had interrogated any of these marchers, I'm sure almost all of them would have sworn to their atheism and, no doubt, attested to their loathing of the Roman Catholic Church, yet here we were, marching toward La Certosa, one of Bologna's most ancient landmarks, the place where all the Bolognese ended up: the rich and the poor, the famous and the obscure. A former monastery, it even had a special section for non-Catholics, almost exclusively occupied by foreigners. But there had been no talk of Paolo Solitudine being laid 'outside the walls'. Like all Italians he had the right and expectation to a proper Christian burial and in the absence, as far as I was aware, of any mention of it in his will, which had left his minor estate (mainly old documents and worthless art as best I could understand) to 'the cause', that was what he was going to get.

We traipsed through the suburbs, the rain falling without relent, the thousands of damp, dark hoodies crowded around the muffled sound system, and ahead of it, I realised, the hearse which must have joined us once we had emerged from the old city. We shuffled forward like a mass of medieval penitents, the muted titian walls of La Certosa finally coming into view, and above the boom-boom-boom still belting out all that urban anger, I began to hear the chime of a bell.

So, this is where it ends for you, Paolo, I thought. For all your philosophy, those lost gaol years, those long evenings of minute-taking, forgotten minutiae. I thought of your mother fainting, your father weeping. I thought of you watching Marta step into the lake, your timidity before you joined her. I imagined you growing old, still stuck in that same groove, and wondering where the years had gone. Then thinking that you had, astonishingly, recaptured them. I pictured you emerging from Manzi's office in the court with that delighted smile on your face, shaking your head in disbelief. I thought of you disappearing through the cellar door. I thought of your bloated body on the mortuary slab.

A mass grumble went through the crowd as a revolving blue light began to wink near the entrance to the cemetery. The dark-blue limousine with tinted windows could only signal one person – Carlo Manzi. At first I was surprised by the absence of additional police (although the standard city police patrol car was leading the cortège, with a few motor-cycle cops stationed at the junctions) but then I realised this was a smart, if ballsy, move on Manzi's part. More police would simply provide an additional excuse for trouble – one man, accompanied by a squad of journalists, a camera crew and photographers was a tougher target. Sure, the whistling, the booing, the abuse began to build up the closer we got to the entrance, but when the priest came to stand beside the Mayor *and his wife* . . . it began to die down. Regardless of any alternative rites, the catechism ran deep in this lot who would sooner display disrespect to their own parents than Mother Church.

Marta Finzi stood as straight as a sentry beside her hus-band. She was dressed entirely in black, her bag clutched in front of her, hair tied tightly back with a jet ribbon, her face powdered ghostly white, dark lines drawn around her eyes. Those pale, bloodless lips. She seemed almost rigid with fear, and who wouldn't be nervous faced by this mob? But perhaps it was something else. Perhaps she was afraid Paolo's corpse would rise up from its coffin and throttle her.

The procession halted, although the rap music played on. I watched a small delegation, including Mario Cento, approach the Mayor and his wife. I tried to keep my eye on Mario at this extraordinary meeting, but I was too far back. 'Come on.' I took Jacopo by the arm. 'Let's see if we can get around the front.'

We skirted the fringes of the crowd and managed to get behind the mob of journalists just as they began to move back, toward the entrance of the cemetery. We had missed the historic meeting and the cortège was on the move again, the priest and his acolytes leading the hearse, and behind them in the front line, the old revolutionaries I had seen speaking before; Marta Finzi walked flanked on either side by Carlo Manzi and Mario Cento.

We found ourselves inside La Certosa, that temple of sad angels and wan Madonnas with its rows of tombs, many of which were badged by snapshots of the occupant in happier times. I was certainly no stranger to the place. Lucia, of course, lay here, marked by a simple plaque and a monument that existed only in my mind, but that was all right – better to be alive in my memories than bone dead here.

'Dan . . . *Daniel.*' It was Jacopo's turn to give me a nudge. 'Shouldn't we get going?' He was right, I had missed my cue: the procession was moving away from us, across the great paved square toward the West Cemetery.

We took a shortcut, tagging on behind the camera crew who were racing to reach the site in advance. It almost reminded me of the old days, trampling unceremoniously over graves to get the big story.

We arrived at the appointed place, covered by an orange tarpaulin bowing with the weight of rainwater, in time to see the procession come around the corner and proceed along the gravel path beneath us. The camera crew pitched their tripod across a neighbouring grave as the hearse pulled in and half a dozen anarchists, a mix of young and old including Mario Cento and Beppe, hefted the coffin upon their shoulders and followed the priest along the narrow path toward the graveside. The front of the procession followed in single file up the path while the great mass of anarchists spread like an invading army across the monument-thick incline and began to converge upon Paolo's grave.

There was no more sound system now, only the bell tolling dully on, through the sound of rain upon stone, rain upon marble, gravel, mud; the umbrellas of the leading mourners, the tarpaulin. Did Marta Finzi see me, stationed behind the TV crew? Did Manzi? Mario Cento? None of them made any sign that they had, and if they had, why should they care? As far as the Finzi-Manzis were concerned, I had little more than a walk-on part in their family drama, while as for Mario – well, I was standing in the right place, with all the other parasites.

The priest gave the nod, and the pair of workers pulled back the tarpaulin, inadvertently tipping much of the rainwater into the grave.

Under the instruction of the undertaker, the pallbearers

navigated the recycled cardboard coffin, which was covered with graffiti tags, pictures, paintings and slogans as dense as camouflage, into the harness above the hole. They stepped back into the crowd that had now massed around the graveside.

The bell stopped ringing and the priest began to consign Paolo Solitudine to the soil, in certain knowledge of his resurrection. As the coffin was being lowered, I examined the faces watching him go. It was a cliché – so doubtless contained some truth – that murderers have a fondness for attending the funerals of their victims, and considering this murderer, if there was a murderer, presumably believed that they had got away with it, why miss the opportunity?

I searched the crowd for Sergeant Romano, who I expected to find looking on with a barely contained smirk, but I couldn't see him anywhere near the Mayor, as I would expect, nor any of the goons I had come to associate with him. Was he among the army of black hoodies massed around us? Perhaps one of those with a scarf across their face? Apparently not – theirs were the eyes of teenage posers.

What about other suspects? How about the old revolutionaries queuing up to toss dirt into the grave as the workers withdrew the ropes? Tired, defeated old men; the debris of history. Did any of this lot have the spirit or wit left in them to commit a murder? They barely looked as if they had enough energy to compete for their spot in La Salaborsa, the public library. Even Mario Cento, bringing up the rear? Admittedly he still appeared to have the heft left in him, but the motive? The opportunity? How could he have gotten down into the canal – even if he had known it was there, which he had denied – if he had been under arrest? And why would he have bothered? Deep down, Mario remained to me, despite that stern Brezhnev face of his, the innocent boy blubbing in the back seat as he and Paolo and 'Antonio' returned from their disastrous raid, and even now tears were falling copiously as he scooped up a handful of dirt and watched it drop down.

Behind Mario came Dolores, who I realised had been made almost invisible by the black hoodie that must have obscured her features amid the crowd, but which was now pulled back, her unmade-up face wet with tears, and then Beppe, the Beard, his Jesus eyes uncharacteristically dry, business-like. That, of course, didn't mean a thing: if we had been in northern Europe, he would have seemed entirely in keeping with the occasion and I wasn't about to finger him for failing to display customary Italian grief in all its broad brushstrokes. Maybe he just hadn't liked the guy. Maybe he wanted to display an aura of strength and leadership to the massed ranks. What set the alarm bells ringing, however, was how, after he had somewhat dismissively tossed his handful of dirt into the hole, he stood slightly back from the others, surveying the crowd. What – who – was he searching for? Then he fixed on somebody in the ranks across the graveside and, as Marta Finzi began to step unsteadily forward, bending down to clutch her contribution to the grave, Beppe gave a small yet discernable nod.

A fraction later I realised what was about to happen, but it was a fraction too late.

Chapter 31

They were probably aiming at the Mayor, who was standing just behind her – but then I realised I had got it all wrong: the people I thought were print journalists waiting outside the cemetery but who had not accompanied me and the camera crew to get ahead of the procession, weren't journalists at all – they were undercover cops. A whole group of them had clustered around the Mayor and were eagle-eyed enough to see, as I had, what was coming – the bucket being hefted by a pair of hoodies toward the graveside, being pitched, even as I was crying out a warning, across the grave.

They were bundling Manzi out of the way as Marta stood upright, sensing something was happening but too slow to react. In fact, quite the opposite: she turned to face it, positioning herself precisely at the point at which to take the full force of the payload – red liquid, paint, I supposed. The ultimate act of political graffiti.

It hit her full in the face. Marta staggered back, blinded and stunned, as an audible gasp went up from the crowd. She stumbled forward, tottering at the brink of the graveside. But it was not Manzi who reached out for her – he had disappeared down the incline amid a huddle of bodies, guns drawn and waving – it was Mario Cento. He took her arm just before she toppled in. Marta steadied herself, her eyes now blinking as white as ping pong balls in that mask of bright red.

Then the booing began, the hissing. Mario let go of her and stepped back, almost as if he was appalled at depriving the audience of that ultimate act of political theatre – Marta Finzi falling into Paolo Solitudine's grave. She wiped at her face, baptised in the anarchist's colours, without even the priest daring to step forward to comfort her.

'*Bastardi!*' she yelled. 'You think you know everything. You know nothing. Nothing!' Her black-clad arms began to wave incoherently, out of time with her words.

'*Vaffanculo!*' Go fuck yourself. A woman's voice. Dolores? No – I was somehow relieved to see her looking ashamed, into the grave.

'You don't know,' Marta shouted. 'You don't know a thing.'

'Fuck off. We don't want you here!'

'I'll do what I like, you cretins!'

I sensed a change in the crowd, a charge of violence. Almost to my surprise, I found myself stepping out from behind the TV camera and pushing through the crowd. '*Marta*,' I said, 'Signora Finzi. Best not. Better to move away.' She swept around, her eyes full of fear and fight. Then she recognised me. The flare seemed to flicker, then die. She let me take her arm. I began to lead her away.

Another TV crew stuck their camera in her face, the reporter barking questions. I shoved the cameraman backwards, so hard he slipped and crashed against a gravestone before dropping the camera, lens first, onto the ground. The reporter, a young woman, brandished her microphone at me like a blade. *'You can't do that!'* I snatched the microphone out of her hand and pitched it into the crowd, which received it with a smatter of applause. The woman chased after it like a particularly shrill terrier.

I led Marta Finzi down the incline toward the car. The crowd parted before us, curious, unashamed eyes peering out from the darkness of their drenched hoodies. They lacked any embarrassment, or hint of empathy, it seemed, as if Marta had got precisely what she deserved, although they couldn't possibly know the truth. But perhaps they did not need to know – perhaps this was the distinction I had been missing all this time: the fault line ran so deeply between the two sides that each took their dues – corruption on one hand, disruption on the other – for granted.

Marta Finzi shivered beside me like a bird snatched from the claws of a cat.

'What are you doing here, Signora Finzi?' I said. 'Why did you come? You didn't have to. Him, perhaps, but you?'

She walked on, without reply.

The Mayor's car was waiting for us, circled by plainclothes cops. As the rear door opened to let her in, I saw Manzi in the front passenger seat, nonchalantly tapping away on his phone and apparently indifferent to the fate of his wife.

Then it struck me: *'Christ.* But it was bullshit, wasn't it, what you said in the tower. You *were* going to leave Carlo. That was your plan all along. None of this let him down gently – Paolo had finally found you a way out, and you were going to seize it.' I shook my head. *'You really did love him.'*

Marta Finzi was bending to get into the car but paused, her eyes lingering on me. She seemed about to say something when a goon moved between us. I heard the door close.

Carlo Manzi looked around at his wife then up at me. His face remained stone sober. He regarded me unblinking but without surprise, almost as if I was already working for him.

Chapter 32

Paint washes off harder than blood. I had to use a kitchen scourer to remove it from beneath my nails, and I thought of Marta, covered in the stuff. Heavy with the weight of the paint, as she was with betrayal, all the betrayals, from her youth to her old age – of her, by her, to herself. The choices we make that mark us, no matter how hard we try to scrub ourselves clean.

Except . . . some people. Some people seem to shine, no matter what. The worst among us. I remembered that cold look in Beppe's eye, a look he shared with Carlo Manzi. I had probably met more monsters in my time than most, throughout a range of professions and, alarmingly, many of them took to me. They seemed to think I understood where they were coming from, that I was like them, but on the contrary – I was just good at faking it. The trick was to stop them finding that out, at least until it was too late.

But I had been played for the fool this time, was reeling from the sucker punch. I'd trusted the Comandante's judgement about Marta, not realising it was tainted by his own guilty legacy. Perhaps he had wanted to believe Manzi *was* behind Solitudine's death; that it might somehow make up for his sacrifice of the young radicals years ago. Perhaps he had felt it was his way of providing Marta and Paolo with a kind of justice, after all. But their story had already been told, and it was too late to add a happy ending.

I turned off the shower and stepped into my gown. Today, I thought, despite the weather brightening up, a fresh wind scattering the clouds and that Mediterranean blue sky beginning to break through, I just wanted to close the shutters and go to bed.

But it was past noon and Rose would soon be home for lunch. Alba would be home to make that lunch. Jacopo, the Comandante . . . it would be business as usual and I would have to chew through our meal as I chewed through life, as if nothing had happened. The world didn't care whether I was happy or I was sad. The sun would continue to shine, the rain fall. Lucia would still be dead, and Rose would carry on pestering me about getting a new iPad.

I opened the closet door and pulled out a clean shirt.

Alba was the first to appear. I heard her come into the kitchen, began to smell the *ragu* she had prepared the evening before – chopped carrot, onion, with a dash of red wine – and she was now heating up. Of course, it was a Thursday – in a city that had gifted the world at least four famous dishes, Thursday in the Faidate Residence meant *tagliattelle al ragu*, which Alba served up as casually as any Briton might microwave a plate of baked beans. We did not own a microwave.

A random thought: I wondered how her internet dating was going, but I wasn't about to ask. I knew she had had a few unsuccessful encounters over the past couple of years and must be growing increasingly desperate as her friends married off and had kids themselves. It was our fault, in a way, Lucia and me. Had my wife not had the bad manners to get knocked over, Alba wouldn't have had to step in to help and could have had more time to enjoy herself and meet someone, rather than assuming the premature trappings of a 'mum' herself. If this had been a generation or two earlier, I might even have been expected to marry her, but although I had adapted to many of the peculiarities of Italian culture, this was at least one that did not appear to be expected of me.

'Oh! Hey, Dan.' She was taking out the pasta. 'I didn't hear you come in.'

'I needed to change,' I said. I recounted the episode at the funeral.

'That's awful,' she said. 'They've no respect. What were they thinking?'

'Publicity, I suppose,' I said, 'presuming they meant to hit the Mayor. God knows what *he* was thinking going there . . .'

'What is it?' said Alba.

I shook my head. 'Something the Comandante said to me . . .'

'Which was?' the Comandante had come in with Jacopo. Despite the crown of his head being wrapped in a bandage the size of a skullcap, which he concealed beneath his trilby, the heavy bruising beneath both eyes and the doctor having prescribed a fortnight's home rest, he had returned straight to work.

'Carlo Manzi – he doesn't do anything by accident,' I said.

'He must have known something like that would happen. "Reconciliation" be damned . . .'

The Comandante shook his head. 'They certainly know how to play into his hands: "damned" is the word, how it will be presented in the press, a faithful attempt at reconciliation spurned. Signor Manzi needs to be seen to be doing everything he can to deal with the reds before the election. He has tried peace . . .'

'It gives him further licence,' I said, 'to use violence.'

'Jacopo told me about this business,' said the Comandante, 'with Signora Finzi. You did well to step in, despite everything.'

I shrugged.

'I will have to call her,' he said, 'to settle accounts.'

I looked at him. 'So that's it?'

'She requested a service and I believe we are perceived to have delivered it. We do not provide our services free, and neither do I believe would she expect us to.'

'But . . .'

'We did what was requested, Daniel,' the Comandante said pointedly, 'and were careful to itemise our time. It is true that she misled us to some extent, but we do not charge for hurt feelings. We do, however, expect to be paid.'

'There's still the other matter,' I said. 'What actually happened to Paolo Solitudine.'

'Which is not for us,' said the Comandante, 'but the police.'

I shook my head. 'I don't think they're likely to do anything soon. To your pal Alessandro, Paolo is nothing but an afterthought. Despite everything, Comandante, I believe we're starting to get somewhere with this. I'd put money on it: Paolo was too nimble to fall into the canal, I can't see it being the cops – what would they have been doing over on that side? It must have happened on Solitudine's way back from his meeting with Manzi. And if Manzi really wasn't behind it, then we're closer to answering the question of who was – who else would be compromised by Paolo's investigation, who else might have known about it, and who else might have known he was down there?'

'Ah,' the Comandante said, 'I can see that you've got the scent, *the solution is just around the corner* . . . but beware, Daniel, there's another corner, then another . . . and it can lead you nowhere, or back to where you began. Believe me, my boy, I know the feeling, and I have learned to grow wary of it. And the question remains – *whose* money will you be putting on it? Who will pay the bills? This is the life we have chosen, Daniel – neither lawman nor reporter. We are no longer paid to serve the truth, but our clients' wishes.'

I thought of what Paolo might think. Paolo, who had lost at everything – politics, love, life – yet who still, somehow, seemed to stand for something. I wasn't going to let this drop and, deep down, I suspected there remained a part of Giovanni that would be disappointed if I did.

'It's already online,' said Jacopo, looking up from his phone.

We were sitting around the table, the meal was almost ready to be served, and Rose had still not materialised. I tried her phone again, and again it went through to her voicemail. I could sense that not only I, but the rest of the family, despite their apparent distractions – phone/*Corriere della Seral* draining the pasta – were also close to arriving at the point, as yet unspoken, of minor panic about our missing thirteen-year-old. 'I'm sure it's nothing,' I said, checking my emails and messages for the third time.

I got up from the table and went to the bathroom. I decided that if she hadn't appeared by the time I returned, I would try Stefania and then her mother, and if there was still no trace, I would go out to look for her.

I was coming back from the bathroom, ready to get my coat, when I saw it. Resting on top of a pile of partially opened mail – bills mainly. A letter from her school.

Class Manfredi has the unique opportunity to attend a performance by theatre group Bakunin-B of Nobel Prize-winning laureate Dario Fo's seminal play **Accidental Death of an Anarchist** *in the courtyard of former hospital Mazzini. The play, which the students are studying as part of their syllabus, is a milestone of Italian literature and the school strongly recommends students are permitted to watch it performed live in the matinee performance offered gratis by Bakunin-B.*

Please provide your permission for your child to attend the performance on the slip printed below.

The slip had been removed.

Chapter 33

'I've just realised,' I said, returning to the table, holding the letter, 'she's out this afternoon – after-school activity.' I picked up my phone and grabbed my coat.

'Aren't you staying for lunch, Dan?' Alba had her ladle poised above the pot.

'And I've also realised,' I said, 'I forgot I'd promised Luca we'd meet for lunch today – what with the funeral and everything, it slipped my mind. I'm sorry!'

'You should phone him and tell him to come to join us,' said Alba, 'now Rose isn't here there's more than enough . . .'

'I would,' I said, 'but he's been going on about this new place in Via Solferino for ages . . . I promised . . .'

Alba assumed the expression of any Italian whose food has been spurned, but didn't look up. Jacopo didn't notice a thing – he was too busy with his phone – while the Comandante, whom I would usually have expected to see through my sub-terfuge, was hungrily eyeing his meal, which would be his first post-hospital *ragu*.

I slipped out of the apartment and crossed the courtyard. When I had closed the main gate behind me, I began to run.

I slowed down as I approached the hospital. I wanted to give myself time to think, as well as get my breath back: *of course* the anarchists planned to hold a performance of their play directly after the funeral, it was the perfect event for the wake. But didn't that damn teacher, Signora Manfredi, realise what she was getting into? Even if there hadn't been any trouble at the funeral? Then it hit me: she was a bloody red herself. I could well imagine her hanging out with Paolo and Mario before eventually getting a proper job. This was about more than farms and plays: *La Manfredi* was indoctrinating the next generation.

'What do you think you're doing?'

'Coming in?' I said.

The pair of youths at the main entrance looked at each other, then the male shook his head. 'Sorry,' he said.

'Look,' I said, 'I'm a friend of Dolores, Mario . . .'

'You're a friend of Dolores?' the female, who looked like a real friend of Dolores with those piercings and tattoos, shook her head. 'I don't think so.'

'Just ask her,' I said.

'Can't. She's tied up.' She nodded at the black and white poster advertising the play. 'Performing.'

'Oh come on,' I said, 'what's one other person? My daughter's in there.'

'Dolores is your daughter?' said the male. 'Pull the other one.'

'What's your problem?' I said.

'What's *your* problem?' said the female. 'There are other performances.'

'Like I said, my daughter—'

'Dolores,' said the male.

'*Not Dolores*. She's with a school party, a group of kids.'

'But I don't get it,' said the female, 'why do you want to go in? Afraid the play might pollute their minds?'

'This is ridiculous,' I said. 'Look, if you must know, I'm worried about her.'

'She's got nothing to be afraid of from us!' she said with an appropriately Dolores-level of consternation.

'It's not you I'm worried about,' I said.

'Who then?'

'The police? They've been here before, remember? And I'm afraid they're going to come again after that stunt you played at the funeral.'

'Stunt?' said the female.

'The paint,' I said.

'I thought I recognised you,' said the male, 'look.' He showed the female the footage on his phone of me accompanying Marta Finzi to the car.

'That's you?' said the female. 'What did you want to do that for?'

'*Do what?*'

'Do you work for her or something?'

'I was just trying to do the right thing,' I said.

'The right thing would have been to leave her be.'

'Look,' I said, stepping forward, 'are you going to let me in?'

They exchanged another look, then stepped in front of me. 'No, we're not going to let you in, parasite. *Fuck off.*'

'*What?*'

'We're not going to let you drag your daughter away,' said the female, 'maybe she'll learn something, before it's too late.'

I thought about forcing my way through. I could probably get past these jokers but I could see others lurking in the background. It wasn't going to work. I backed off, walked away.

'But feel free to come and see one of the other performances,' the male called, '*you* might learn something too!'

I turned the corner and went down the lane to the gates, which opened on to the 'farm', but they too were bolted closed. I went back along the lane, trying to call Rose but still only getting through to her voicemail.

Okay, I thought, perhaps I was overreacting, getting worked up over nothing. In a sense, the *stronzi* on the door may have had a point – Rose would be furious if I pulled her out of the audience as if she was a naughty schoolgirl. I needed to calm down. I was probably still shaken from the funeral myself. I could go to a nearby bar, wait it out.

I passed the boarded-up doorway I had tried when I first visited the hospital but found locked. Well, it was worth a go. I removed the boarding and gave it a tentative shove.

It swung open.

I was in a dark, seemingly deserted corridor with a high ceiling and polished stone floor. Wide doorways were covered with multi-coloured Indian-style cotton hangings or banners, ranging from classic red and black anarchist symbols to gaudy prints featuring Che Guevara and the ubiquitous *PACE*. Behind them I glimpsed bedding, sleeping blankets, camping stoves. These were the former hospital wards that were now being used by the anarchists as dormitories. I followed the corridor along to a pair of double doors. I pushed through them and stepped into a long portico, which, in turn, looked onto the courtyard.

Mario Cento and his helpers had made a lot of progress since I had last been here: there was now a stage raised above the audience, which was sat upon mats and cushions on the floor in a crescent. I could see, simply by the colour scheme, that Rose's class of teenagers had been placed at the front, while the predominantly black-clad anarchists and their followers – those that weren't participating in the production at any rate – were sitting further back. Even from the portico I could hear the dialogue loud and clear – one of them was obviously an audio whizz and they had microphones hooked up, with the great amplifiers I had seen as part of the mobile sound system in the funeral procession raised up on either side of the stage.

The stage itself was set as an office, a tatty 1970s-style office with a huge, wooden desk placed in the centre, a potted plant, a coat stand and a few plastic chairs scattered about. In the background were photocopied wanted posters and a large window, closed by a pair of lurid orange curtains.

And talking of lurid: there was Rose's purple and green *Fedez* backpack, placed between her and Stefania near the rear of the class.

What the hell, I was here now. I picked my way through the anarchists, variously cross-legged, stretched out, hair braiding, dog stroking, spliff smoking, Tennants-supping, to crouch down beside her.

'Dad!'

'You can't keep away from this place, can you.'

'What are *you* doing here? *Again.*'

'Working, *again*. I hadn't realised there was the play. Is it any good?'

'It's . . . all right.'

'What's it about?'

'*Dad.*' She rolled her eyes.

'What?'

'*Everybody knows* what it's about. It's about the death of the anarchist, isn't it. You see – that one up there? That's "the Maniac", although no one actually knows he's mad, or a fraudster in any case, but he was arrested by the Inspector earlier on, who did know, but who had to go out, and now he's pretending to be the judge who's come to investigate the "accidental" death of the anarchist.

'So you see, now he's questioning the policemen involved and helping them to make up a story to cover themselves, while, in fact, cleverly getting them to admit that they did, actually, murder the anarchist. And look, there's Dolores!'

I had to look hard, but then I got it: beneath the blonde curly wig, her eyes heavy with blue and silver make-up, wearing a tight-fitting seventies dress and high heels, swinging a fake D&G handbag, it was indeed Dolores. She was playing Feletti, the reporter, and with some aplomb: Dolores' Feletti was astute yet morally compromised, part-crusader and part-hack, but which instinct would prevail? That was one of the questions the author would leave open at the end of the play.

'What's that accent?' I said.

'What do you mean?' said Rose.

'Is that supposed to be an *English* accent she's putting on?'

'*No.* Is it?'

Either way, the girl could act. The Maniac, played, of course, by Beppe, the Beard, should have stuck to rapping at funerals: he acted much the same way, declaiming like a Shakespearean chorus rather than a character in a play, while Mario, as the Inspector, reappearing toward the end of the play to unmask the Maniac, kept fluffing his lines.

The performance drew to a close. But instead of a curtain coming down, the cast unfurled a giant banner across the length of the stage bearing a photo of Paolo Solitudine. Written underneath in painted red capitals (the same red, I wondered, that had been pitched at Marta Finzi?) was MURDERED BY THE POLICE. The audience, including my daughter and her class, rose to their feet in applause, their teacher, *La Manfredi*, the most enthusiastic of the lot. Her expression only faltered when she saw me.

'Signor Leicester.' She struggled to keep the dismay from her voice. 'It was magnificent, no?'

'A very . . . passionate performance.'

'Passionate . . . yes!'

'What did you think, kids?' I asked.

'It was good,' said Rose. 'Dolores was great!'

'Stefania?'

'Good,' said Stefania, giggling. She looked down at her smartphone.

'You've got a fan,' I said to Dolores, who had arrived beside Signora Manfredi.

'You were wonderful, darling!' said Signora Manfredi, taking her face in her hands and giving her a big kiss.

'I actually meant my daughter,' I said. Dolores grinned.

I had never seen her look so unabashedly happy. Although she still had on that cheap blonde wig, the crude make-up, I had a glimpse of the girl Dolores could be. Strip away all the anger, piercings and shorn hair; show her a bit of encouragement, give her an opportunity to shine, and she could be worth so much more than the Chiara Delfioris of this world. She deserved better.

'Did you see? I missed my cue in the scene with the fake bomb,' she said.

'I didn't see anything, darling!' said *La Manfredi*. We all shook our heads.

'You seem to know each other well,' I said to Dolores.

'Signora Manfredi was my teacher,' she said.

'Ah.' I wondered how many other black-clad kids here *La Manfredi* had fostered. The teacher seemed to sense what I was thinking.

'You were one of my star pupils, Dolores, darling,' she said, 'I'm so very proud of you. And I hear from your lecturers you're now doing very well.'

'I do wonder what the point of it is, sometimes,' she said.

'With the marks you're getting, you could do a doctorate. I could help you apply for a scholarship.'

'And then what, *signora*? You know as well as I do, all the university jobs are sewn up. You need the connections. No one's going to hire me – they keep it all in their families.'

'Well, darling, you could always become . . .' I knew what she was going to say: a teacher. So did Dolores.

'Anyway,' she said, 'farming is the future.'

'Farming is the future!' said Rose, giving a raised fist salute. Stefania followed suit.

'You realise, don't you,' I said to Rose, 'you have to get up at five o'clock in the morning to milk the cows.' Dolores shook her head.

'Desdemona's a late sleeper. We don't start until eight.' She smiled at Rose. 'You could come and help me out if you like. Why don't you ask your dad?'

'Dad?'

'Sure,' I said. I looked at Dolores. 'We'll see how long it lasts.'

'You'll see,' said Rose. 'He's always putting me down,' she said to Dolores.

'You know that's not true,' I said. Signora Manfredi and Dolores were scowling at me. 'It's just . . . she has these enthusiasms . . .' Mario Cento came to stand at the centre of the stage and began signalling to someone at the back. The sound system began to blast out the usual Italian rap.

'Well, we ought to be going,' I said. I indicated to Rose and Stefania to get their things. Rose looked ready to argue, so I said, 'I've got a treat in store for the pair of you.' Whatever *that* was: I would worry about it after I had got them outside. 'There was just one thing, Dolores, I was wondering: what role was Paolo playing?'

'What?'

'In the play. I couldn't help thinking when I was watching it, what role Paolo Solitudine was down for.'

'The Inspector,' said Dolores.

'Ah,' I said, 'that would explain it – why Mario wasn't so . . . polished.'

The girls had already got their coats on and their backpacks at the ready. It was amazing what the prospect of a treat could do.

'That role, the Inspector,' I said. 'He comes in at the beginning, then again at the end, correct?'

'That's right.'

'And the raid, when it happened. I was told it was during a run through of the play.' Dolores nodded. 'What part?'

'Part?' she said.

'The beginning, the middle or the end?'

'I suppose you could say the middle. It was the bit when the Superintendent turns up.'

'So, when you said he was at the rehearsal, at the time the police raid actually took place, Paolo wasn't on stage.'

'No, but—'

'But my point is, Dolores – you didn't actually *see* him, did you? When you said he was there, you had just presumed he was present.'

'All right, I didn't *see* him, not all the time. I was playing my own part. But I saw him hanging around . . . why?'

I shook my head. 'It's not important.' I could have told her that I already knew where Paolo had got to, that seeing it up there on stage had simply helped clarify matters. That access to the canal via the kitchens had provided Paolo with the opportunity to slip away unnoticed for his meeting with Manzi. But then, on the way back . . . Still, I wasn't about to get into that in front of a pair of teenage girls and their politically subversive teacher.

'Come on, kids,' I said, wondering if a gelato would suffice, then I heard it, we all did – ripping across the courtyard, cutting through the bass-heavy rap in terrified treble. A woman's scream.

Chapter 34

They poured out of the portico, batons raised, visors down, round shields at the ready, hitting out at everything, everyone. Fortunately for us, the outer-circle of anarchists took the initial impact. By this time, the lucky ones had managed to get to their feet, but there were still a fair number zonked out on the floor and the best they could do was try to cover their heads as the blows and kicks rained down. As for the ones standing up, it would have been funny if it hadn't been so painfully real: they didn't even have chairs to defend themselves with and when they weren't trying to hold off the cops with their arms and legs, they were hitting back at them with cushions and pillows they had picked up off the floor. It seemed one hell of an uneven battle.

Rose's class, except Rose herself and Stefania, who were hiding behind me, had clumped together around Signora Manfredi. The girls were screaming, the handful of boys rooted to the spot. I grabbed Dolores, who had wrenched a piece of wood from the stage, thrown off her wig, and was heading toward the throng, ready to do battle.

'Wait,' I said, 'you've got to help us.'

'We've got to fight!' she said.

'We've got to get these kids out of danger,' I said. We watched a wheelchair carrying an old hippy being tipped onto its side by a cop who began dragging its occupant across the courtyard by his hair.

'This way,' said Dolores. By now most of the portico around the courtyard was crawling with cops, along with the prone bodies of those anarchists who had either been in the wrong place at the wrong time or dragged inside for an extra beating, but they had yet to reach the far corner of the complex. 'Quick,' Dolores said. We crossed the portico and went through a doorway I recognised – it led to the kitchens.

'You're not thinking of the canals,' I shuddered at the thought of being trapped down there with all these kids.

'No.' She ran ahead and unlocked another door – it opened onto the farm. She peered out. 'They're not here yet. If we can make it to the gate, it's bolted from inside.'

I nodded. 'Kids.' I turned around. 'I know you're scared but just do everything we say and you'll be all right. Okay?' They nodded at me wide-eyed, while in the background all we could hear were the sounds of fear, pain, and violence. 'Let's go,' I said. There was no time to waste.

We kept low, crouching behind the old hedges and trees that bordered the 'urban farm'. Across the field – in reality, more like a series of allotments – we could see smoke beginning to billow upwards from the courtyard. White-grey smoke. Wood smoke: they were setting fire to the stage.

Squatting behind an old iron bench ahead of us, Dolores raised her hand and, behind a hedge myself, I stopped. One of the girls stood up to take a look at what was happening and I waved to their teacher, who pulled her unceremoniously down. Then I took a peek myself.

A couple of cops had come outside, dragging a protestor between them. They began beating him – wordlessly, almost mechanically, the thud of their batons audible across the field while he lay in a foetal position trying to cover his head. 'Keep them down,' I hissed at Manfredi. I didn't want the kids to see this.

Above us, a helicopter began to circle. We couldn't stay here – it was only a matter of time before we were spotted either from above or below.

A shrill, electric whistle. Barked instructions over the police radios. The thudding ceased. When I looked over the bench again, the police had disappeared. Only a black shape was left on the ground, beginning to unfold itself. The man let out a low moan. Dolores raised her hand and beckoned us on.

By the time we made it to the gate, we had broken into a run. I realised we must have been seen by now, at least from above, but I was gambling that after Dolores had opened the gates it would be too late.

She fell against it, slamming her palm against the old iron bar and lifting it up. 'Quick,' she said. We both leaned against the door to push it open. The kids crowded around us and pushed too. We spilled onto the lane – straight into a wall of flashing blue lights. A line of riot police raised their shields and drew their batons. 'Wait!' I held out my hands. 'These are kids! School kids!' Behind them, atop a satellite dish-festooned van there was a camera crew. 'Schoolchildren!

Please.' My hands were raised above my head now, Rose and Stefania clinging onto either side of me.

He stepped from the police ranks and raised his visor. It was Sergeant Romano. 'There's no getting rid of you, is there,' he said softly. Then he turned to face his colleagues, and the cameras. 'Rest easy, lads,' he announced, 'these are just schoolchildren. We're here to make sure they don't get hurt. Is there someone from the Red Cross around? Quick, corporal, see if there's someone from the Red Cross.' He asked me loudly, solicitously, 'Did any of the anarchists harm you or the children, sir?'

'Come on, kids,' I said, 'it's all right.' Romano nodded and the police line began to part in a rattle of plastic armour. The children shuffled through, dwarfed by the forces of law and order.

Signora Manfredi brought up the rear, her face a portrait of anguish. She tried to say something to me, but nothing came out. I turned to grab Dolores – this would be my only chance to get her out in one piece – but she was hanging behind, looking in the direction of the farm. 'No,' I saw her mouth. Her feet begun to carry her back inside.

'Dad?' Rose was tugging at my hand. 'Dad?'

'You go,' I said, pushing her gently forward, 'with Signora Manfredi.'

'*Dad*, I can't leave you here!'

'Go, Rose,' I said, 'you'll be safe now. Please, do as I say.'

'But what about you?'

'I'll be fine,' I said. 'I've just got to check that Dolores—'

'*Dad.*'

I called back Signora Manfredi and placed Rose's hand in

her's. My daughter, who was wearing, I noticed for the first time, her mother's olive turtleneck jumper beneath her puffa jacket, began to move away from me. I watched the pair of them pass between the police ranks. Rose looked mournfully over her shoulder before they closed behind her.

'You're not leaving with them, Englishman?' Romano said. 'It would be better for you if you did.'

'My friend,' I mumbled, stepping backwards.

'Your friend?' He caught my shoulder as I tried to go through the gate. '*Don't*,' he said, but I pulled away from him and crossed the threshold.

Chapter 35

They were holding burning torches. They must have lit them from the fire in the courtyard – lengths of wood wrapped with material taken from those lurid curtains, maybe even the banner that had hung above the stage proclaiming their culpability. Now it was being used to torch the buildings and structures outside.

They didn't see Dolores approaching them – they wouldn't have been expecting anyone to come from that direction and, in any case, they were thoroughly absorbed in their work, doling out armfuls of hay to start burning the empty shelters, gathering up farm implements and other combustible materials, or simply standing back to enjoy the spectacle. Dolores moved among them, seemingly invisible, as if it was the most ordinary thing in the world for a slender, shoeless girl in a seventies dress to pass through their ranks while they laid waste to the farm.

She entered the cow shed, which was already billowing black smoke from its corrugated roof, yet still, no one seemed to see her. It was only when she emerged, coughing, blackened by smoke herself, her arms around Desdemona's neck, trying to haul the cow forward, that they first took notice.

Desdemona was in a bad way, crazed by the flames. Her head lurched from side to side. Her body heaved. She stumbled forward and her legs buckled. She got to her feet.

I had reached the police lines myself by now, but all eyes were on the spectacle of Dolores and Desdemona in front of the burning building.

'Water!' pleaded Dolores, 'bring us water!' I spotted a tin bucket by a tap and made for that. It was already full, but as I tried to deliver it, a cop caught my arm.

'They're for burning,' he said.

'It's not for the buildings,' I said, 'it's for *them*.' He let me go and I barged through the ranks. 'Here,' I said as I reached them. The cow had begun moving in terrified circles.

'Put it to her mouth,' said Dolores, 'try to get her to drink.'

I raised the bucket, but the cow batted it out of my hands and onto the ground. She bolted backwards towards the burning shed and carried Dolores with her. I went after them, but Desdemona soon felt the heat and rushed forward again, leaving Dolores facedown on the ground. The cow was free now. Confused, crazed, the sheer bulk of her out of control.

Then I heard it, the pistol crack.

Desdemona froze. There was another bang, and her front legs went under her, then her back. She remained upright for a moment before tipping sideways. She lay on the ground, her vast brown and white belly heaving.

Desdemona lifted her head upwards. The heat, the smoke, the chaos – it must have seemed like a circle of hell through those huge uncomprehending eyes.

Sergeant Romano came to stand above her. He pointed

his pistol downwards. Another pair of deafening cracks. The cow's head fell flat onto the dirt. Her belly heaved a final time.

Then Dolores was there, kneeling to cradle the cow's head, blood soaking into her dress as she rocked back and forth.

'Stupid bitch,' said a voice.

'What did she think she was doing, keeping that animal here?'

'These people, they're all the same – they think they can do anything.'

'Bet she was breaking a stack of laws.'

'Stupid bitch.'

'It had to be done,' said Romano. He looked down at the gun in his hand, smoke still seeping from its barrel. 'She was on the rampage, she could have killed someone.'

Dolores looked up at him, her cheek smeared with Desdemona's blood. 'Murderer.' She shook her head. 'You're all murderers.'

'When will you learn, love?' said Romano. 'It goes like this: dead humans, well, that can equal murder unless, that is, they're just stupid, sloppy bastards like your pal and fall into the canal. Dead cows on the other hand . . . well, I'm sorry, darling, but that means burgers.'

It was only when Dolores came at him I realised what she had in her hand – a machete she must have plucked from a nearby pile of wood and farm implements. I don't think even Romano understood until the last moment, otherwise he might well have thought about raising his pistol and simply shooting her, but as it was he blocked her falling blade with an upturned forearm lined by polycarbonate, then smashed her around the face with the side of his gun. Dolores dropped to the floor, out cold.

Romano shook his head. 'Silly, silly girl,' he said. 'And that, gentlemen, is what we call "attempted murder".'

Chapter 36

We stood in a circle around the unconscious girl until, after an almost indiscernible tilt of Romano's blue helmet, the machinery of the state reanimated. A pair of lumbering cops knelt over her, slapping her around the face until she blinked dazedly, then lifted her to her feet and secured her hands behind her back with plastic cuffs. Another pair were about to do the same to me when Romano raised his hand.

'Leave him,' he said. They let me go. 'Next time,' he said, 'you'll do what I tell you. Except there won't be a next time, will there. You should look out. You're not even fucking European any more – I can have you on the next plane back to your crappy island.'

I watched them lead Dolores away, still only half-conscious. The cowshed was fully ablaze now, belching smoke into the sky while the police trampled back and forth over the carefully cultivated crops, swiping at the vines with their batons and gathering up anything combustible for the fire.

One thing was for sure: it was all over for the kids at the old hospital.

*

I took my time returning home, the time necessary to collect my thoughts before facing Rose, but when I arrived at the Faidate Residence she was in none of her usual places. I called her mobile – and heard it ringing in the next room. I plucked it off the kitchen table.

'Rose!' I called. Then I noticed her backpack and jacket in a pile next to her shoes in the cubby beneath the stairs. The stairs led to only two places – a terrace, but she was unlikely to have gone outside, or the attic. And that was where I found her.

She was in the room beneath the eves with its window that looked out over the chimneys and towers of Bologna. This place . . . I knew this place – it was where I had retreated in the days and weeks following Lucia's death, a largely forgotten corner of the family fortress used to store battered old cases, dusty legal journals, children's games; a room that had once, presumably, been servants' quarters, at the edge of the roof that ran across the building and was still supported by the trunks of trees felled hundreds of years ago, beams that had probably witnessed countless dramas played out below.

Rose was curled up among Lucia's old clothes. Her head was resting upon a pile of jumpers, her body covered by an old purple faux-fur coat. It had been the early days in London, one freezing morning at Camden Market, when I'd bought it for Lucia to stop her shivering. We had hiked up Primrose Hill and embraced hotly, like the young lovers we were, then gone down to the centre to see a film, and I knew that, as we walked, wrapped around each other through the park, that fake fur pressing against my neck, I would marry her.

'Dad.' Rose was looking drowsily up at me. 'You're all right.'

I sat down beside her. 'Look, Rose, I just wanted to say—'

'You smell of burning.'

'There was a fire.'

'And Dolores?'

I broke the news as gently as I could, although there was no easy way to soften two essential truths: that Desdemona was dead and Dolores had been arrested.

I held Rose as she sobbed, reached for Lucia's coat and wrapped it around the pair of us.

'I can't take it,' said Rose.

'What can't you take, darling?'

'These deaths.'

I closed my eyes, but this time it was no good – the tears came anyway, although Rose didn't seem to notice, or in any case, mind.

'I'm sorry,' I said. I didn't know what else to say.

'I think of her, you know – Mum.'

'I know you do, love.'

'I know it doesn't seem like it, but I do. Every day. Well . . . almost every. Sometimes I forget. And then I feel guilty.'

'You shouldn't feel guilty,' I said. 'She'd want you to be happy. She'd want that most of all.'

'That's why I tried on her clothes. I thought she would like that.'

'She would. She'd love it. I'm sorry if I seemed . . . I don't know . . .'

'That's okay,' she said. 'I should have asked. I'm sorry that I'm bad sometimes.'

I shook my head. 'I'm sorry, too. That I'm bad sometimes, I mean.'

She looked up at me and dabbed my tears with her sleeve, Lucia's sleeve. 'That's okay,' she said. 'Mum would want you to be happy, too.' Rose rested her head back against my chest, and we stayed like that until it grew dark.

Chapter 37

A pall hung over the city, the plumes from the fires in the old hospital seemingly contributing another layer of grey to the dreary, blanket sky, the smell of burned wood assuming a particular potency in the area around Via Mazzini.

The Battle of Ospedale Santa Maria Maddalena, as it had been billed in the *Carlino*, was over, and the 'anarchist band', as the paper put it, had been 'scattered to the winds'. Some were in hospital, others had fled, more were in gaol for crimes 'ranging from obstruction to attempted murder'. 'We are devastated that this had to happen,' said Mayor Carlo Manzi, 'but we cannot stand by and allow our progress, and the well-being of all Bolognese, to be blocked by a tiny minority bent on obstruction and destruction', although, as every reader of the *Carlino* knew, the real reason for 'the battle' was revenge for the attack on the Mayor's wife at the funeral, and quite right too, many of them had probably muttered. The Mayor was a man like anyone else, and did what he had to do.

I was getting ready to visit Dolores when Rose asked if she could come.

'I'm not sure they permit children, darling,' I lied.

'No, you cannot,' said the Comandante, looking up from his morning paper. Both my daughter and I were startled: he had never told Rose 'no' to anything. 'I am not having my granddaughter visiting a red accused of the attempted murder of a policeman,' he said.

'Even a corrupt one?' I said. He glared at me.

'But she's my friend!' said Rose. She began to furiously dab at her phone.

'Dolores didn't mean it, Giovanni,' I said, 'you know that. And it was her that got us out of that mess.'

'You wouldn't have been in it in the first place had it not been for her and her friends and their disgraceful behaviour at the funeral.'

'I'm increasingly beginning to have my doubts about that, which is one of the reasons I want to visit her,' I said.

'Oh?' he said, then he realised it referred to the Solitudine case. 'Oh,' he said.

'It says here that anyone can visit,' said Rose, holding up her phone, 'people who are under "pre-trial preventative detention" can see whomever they like. I could go on my own if I wanted.'

'You are not going on your own,' said the Comandante.

'I could – she's my friend and you can't stop me!' The pair of them glared at each other across the table. This was truly something to behold – our very own Battle of the Faidate Residence.

'You can come with me, Rose,' I said, looking at the Comandante, who scowled and picked up his newspaper, 'if you get a move on.'

*

'What was wrong with Granddad?' said Rose as we pulled out of the courtyard.

'Wrong?'

'He was so angry. I've never seen him so angry.'

'He just worries about you, darling, that's all,' I said.

'Why should he be worried?'

'Because he doesn't realise,' I said, 'what a tough cookie you are. It's your bulldog spirit.'

'My what?'

'Bulldog spirit,' I said, 'it's a British trait. It means you're fearless.'

'Oh,' said Rose. She twisted around. 'Can we get one?'

'What?' I said, knowing exactly what.

'A bulldog!'

'*No,*' I said. 'It's a big commitment—'

'I'll walk him,' she said.

'That's why it's a commitment,' I said, 'because it'd be me who'd be doing the walking, after your excitement had worn off.'

'Dad . . . *please* . . . say you'll think about it.'

'I know what you're doing,' I said, 'do you think I'm stupid?'

'You're great!'

'Didn't you hear me?'

'We can call him Lorenzo,' she said. I glanced at her. I wasn't going to fall for that one, either. Some mysteries were better left unsolved.

We took Via Stalingrad, out toward La Dozza, past the prostitutes standing beneath their umbrellas, then crossed the outer ring road – the Tangenziale – onto Via del Gomito. The prison finally loomed into view.

'It doesn't look like a gaol,' said Rose, as we swung into the car park, 'are you sure this is the right place?'

'What's a gaol supposed to look like?'

'I don't know, older, with big walls . . .'

'Like a castle?'

'Yeah,' she said, 'sort of?'

'This is worse,' I said, parking the car with the great grey seventies prison blocks in the rear mirror. 'At least a castle would look cool, no?' Indeed, if La Dozza resembled anything, it was the city's main hospital, Maggiore, thrown up around the same time on the other side of the city – another oversize tower block that told nothing about the pain and sorrow contained therein.

I felt Rose come close to me as we approached the reception, although she didn't take my hand in the girlish way she still sometimes affected when we stepped out. This was serious business, grown-up business.

We were processed no more or less efficiently than at any other organ of Comune bureaucracy. The insides of the building too bore little of the Victorian gloom of some slammers I'd visited in the UK. The sour-cream-coloured walls, the noticeboards, plastic bucket seats, the scuffed linoleum floor, could be out of any Italian school, hospital or government office. Only the uniforms, and the preponderance of white-painted bars on the windows, doorways and at intervals along the corridors, gave the game away.

As Dolores came toward us in that formless pale blue tracksuit and flip flops, she looked little different to the rest of the young women – hustlers and whores, I guessed, mostly of Eastern European descent. Dolores seemed particularly young and scrawny, I thought, stripped of her piercings, the punky outfit that projected her personality. She belonged to the state now, and its first priority was to deprive you of your individuality.

I thought of the joy I'd glimpsed beneath that blonde wig just a couple of days earlier, looked at the girl pulling back the orange plastic chair, sitting on the other side of the table: the black and yellow bruising running from her cheekbone down to her jaw where she had been whacked by Romano's pistol, her head animated by a nervous twitch, her hands clasped restlessly in her lap – clenching, unclenching – only those hazel eyes relatively still, looking at the pair of us as if searching for something, anything, to hold on to.

I pushed a packet of cigarettes across the table. Dolores took them, saying an almost inaudible thank you before placing them, unopened, on her lap.

I looked at Rose who had, after all, been so keen to come, but who was now sitting there dumbly, overwhelmed, no doubt, by the thundering adult reality of it all.

'I've got some questions,' I said. Dolores' glance flickered between the pair of us. She tore open the cigarette packet, took one out. She leaned over to the woman on the next table and got a light.

'Go on,' she said, bereft of her usual cocky charm.

'Did you know your boyfriend, Beppe, was going to pull that trick with the paint?' Dolores looked surprised. She shook her head.

'No,' she said, 'why?'

'Because it was obvious there would be a response, no? It was like an invitation to attack the hospital.'

Dolores took an agitated drag. 'It doesn't work like that,' she said, 'if we had to worry about how the authorities would respond, we would never do anything. It's like the partisans—'

'The partisans?' said Rose, who had been studying them in class.

'If the partisans had been worried about reprisals they would never have fought back,' said Dolores.

Rose nodded as if that made sense. She looked at me. I wondered what on earth I was doing here with my teenage daughter.

'They didn't do suicide missions though, as a rule, Dolores,' I said. 'Now your group has been evicted from the hospital. You're in prison. Desdemona is dead.'

'I . . .' Dolores' eyes welled with tears. Rose gave me an admonitory look.

'How long have you and Beppe been dating?' I said.

'How long? Dating?' She shrugged. 'We don't really—'

'How long have you known him?'

'About three months. Why?'

'He's on your course?'

'No, he's older than me. He's doing a post-grad in politics.'

'But would you say that you knew him well?'

'I . . . well, yes. Of course!'

'Did you tell him about the journal?'

'I . . .' She bit her lip, shook her head.

'Why not?'

'It . . . just didn't come up.' She thought about it. 'All right, maybe I didn't want him to know I was helping you. That I gave it to you. He didn't like you. He didn't trust you.'

I nodded. 'And the keys. Paolo's keys. What did you do with them after we had used them?'

'I . . .' She looked at Rose. She looked at me. 'I gave them to Beppe. Why?'

'The police got in through the door I used. It was locked before, when I visited you the first time. This time it was open. Someone must have unlocked it.'

Dolores was shaking her head. 'What are you saying?'

'That Beppe let them in,' said Rose.

Dolores looked at Rose. 'No,' she said.

'That's what you were saying, wasn't it, Dad?' I just looked at Dolores.

'No,' she repeated.

'Has Beppe come,' I said, 'to visit you?'

'What's that got to do with it?'

'Has he been in touch?'

'What are you trying to say, Daniel?'

Rose looked about to tell her, so I held up my hand.

'You read the journal,' I said, 'at least parts. You could see how Paolo's group was manipulated, betrayed. How they were infiltrated.'

'You're saying Beppe's . . .' Dolores sunk back in her chair.

'I don't know, Dolores,' I said. 'But something's not right. Did you know that Paolo was looking into the Comune's property sales?'

She shook her head.

'How does your group select new properties to occupy?'

Dolores thought about it. 'Mario and Paolo would usually come up with a proposal, scout it out. And . . .' She swallowed. 'Beppe, too.'

'So Beppe was involved in this process?'

Dolores nodded. 'We don't have hierarchies, but it's true, Beppe is the one they go to. In fact, Beppe found the hospital. And some of the ones before.'

'Like the court building?'

Dolores nodded. 'I think so. But you don't think he could have had something to do with it, do you? Paolo's death?'

I could feel Rose's eyes on me, rapt. 'I'm just trying to tie up some loose ends,' I said. 'But let's keep this conversation between the two,' I looked at Rose, 'the *three* of us, for now, okay? Please don't say anything to Beppe, if he does show up, just to be on the safe side. In the meantime, what's being done to get you out of this place?'

Dolores shook her head. 'Forget it,' she said. 'I'm fucked,' then looked at Rose. 'I'm sorry,' she said.

'It . . . may seem like that,' I said, 'but you're young. You're strong. If you stay strong you can get through this.'

'*How?*'

'Have you spoken to a lawyer?'

'The lawyer?' She rolled her eyes. 'They gave me a lawyer. He doesn't give a shit . . .'

'What did he tell you?'

'That I was fu— that it was best if I just pleaded guilty, maybe then they'd let me off lightly.'

'It's not so open and shut,' I said.

'How so? I hit him with a machete!'

'But did you mean to?' I said.

'Of course I meant to!'

'Maybe you didn't realise it was a machete. Maybe you thought it was just a piece of wood.'

'No – I knew it was a machete. I wanted to split that bastard's head in two for what he did to Desdemona.' The blood was returning to her cheeks. I had a glimpse of the old Dolores.

'But you get my point, don't you, Dolores? It's their word against yours. There were piles of wood lying around they were building fires with. When you picked it up you just thought it was a piece of wood.'

'No one will believe me. He's got all those witnesses, all those *pigs*.'

'And me,' I said.

'What? You too?'

'No, what I mean is – I was there too, I could speak on your behalf.'

Dolores eyed me suspiciously. 'Why would you want to do that?'

'You say I'm a cynic,' I said. 'Maybe it's in my interests. You're not much good to me here, but outside, well, maybe together we might just get to the bottom of this.'

Dolores shrugged, then nodded. She might not believe me, but what did she have to lose? 'And anyway,' I said, 'it'd be worth it to wipe the smile off that fucker Romano's face.'

'Murderer,' intoned Dolores.

'Murdering fucker,' said Rose.

It was good to leave Dolores looking more like her old self, and Rose was in fine fettle too. 'We'll show the fucker,' she said as we got in the car.

'Rose,' I said, 'please, *basta*. I should never have used that word.'

'You think I don't use those words?' said Rose. 'I know worse ones—'

'I'm sure you do, but are you old enough to know how to use them?'

'What does that mean? Of course I am! Do you want me to explain what they mean?'

'*No.* No, thank you. What I mean is, one of the reasons we don't use swear words in front of you is . . . well, apart from the fact you're still a child—'

'I'm thirteen!'

'All right, a teenager, is that you might use them in the wrong place, and it might upset people, like your grandfather, for example.'

'It wouldn't take much.'

'You should cut him some slack. He's been under a lot of pressure recently.'

'About this job you've been doing with Dolores?'

'Sort of.'

'Because it has "raked up the past"?'

'Yeah,' I said, 'something like that.'

'Was it really like *Accidental Death of an Anarchist*?'

'Those days?' I said. 'It would seem so, only without the jokes. It was a tough time for your granddad. To leave the house every day, not knowing if he would return that evening. It must have been very stressful for everyone.'

Rose was silent for a while, then she said, 'You'll always come back, won't you, Dad?'

'Of course,' I said. 'Those days have passed. Don't worry, darling.'

She turned to me. 'But they haven't really, have they.'

Chapter 38

'We are not getting her a lawyer!' said the Comandante. 'Do you want to destroy us?'

'I'm not saying we pay for one, Giovanni,' I said, 'only that we ask around, see if we can get someone a bit sharper to represent her.' We were in the office on Marconi. Outside, the fog, which had been hanging like a veil since morning, had begun to thicken.

'Do you realise how this will be viewed?' said the Comandante. 'As if we are taking sides – the wrong side. Ours is a very tribal business, Daniel, people close ranks, and are expected to. To be seen to be protecting someone who tried to murder a police officer would be the end of it for us.'

'It was the heat of the moment,' I said. 'Sergeant Romano had just killed her cow.'

'Her *cow*, Daniel. Just a cow, a rampaging animal. He did what any responsible officer would have done.'

'You had to be there,' I said.

'I doubt very much that I would have been there,' he said. He didn't need to add – and neither would my daughter.

'Spare me the sanctimony, Comandante,' I said. 'You're defending a cop who's corrupt to the core.'

We sat facing each other in mutual incomprehension. 'Perhaps you misunderstand me,' he said slowly. 'When it pertains to the survival of our business, it is not a case of morality. It is neither here nor there if Sergeant Romano is corrupt.'

'Because we – or at least *you*,' I said, 'are implicated in this whole dirty business. You're afraid.'

'How dare you! I have proved my courage many, many times over, young man.'

'But as one gets older, one starts to feel more vulnerable, isn't that so, Comandante?'

'And you,' the Comandante said, '*brim* with the pitilessness of youth.'

'On the contrary, Giovanni, I am not so young, and I am full of pity.'

'Catastrophically misplaced,' he said, 'in my opinion.'

'These people tried to kill you, Giovanni. I think if anything is misplaced it's your loyalty.'

'We don't know that,' he said.

'We don't know a lot of things,' I said, 'but we can make some pretty good guesses.'

'I am *not* afraid,' said the Comandante. 'Perhaps you are right, perhaps it *was* an attempt on my life. Or a warning. But either way, *I am not afraid*, of any of that. We all have to answer for our actions sooner or later, either in this life or the next.

'But I *am* afraid for you, Daniel. For Jacopo, for Alba. For Rose. I'm afraid for the family, the business. Of the direction you wish to take us in – as some kind of campaigners for social justice it seems – at the cost of our contacts, our friends. These hippies won't pay the bills. And when I'm gone, where will you be? What will Jacopo do? Who will provide for Rose? Yes, I am afraid, Daniel. I am afraid for the future.'

'I am only asking,' I said, 'to give the girl a helping hand. Discreetly. We really do owe her that much.'

The Comandante shook his head. 'The only debt we owe, Daniel, is to this family. I hoped you would have understood that by now.'

I stood up, left his office, went for my coat. I heard the Comandante call after me but kept going – out of the building, and into the gathering fog.

I went looking for Beppe, the Beard.

The fog might have been eulogised in this part of the world for its stillness and obscurity but as I stepped outside it wasn't the bucolic Emilian countryside it called to my mind, rather the smoke that had risen up from the old hospital in Mazzini and fallen upon the city like a belated reproach.

I headed down Via Marconi then cut towards the university zone, the confrontation with the Comandante dogging me even as I tried to place Beppe front and centre. I was angry for losing my temper with Giovanni when I knew he only had our best interests at heart. I was angry for walking away. But I was angry, too, with him for not revealing the whole story, for being tied up with this black fund, for the taint it left upon us all.

The paint, I thought, sticks to everyone in the end.

The fog kept thickening, driving people inside. One like

this could swallow a city – even a city as large as Bologna. I kept to the porticoes, like a good Bolognese. The few cars were snailing forward in a haze of reflected headlights, the remaining cyclists nervously pinging their bells. The porticoes had become like tunnels bored through dirty, watery snow.

I didn't know where Beppe would be living now the squat had been closed down, but I knew where he was supposed to be studying.

The political science faculty was buzzing even more than usual, the students crowding the corridors, averse to venturing outside. Without a great deal of hope, I went to the lady at the reception desk. 'I'm looking for Giuseppe Farinelli,' I said. 'He's a post-graduate student.' Dolores had not been able to tell me the name of his professor, only his field of specialisation. 'He's writing a dissertation on the politics of urban planning.'

'Ah,' said the lady behind the lady I was speaking to, 'that will be Gotti.'

'Ah yes, try Professor Gotti on the first floor. There, up the stairs on the right.' I mounted the staircase – the same one I had taken to the office of Marta Finzi. But this came as no surprise, she was a professor in the same faculty. Ditto that she was on the same floor, the same corridor . . . but next door to Gotti? I stopped outside her closed office door. Possessed of little more than recklessness, I tried it. It was locked.

I moved to Professor Gotti's door and knocked.

'Come.'

At an untidy desk in front of the window sat a rather corpulent male professor with a green and white spotted bowtie.

At a smaller desk pressed against the partition with his back to me, was a dark-haired student bent over a laptop.

'I'm sorry to bother you,' I said, 'I'm trying to track down one of your students.' The student looked around – it was Beppe.

'In fact,' I said, 'I've found him.'

'You two know each other?' said the professor.

'I wouldn't exactly say that,' I said.

'You're not one of his rabble-rousing associates then?' The professor looked me up and down. 'But not the police, either, I hope!' He gave Beppe a reproachful look. Beppe shook his head.

'No, Professor,' I said, 'not the police.'

'So what do you want him for then?' The professor appeared to have assumed the role of Beppe's advocate.

'Really,' I said, 'it's nothing. I was just wondering if he had had a chance to visit his girlfriend yet?' Beppe looked startled. 'When I went she looked like she could do with seeing a friendly face.'

'What girlfriend is this?' said the professor. 'Is there something wrong with her?'

'You could say that.' I glanced over Beppe's shoulder at his computer. He realised what I was doing and pulled the lid down.

'Of course,' he said, 'of course I have.'

'Of course you have,' I said. I stood looking at him.

'Is that it?' said Beppe. The professor pulled out an unlit pipe and began to fill it. He looked curiously at me.

'That's it,' I said.

I closed the door and left the building, stepping into the busy portico. It was even louder than usual with the noise of the students bouncing off the fog. I headed to the Cluricaune. The pub was large enough for me to go unnoticed. Or so I thought.

'That will be three euros, Daniel *Lest-her*,' said Giorgio, the barman.

'That joke could quickly wear thin.'

'To you, maybe, Daniel *Lest-her*.'

I took my Guinness and headed for a quiet corner. I thought back to meeting Marta Finzi in her office, the partition that hadn't quite reached the ceiling or the ends of the walls. Beppe would have simply had to position himself close to the gap to hear everything we were saying. And of course I had been picked up soon afterwards. My instinct had been to blame Marta once I learned of her involvement in the Omega scam, but that hadn't really added up – why alert her husband's associates when my investigation was meant to remain a secret?

So it *had* been Beppe, then. Beppe who was Romano's inside man. Beppe who was now playing the part once occupied by Carlo Manzi – the *agent provocateur* – among these modern-day revolutionaries. And what about Dolores? Was she supposed to become the new Marta Finzi?

I found Ispettore Alessandro's number in my contacts. My finger hovered over it. If it was true Romano had gone rogue then I had nothing to fear. But was the *ispettore* telling the truth?

I pressed the message icon.

We need to speak, I wrote.

Alessandro responded almost immediately.

Ex-Monastery of the Capuchins, 16.30.

It was three o'clock. I started walking.

Chapter 39

The Ex-Monastery wasn't far away – the distance from the centre of the city to where the last, or furthest, of the old perimeter walls had stood before it had been torn down to make way for the Viale – but I wasn't going to stroll into a meeting with Ispettore Umberto Alessandro without scouting out the location first.

When I checked out the building on my phone, I was pretty sure I had landed on the same web page Beppe had shut down when I had been in the office. An estate agent's site, focusing on property developers. The site explained that the old monastery had been disestablished during Napoleon's short-lived rule of the city. After Boney had been given the heave-ho it had been retained for public use, most recently by the Comune for meetings and special events. But of course the Comune was now trying to get rid of it, for offers above three-million euros.

The Ex-Monastery of the Capuchins had a great deal of potential for luxury development, not least because of the frescoes by the Carducci brothers that still graced the porticoes at the entrance, and the high wall that ran for half a kilometre along the length of the Viale, concealing a space where the monks had once cultivated wine and olives, and that had subsequently been used for barracks by the Germans during the Second World War. It was now a mix of derelict wooden buildings and abandoned greenhouses.

It would provide the anarchists with a perfect replacement for the old hospital on Mazzini, I thought. The land, even, for their farm. The only problem was – like the hospital – it would be short-lived.

If Beppe was Romano's inside man, he was taking his orders about what property to target next. That was what Solitudine had worked out: that the anarchists were being used to beat down asking prices. After all, who was going to buy a building occupied by a bunch of *punkabbestias*? The irony – those devoted anti-capitalists were being manipulated by the police not out of fear of revolution, but to fix the property market.

This was why Beppe's antics at the funeral made sense. The anarchists' occupation of the old hospital had outlived its usefulness. Now, it seemed, they were about to have somewhere new to go.

Was that the answer then? Had Beppe realised Paolo had got wind of what he was up to and decided to get rid of him? Did this explain the first attack on the hospital – which Beppe must have been aware was coming? Had Solitudine known Beppe was the police mole? Had he confronted him? And where did the meeting with the Mayor fit into all this?

And what was Alessandro's part? I had contacted him because I had taken a gamble – that the Comandante was right and he could be trusted. But it was a gamble sure enough: the *ispettore* had beckoned me into the very heart of the conspiracy.

The fog had finally begun to thin as I left what would have marked the limits of the old city and I crossed the Viale, walking through the small piazza which was now used as a car park in front of the former monastery. Sure enough, there were the famous frescoes that ran the length of the building – patchy, filthy from accumulated grime and exhaust fumes, but more or less intact. Beneath them were rolled up sleeping bags, flattened cardboard boxes and the assorted paraphernalia of the rough sleepers who occupied this place at night, knocking back their booze and feeding their dogs.

I walked to the far end to the gateway and found a door set inside the old oak gate that had been secured with a meaty-looking padlock. It was a combination lock, which was commonly used in the construction industry for properties that required multiple access. Bog standard, twenty euros. Big and ugly enough to deter drunks and druggies but, supposedly, not to keep out someone with basic lock-picking skills. I pulled out my set and bent forward, glad Dolores wasn't standing over me this time.

I pushed the shackle of the lock forward to release the tension on the plate that kept the combination dials in place, then dug my probe into the first slot, moving it either way to see if it caught. No luck. I tried the second. There was a click and the shackle jumped out. I straightened up, looked around. No one appeared to have seen me. I pocketed the lock and pushed the door open.

The gateway led directly into a courtyard-cum-cloister ravaged by graffiti. An abandoned bell tower stood above me like a tombstone to a lost world.

Directly ahead was another, ungated, archway that

appeared to lead onto the open space remarked upon by the website. I walked beneath the arch and, sure enough, visible through the wasting mist, was an expanse of prime real estate, populated by the ruins of greenhouses and burned-out barracks. Long grass grew between the buildings, and rubble and trash were strewn all around. I could imagine Dolores – an army of Doloreses – clearing this site, recycling the materials, turning over the land, introducing livestock . . .

Farming is the future!

And yes, I could also imagine the wealthy Bolognese pulling up their SUVs between these cloisters before strolling to their luxury condos hidden behind the centuries-old walls.

What a racket.

That was when I heard it. The sound of an empty drinks can being punted across the courtyard behind me. Then – nothing. Whoever it was had frozen, fearful of being heard. I froze too, stuck here in the open, mid-way between the gateway and a line of derelict greenhouses.

Both of us waited for the other to make the first move. I figured that unless they had actually followed me, which I doubted, they – whoever they were – had discovered only that the lock had been removed. And anyone could have done that: one of the druggies could have got smart. It could have been a contractor who had pocketed it as I had, then perhaps forgotten to replace it on the way out. These thoughts would be running through their mind, while there was only one on mine – there was someone coming and I wasn't supposed to be here.

They moved first. Now I heard them, stepping softly beneath the second gateway toward me. And I moved when they did.

To the side of the gateway there was an old, larger than life-size statue of the Madonna. Piled beside it: an iron bath, a toilet and some masonry. It would have made the ideal hiding place but it was too dangerous – I would have to cross their sightline. Instead I made for the greenhouses and crouched down, just in time to see them step out of the gateway.

Standing in the threshold, Beppe looked slowly around.

I shrunk back, pressing myself against the rotten, damp wood. I heard his tread on the gravel as he moved toward me.

I barely breathed. I was waiting for him to arrive, working out what I was going to do when he did. I decided to go on the offensive, say what the hell are you doing here, confront him, as I'd planned to do earlier that day, not give him enough time to think, and maybe, in this private space with the sound of the traffic from the Viale thick enough to muffle any loud noises, grab him by the collar and shake him up a bit. God knows he could do with it.

Then the footsteps grew quieter – he was moving away.

Still, I remained crouched, straining to hear every sound. I finally leaned forward. Beppe was nowhere to be seen, but I stayed where I was as watery-white particles drifted around me.

I checked the time, which could play tricks on you at moments like this. It was a quarter to four. I would give it a few more minutes before making a move.

I heard conversation in the courtyard. Unhurried, unselfconscious, discursive, definitely not wary or afraid. Footsteps scraping across the trash-strewn stone, a cough. The men emerged out of the second gateway: Romano and Alessandro.

They were too far away for me to make out what they were saying, but Romano seemed to be taking the lead, waving his hands expansively, presumably expounding on their plans for the site. Alessandro's hands, meanwhile, remained firmly in his smart overcoat pocket. His expression was neutral, watchful, attentive, but in the manner of a leader rather than follower. He would ask the odd, short question, and Romano would provide him with a long answer. This was a pitch, I realised.

Finally Romano began to dry up and the *ispettore* stopped asking questions. The two men stood there, just in front of the gateway, looking at each other. Alessandro said something, softly, and pointedly, to Romano, who nodded, as if he understood.

I watched Romano step sideways, then Beppe emerge from behind the Madonna. He had a pistol in his hand. He pointed it at the back of Alessandro's head.

Something lifted me, like an invisible hand, to my feet.

I was standing up, almost as surprised as Romano and Alessandro, who had turned toward me. Then I saw Beppe squeeze the trigger.

Nothing happened. Now the two men followed my gaze. Beppe was still pointing the gun at Alessandro, repeatedly pulling the trigger but without effect.

Romano nodded furiously at Beppe, but now his gun appeared to have jammed completely. Beppe began fiddling with the weapon as if it was no more sinister than a stuck desk stapler while, in the meantime, I noticed Alessandro remove a small pistol from his overcoat pocket and casually aim it at Beppe's belly.

'Daniel,' he called out. 'Come, join us.'

Beppe was still trying to unjam the pistol, seemingly oblivious to the gun in the *ispettore*'s hand.

'Give it a rest, son,' Alessandro said, 'it'll do no good. Didn't the sergeant tell you? The weapons we distributed to our creatures were invariably duds. Or –' he looked at Romano, staring at him like a rabbit in headlights '– perhaps the sergeant inadvertently provided you with one?' Romano looked about to say something, but Alessandro shook his head.

He raised his pistol so it was now pointing at Beppe's chest. 'This one, on the other hand, is drawn from another source. It is one of those, well, I hesitate to say it in the presence of our English detective here, but it's what they call a "throwaway". Like that piece of junk in your hand, we used them in the bad old days, when we had to take certain measures in the defence of the state we did not wish to be traced to an official source. They could have come from anywhere, you see, or nowhere. But this one, I can assure you, most certainly does function as required.'

'Please,' said Beppe. 'Ispettore. I'll . . . tell you everything.'

'You'll tell me everything,' said the *ispettore*, 'that's very good of you. But what can you tell us that we don't already know? I don't know about you, Daniel, but at this point I'm beginning to feel pretty up to speed. The sergeant here,' he said, nodding at Romano, 'decided to get rid of me if I didn't fall into line with his plans, and you, Beppe, were the means. A tool, in other words. There's little more to it than that. What more do we need to know?'

Beppe had turned chalk white.

'He's young, Ispettore,' I said, 'an idiot. He was used, like you said. But I'm sure there's still more he could tell us.'

'There is?' said Alessandro.

'About the murder of Paolo Solitudine,' I said.

'Oh,' said Alessandro, 'that.' He looked at Romano. 'Well, what do you say, Sergeant?'

Romano opened his mouth to speak but Alessandro turned his pistol on him and pulled the trigger. The noise from the Viale may have muffled the sound of the gunshot outside, but inside the walls of the ex-monastery my ears rang.

Sergeant Romano sank to his knees, then fell backwards onto the ground. A shiver, like a bolt of electricity, ran from his shoulders down the length of his arms to the ends of his fingers, then he was still.

'On the other hand,' said Alessandro, looking down at the corpse, blood bubbling from the neat hole in the centre of Romano's forehead, his eyes bulging with blind surprise, 'don't bother.'

Chapter 40

You would think a slaughterhouse smells of blood and shit, but mostly it reeks of bleach, or at least the industrial quantities of disinfectant used to meet today's health and safety standards. Everywhere, that is, except the killing floor. I was working in the pre-slaughter section when I was undercover, which was precisely where I wanted to be – the point of my piece was to demonstrate certain abattoirs were still using prohibited technology in the 'stunning' room, in particular 'penetrating' bolt pistols which actually punched a hole in the cow's head, destroying a part of its brain. These were now outlawed because of the danger of spreading diseases. And yes, I did – I lasted precisely three days blasting holes into the foreheads of frightened bovines just like Desdemona, pulling the trigger until my index finger ached, the bolt burned hot. And despite the mask, the goggles, that stench always got through – of scorched blood and hair. The same stench that rose upon the particles of mist hanging around us as Romano lay inert on the floor like any other hunk of dead meat, and I realised in that odd, matter-of-fact way you can in extraordinary circumstances, that burned bone must smell the same as burned hair, because the bullet had entered through his forehead, which, along with the rest of his skull, was completely bare.

I became vaguely aware of Beppe coming down from behind the statue, Alessandro grabbing him by his beard, then stepping back with disgust as the young man instantly threw up. He remained bent on his knees, heaving, until Alessandro had had enough and hauled him to his feet. Nothing was said. What was there to say? A corpse was at our feet and Ispettore Alessandro of the Special Operations Group had gone from behaving like an actor in a commercial for upmarket clothing to a hands-on killer. I followed him and Beppe out to the car park.

'This, of course, is the point where you were supposed to come in,' he said to me. 'I didn't expect you to witness any of that, but perhaps it is better that you did. It saves me having to fill in the gaps.' We went to stand by the *ispettore*'s limousine. 'You didn't trust me, so you thought you would "case the joint" first. Bravo. I would have done the same. As you said, you've known me for little more than a week. I admire a man who relies on his own judgement, it is the best way. You don't mind driving, do you? I appear to be a man down.'

The *ispettore* had a hand on the arm of Beppe, who was standing wretchedly beside him. 'You know what, hold on a moment, Daniel,' said Alessandro, 'you see that handle there? Would you mind popping the trunk?'

Beppe's eyes widened as he was led around the rear of the car, but instead of bundling him inside, the *ispettore* pulled out a beach towel. 'I always carry a couple,' he said, 'for the summer. Still, you see – you never know when they might come in handy. You,' he said to Beppe, opening the rear door, 'make sure you sit on this. I don't want my seats to reek of any other . . . ejaculations.'

I got into the driver's seat and began to familiarise myself with the controls. I looked questioningly in the rear mirror. The *ispettore* waved his hand as if I was, indeed, just another driver. 'The Viale,' he said.

I eased the car onto the ring road.

Chapter 41

I took it slow, as if I had a crate of crockery on the back seats instead of a killer cop and his would-be assassin. The road ahead was uncommonly empty, or at least any other vehicles were obscured by the drifting fog, lending it a dreamlike quality, although I was keenly aware that this was reality – in fact, too bloody real. For all the tight spots I'd been in, criminals I'd encountered – even the ones who had gone on to commit, and be convicted, of murder – I'd never actually witnessed a murder before, let alone in cold blood, let alone of a cop by a cop. Driving along that shrouded highway I felt as if I had taken a road that there would be no getting off, and no going back. An extrajudicial killing is not something easily forgotten – disclosure can be as risky for the witness as the perpetrator – and the paint most definitely sticks.

'Now, young man.' Alessandro patted Beppe's knee as if he was his wealthy uncle. 'I believe you were going to tell me why I shouldn't kill you.'

'I can tell you everything,' said Beppe.

'But the question remains,' said the *ispettore*, 'is your everything worth anything to us? Or will it simply be more expedient for me to put a bullet in your head? After all, you wouldn't have hesitated to put one in mine.'

'You want to know about Paolo Solitudine,' he said, 'I can tell you about Paolo.'

'Paolo Solitudine,' said the *ispettore*, 'your pal Paolo. Poor Paolo, everybody's fall guy, right, Daniel?'

'It would seem that way,' I said.

'What about Paolo?' said Alessandro.

'I know who killed him.'

'What? You mean, it wasn't you?' Alessandro shifted in his seat, a sly smile appearing on his face. 'You hear that, Daniel? Our erstwhile assassin here is innocent. Enlighten us then, young man. We're all ears.'

'It was during the first raid,' he said, 'on the hospital.'

'We worked that out,' I said.

'It was a set up.'

'The raid?' I said. 'That much is plain. You conspired with Romano to stage the raid so you could bump off Solitudine,' I said, 'who had found out about your plans.'

'*No*,' he said. 'No. It wasn't like that, not at all. I knew Paolo was going to see the Mayor. I knew about Paolo and his wife. I had seen them . . . followed them. Mario hated the Mayor, he hated the Mayor with all his heart.'

'What's Mario got to do with it?'

'Mario told me about what happened. In the past. Why him and Paolo were sent to gaol . . . how the Mayor, Carlo Manzi, betrayed them. How he was an informer, both him and his wife.'

'An informer,' I said, 'like you, you mean?'

Beppe hesitated, nodded.

'Rudy . . . Sergeant Romano, that is, had a tap on Paolo's phone. He discovered there would be a meeting between them, between Manzi and Paolo.'

'So,' I said, 'you had this raid staged to coincide with the meeting. Why?'

'Rudy arranged it to disrupt the rehearsal, to provide a distraction. I needed to be able to get Mario away, over to the court building. Sergeant Romano was clear – he wanted Mario to witness Paolo and the Mayor together.'

'Dolores said Mario was arrested.'

'That's what he told Dolores afterwards. Instead, the sergeant had arranged for one exit to be left clear. I grabbed Mario and that's what we made for. When we were outside, I told him – that something was troubling me, it had been playing on my conscience; that, in fact, even as the raid was taking place, at this very moment I knew Paolo was secretly meeting the Mayor. I couldn't tell him what for, but given Mario's suspicions about the Mayor, I didn't really need to. I took him to the courthouse so he could see it with his own eyes. We waited across the courtyard – saw them both exit the office.'

'He didn't ask you how you knew about this?' I said.

'I told him a sympathiser in the Mayor's office had tipped me off.'

'And what did you hope to get out of it?'

'To divide them,' said Beppe. 'Rudy, the sergeant, wanted to drive a wedge between them so I could have more influence.'

'Always ambitious,' said Alessandro, 'even for his creatures.'

'But how does this lead to Paolo's murder?' I asked.

'Mario lost it,' said Beppe. 'I'd never seen him so angry. He was going to go after Paolo there and then, in the courthouse, but I held him back – I was frightened it might get out of hand.'

'And then?' I said.

'He broke away from me, ran outside.'

'And you didn't go after him?'

'I did, but not straightaway . . .'

'His work was done, Daniel,' said Alessandro, 'he had sown discord. Isn't that right, young man?'

'That's right, Ispettore,' said Beppe, 'but when I got back to the hospital, I went to the kitchen and found Mario washing the blood from his hands.'

'Blood, you say,' said the *ispettore*.

'Yes,' said Beppe. 'I said: "Mario, what happened?" and he said, "I waited for that bastard and gave him what for, that's what happened."'

'And when Paolo didn't reappear,' I said, 'what then? Did you speak to Mario about it again?'

'Not until they found his body. Until then, I just assumed Paolo had gone off somewhere. Then I asked him – "Mario, what really happened?" And he appeared to be in shock – he said, "I was waiting for him, in the dark. As soon as he came through the doorway I tried to grab hold of him but he managed to break away and run back the way he came."'

'And what about the blood?' I said.

'I asked the same thing – he said, "I might have punched him just the once, in the tussle, but it was nothing."'

'And you believed him?' I said. 'When he said "just the once"?'

'I didn't know whether to believe him or not.'

'What did Sergeant Romano say?' I said.

'I . . . I told him, straight afterwards, I mean, about the fight, and he was pleased. Then . . . when Paolo was found dead. Well, I didn't say anything . . . I was afraid.'

We drove around the Viale in silence while that sank in.

'And Mario,' I said, finally, 'when I spoke to him, he seemed pretty clear about the blame lying with the police, how did that come about?'

'A few days later he called me into his office. He'd been drinking. He said it must have been an accident. That Paolo must have become disorientated, fallen into the water . . . but we shouldn't waste his death, he wouldn't want that. We'd blame the police.'

'And you still believed him?' I said.

'I . . . I don't know.'

'And the key – the key to the canal we found at Paolo's place?'

'When they found his body, I went down for another look. It was still in the lock, so I took it out and returned it to his apartment.'

'Was that before or after you had ransacked it?' I said.

'I don't know anything about that.'

'And tell me, Beppe,' I said, 'when did you find out that Paolo had discovered about your plot with Romano to target the properties for occupation?'

Beppe shook his head. 'I had no idea he'd found out.'

'What do you mean, no idea?'

'Not until you mentioned it, just now.'

'Really?' I said. 'Well, that's convenient.'

'Why?' he said.

'Well, young man,' said Alessandro, 'for a start it removes your motive.'

'*I swear*—' he said.

'Do you think there's more to it than simply wanting to undermine Paolo's authority and put this one here in charge?' I said. 'Do you think Sergeant Romano was betting that if Mario discovered Paolo's deal with the Mayor it might result in more than just a falling out – it could drive Mario to murder?'

'He certainly liked to get others to do his dirty work for him,' said Alessandro. 'Either way it would be win-win for Sergeant Romano. Paolo couldn't explain what he was doing with the Mayor without confessing to the deal he'd made – for the sake of "love" no less! I can't imagine that going down well with Mario . . . whether they fell out or he bashed his head in, what had he got to lose?

'Ah, yes, my sergeant certainly didn't lack for ambition, and, of course, once I was out of the way . . . You know what they say about filling dead men's shoes, Daniel? In this country it can be taken literally. Okay, driver,' he said, 'if you could be so good as to take this turning here.' It was the sign for Bolognina.

Chapter 42

Bolognina, where the old world ended and the new one began. Over the bridge, across the railway tracks, to where the city had risen from the ashes of the Second World War – the poor part of the city, that is, where the workers had traditionally lived and toiled, and that had been flattened by Allied bombs during the war as the price the old, wealthy part of Bologna paid to remain pristine. Out of the ruins: block after block of shabby apartment buildings and industrial units with the odd scrubby park in between, where the poor played basketball, nursed babies and were significantly more multicultural than the people inside the walls.

'Where are you taking me?' said Beppe. Alessandro ignored him.

'This is where we spend most of our time, Daniel,' he said, 'invisible. It is remarkable how *invisible* this part of the city is, and yet how much business it generates, for policing, I mean. Still, by keeping all . . . *this* on the right side of the tracks, or perhaps that should be the wrong one, the powers that be leave us alone to do what is necessary. Pull in here.'

It was a rusty metal gate bordered by brick walls. Alessandro produced an electronic key, pointed it, and the doors yawned open. I drove in. It was some kind of factory, built in the fifties – grubby white walls, broken windows. Visible through the open doors: the wreckage of pilfered machinery, smashed furniture.

'We seized this place,' said the *ispettore*, 'it was being used by organised crime for distribution. We were trying to sell it, actually – you see that?' He meant the half-built apartment buildings on the other side of the walls. 'They were keen to buy the land, but went out of business. It seems that while there's plenty of demand for hotels and luxury apartments in the city, not so much for the ordinary ones. Come on,' he said.

Alessandro went around to the other side of the car and pulled Beppe matter-of-factly out, the spindly young man hanging in his grip. He began walking him toward the factory while I followed on behind.

I wasn't feeling half as cool as I was making out, but I knew enough to keep a clear head and leave the worrying to later. Most of all: to make sure there was a later. Alessandro had absolute control of the situation. This was definitely a man who had not been thrown by events, and for now I had to focus on that, and not allow him to exploit my sense of disorientation. Did I think he was about to kill me? Probably not. The kid? Quite possibly, and if I couldn't prevent that, I didn't want to get implicated if I could avoid it, either.

'Sit here,' said Alessandro. He pushed Beppe onto an old wooden chair facing a shuttered door. On either side of us were workbenches with the remnants of old machinery.

Placed seemingly at random across the benches and the floor were little luminous green and orange stickers. I knew what these indicated: crime scene, forensic evidence markers.

'Take off your shoes,' Alessandro told Beppe, 'and your socks, while you're about it.' Beppe looked up at him questioningly but did as he was told.

'This is where they used to take them,' Alessandro said to him, 'the *Camorristi*, when they wanted to make a point. They'd sit them in this very chair, the one that you're sitting on, Beppe, and cut little pieces off them until they would talk. Or just for fun. I was speaking to one of them and I asked him: why do you always cut off the fingertips? And he said – *come on*, have you ever tried pulling out a fingernail? Do you have any idea how much *effort* that takes? Much easier to – and he made this scissor movement, right? – "snip, snip, snip".'

Alessandro leaned against a bench and pulled out the gun he had used to kill Sergeant Romano. 'But we are not barbarians like them.' He cocked the pistol with a well-oiled snap. 'We're the good guys.'

'I beg you,' said Beppe.

'Ispettore,' I said, 'you don't have to. I'd say the kid has learned his lesson.'

'As a student of politics, Beppe,' said the *ispettore*, 'do you know your history? Uncle Joe Stalin had a saying: "no person, no problem". This could certainly apply to you, could it not? After all, you have just witnessed the slaying of a policeman, that most grievous of all crimes.

'If I do away with you, a known troublemaker with a grudge against the police, make it appear like a suicide, perhaps place the gun in your hand, then it would certainly wrap things up, would it not? Particularly from the perspective of the investigating officer –' he looked around '– who would be me.'

'I only tried to do what was required of me,' said Beppe, 'I thought I was working *for* you.'

'Even when you set out to murder me?'

'That was a mistake,' said Beppe, 'Rudy, the sergeant, said you knew too much . . .'

'Well, he was right about that,' said Alessandro.

'I tried to say no, but he wouldn't have it. He said if I didn't get rid of you, he would have me killed.'

'You were placed under duress?'

'Duress, that's it . . .'

The *ispettore* glanced at me, then back at Beppe. 'Still, I'm looking for a reason not to kill you, myself, son. How do I know I can trust you?'

'You can trust me, sir,' said Beppe, 'of course you can trust me. I always did whatever the sergeant requested.'

'Well, that's true enough, including trying to murder me.'

'I . . .' Beppe hung his head. There was the heaviest silence as I – as we, I suppose – waited for the gunshot.

'If I was to give you another chance,' said Alessandro, 'what would be in it for me?'

Beppe looked up. 'My loyalty,' he said almost breathlessly. 'My unswerving loyalty.'

'Even when,' said the *ispettore*, 'in the course of events, you move into mainstream politics and become a person of some influence?'

'Naturally, of course . . .'

'To the extent that you would follow my instructions to the letter?'

'Yes . . .'

'Because, if you were to refuse, you would know that I had in my possession a murder weapon with your fingerprints upon it, which could be immediately "rediscovered" and implicate you in the killing of a police officer?'

'I . . .' Beppe realised what was happening, but also that he didn't have a choice. He nodded. Alessandro looked at me.

'What do you think, Daniel?'

'Sounds like a deal to me,' I said, perhaps a little too quickly. Alessandro smiled. He looked down again at the pistol, then back at Beppe. He cracked out the magazine. Began to wipe the weapon with a handkerchief. When he had finished, he held it out to Beppe, who hesitated.

'Take it,' I said. Beppe took hold of the weapon and began to thoroughly incriminate himself.

'Far simpler than using all that expensive equipment, eh?' said Alessandro.

The *ispettore* had me pull up the shutters. We looked out at a wasteland of disused ground. Mud and grass, stones and broken glass. And beyond that: the unfinished housing project beginning to glimmer as the sun burned off the last of the fog.

'Off you trot, then,' said the *ispettore*. Beppe looked at him, then down at his bare feet. The *ispettore* nodded at his boots and socks.

'We'll hang onto those,' he said.

Beppe looked at the *ispettore* then at me. He was about to

say something but I shook my head. He stood up, stepped gingerly between us, then through the doorway. He began to pick his way across the barren land.

'Why did you keep the boots?' I said as we watched him go.

'Evidence,' said the *ispettore*. 'Footprints.'

'And the socks?'

The *ispettore* shrugged. 'Damned if I know,' he said, 'but the little shit tried to shoot me. Why make it easy?'

The sun had finally broken through and I had to tilt the visor down. In the seat next to me, Ispettore Umberto Alessandro had put on his sunglasses.

'You're looking a little peaky, Daniel,' he said. 'Would you like me to drive?'

He had a point – it was, after all, his car, but until that moment the thought hadn't even occurred to me.

'You just killed a man, Ispettore,' I said as I started the engine and pulled out. 'And threatened another with torture. That's not something I see every day.'

Behind those dark glasses, Alessandro seemed to think about what he wanted to say. 'I'm sorry,' he said finally. 'But there you were – at the wrong place at, quite literally, the wrong time. Thank you, by the way.'

'For what?'

'For trying to warn me, about the young man.'

'Was that why you didn't shoot me, too?'

Now he tilted his sunglasses onto the bridge of his nose and gave me a frank look. 'Are you serious?'

'You tell me.'

'I would never have harmed you, Daniel. You did nothing wrong. You're the Comandante's son-in-law, for Heaven's sake.'

'So it was nepotism that saved my skin,' I said. 'How Italian.'

Alessandro smiled. 'You know, don't you, it's not just Italy – in every country, there are people like me, and your father-in-law.'

'What do you mean?'

'Do you think the Comandante would have acted any differently?'

I was startled by the question, but managed to splutter, 'He would have had him prosecuted.'

'*Dai*. Really? He would have destroyed the reputation of the nation's security services and exposed a top-secret fund to "bring to justice" one traitor? For an act of treason like this, there can be only one punishment. Everyone understands that. Even Sergeant Romano, I'm sure, from his particular corner of Hell.'

'So you were judge, jury and executioner.'

'It comes with the job description.'

'I doubt it.'

He shook his head. 'There's no shortage of people who abhor cruelty to animals but enjoy a nice *cotolleta* without wanting to know where it came from.' He smiled. 'Or reporters writing articles about injustice on computers made by Chinese slave labourers. People are perfectly happy for someone else to do their dirty work, so long as it doesn't get in the way of their sense of self-righteousness.'

'And they call me cynical,' I said. 'So, you believe this story about Mario Cento?'

'Your friend seemed pretty convincing to me, Daniel.'

'He's certainly not my friend,' I said.

'You were keen enough to save his life.'

'You're not telling me now you intended to kill him.'

'It's true,' Alessandro said. 'Despite fully intending to murder me, I had decided the little prick deserved a second chance. After all, the church teaches us that we should all be given an opportunity to repent.'

'You're a religious man?' I said.

'Deeply. How do you think I sleep at night?'

'So what are you going to do about Mario, then?'

'I will pull him in for questioning, hear what he has to say. Present him with the evidence . . . contrary to the impression you may have, Daniel, I've always had a very strong impulse to avenge the innocent.' I gave him a sideways glance. 'The guilty can look after themselves.'

'Still, I'm not convinced Mario was responsible,' I said. 'I went into the canals with him. For a start I can't see him getting across that overflow pipe. He'd have been more likely to end up in the water himself. And if Paolo was nimble enough to get across that, then he probably wouldn't have fallen into the water on the other side.' I shook my head. 'I can't see Mario beating him to death, either, come to that – he's all bark, no bite. All right, maybe landing a punch in the heat of the moment, but murder? No. For all his talk, he's a big softy. I think he was telling Beppe the truth.'

'Pull in for a moment,' said the *ispettore*. I turned off the main road onto a private street. 'After speaking to the Comandante, I took a tour of the canals myself,' he said. 'Close to where you found Signora Finzi's scarf, I found this.'

The *ispettore* reached into his pocket. He pulled out a silver medallion of the Holy Family.

'What's so funny?' he said.

'That's not proof Mario did it,' I said, 'it proves that he didn't.'

Chapter 43

The Osteria della Luna was catering for the early traffic – shop-keepers popping in for a quiet *aperitivo* before heading home, students laying an early claim to a picnic table, and the usual old drunks securing their seats for the night, among them Franco. He was precisely where I expected he would be: in the same seat I had found him slumped dead drunk the time before.

Only this time he had not yet sunk so low, was sitting relatively upright, a glass of wine before him, gazing up at one of the old photos.

'Reminiscing,' I said, 'about old times?' He looked vaguely up at me, not so much drunk, I thought, as shifting from the past to the present.

'It's you,' he said. 'Still playing stooge to the bourgeoisie?'

'What about you?' I said. 'That notice at the entrance call-ing for volunteers for the Mayor's regeneration programme, that's what you meant, wasn't it, when you said you were *still* an engineer. You'd signed up.'

'So what if I had?'

'Opening the canals, is it?'

'Seeing as I was one of them that covered them up in the

first place,' he shrugged, 'and they were looking to know how it was done. Why not? Seemed the right idea at the time, and the right one now, too – give the kids some work, even if it is as fake bloody gondoliers . . .'

'That lady,' I said, pointing at the photo Mario had been staring at – of a group arm-in-arm at a dance, a great hammer and sickle banner hanging behind them, 'in fact, that rather jolly-looking chap standing beside her, it's you isn't it, and the lady – she's the one I saw you with, watching the funeral procession, in the wheelchair.'

'Like I said, I volunteer. You've got to give something back.'

'But her,' I said, 'that lady in particular . . .'

'Francesca. I came across her again in the home. There, in that picture, she was young, of course, full of potential. I think she was studying medicine or something – anyway, I remember thinking at the time: that one will go far. But then I met her all these years later, and she was . . . well, I mean, she was all right, she liked to read books and that, but she didn't have any feeling on her right side, had been paralysed ever since she got clocked . . .'

'You mean during the attack at the dance.'

'That's right,' he nodded. 'That had been the end for her. No career, no marriage, no kids.'

'So is that why you did it, Franco? You were heading back, along the canal, when you came across Paolo . . .'

Franco turned and looked me full in the face, a broken grin, more like a leer, playing on his lips. 'What's that you're suggesting?'

'Let's face it, you almost came out with it that first time we met.'

'You've got nothing on me,' he said.

I lifted the medallion out of my pocket and dangled it from my finger. It swung gently back and forth.

'Found God?' he said.

'No,' I said, 'but this *was* found somewhere it shouldn't have been. Good try,' I said.

'Nothing to do with me,' he said. 'Any idea who it might belong to?'

'You know who it belongs to, Franco,' I said, 'because you placed it there. In fact, it was you who was down there that day, with the light, sniffing around.'

'This medal,' said Franco, pointing a stubby finger, 'proves Mario Cento murdered Paolo Solitudine.'

I shook my head. 'Mario Cento never found the medallion he dropped the night of the dance, and neither did the police. That's because you picked it up off the floor. You were the treasurer, the one who tried to stop them.'

Franco licked his lips. 'I tried to reason with them,' he said, 'but they wouldn't listen to reason. Chose violence, and got what they deserved.'

'But why Paolo, Franco? It was such a long time ago.'

'A long time? Too true – a bloody long time for Francesca, her life ruined, every day a reminder of what happened, what she had lost, while that lot . . . well, they were treated like heroes.'

'So you came across him, and what?'

'Nothing.' He shook his head. 'He was lost, had gone the wrong way, I offered to help him out, it was only when he said . . .'

'What?'

'Comrade. Thank you, *comrade*. Something snapped. I belted him with the lamp and he went over. End of story.' He gulped his wine, gave me a defiant look. 'No regrets,' he said.

'But he didn't do anything, Franco. He didn't harm Francesca.'

'He was on the raid, wasn't he. *Collective responsibility.*' He took another sip. 'Cheers,' he said.

'You're going to gaol,' I said.

'What?' He looked surprised. 'You're not actually going to turn me in?'

'It wasn't me who found your "evidence",' I said. My eyes drifted to the pair of undercover cops sitting on the table behind us.

'But it was you that made the link,' he said, 'why couldn't you just leave it?'

'Because I made a deal, Franco,' I said. 'I traded your past for someone else's future.'

Chapter 44

I had taken the precaution of booking a table in the back room at Leonida for the lunch, formally to celebrate Alba's thirty-fourth birthday – and for once save her doing the cooking – informally to draw a line under the Solitudine case and mark the reconciliation between myself and the Comandante, although, to be fair, we were never at serious risk of a permanent falling out. We were family.

The *trattoria*, hidden away in Vicolo Alemagna, had been serving up high class Emilian cooking since 1938, and the décor hadn't noticeably changed since, although it had managed to remain remarkably spick and span – I might have found it hard to believe you could still source new replacements for eighty-year-old fittings had I been anywhere but Italy.

Alba and Rose had arrived together, and moving through the restaurant I realised that this time my daughter was wearing one of Lucia's best black dresses, only it had been adjusted to fit her. Both were made up and looked as crisp as the bright autumn day.

I glanced anxiously at the Comandante, who broke into a rare smile.

'It looks *lovely*, my darling,' he said to Rose. 'Alba – your friend did a splendid job. And of course, you are looking beautiful, but then you always do. Happy birthday!'

'You old charmer,' I said as they went to hang up their coats. 'I was worried about what you might think.'

'She's the image of her mother,' he said wistfully.

The ladies sat down and the *padróne* materialised to take our order. I didn't need to look at the menu to know what I'd be having. In fact I rarely looked at menus these days, not least because in almost any restaurant you could ask the kitchen to whisk up whatever you liked, so long as it was in the Italian culinary canon, and for me, as with many locals, particular *osteria* and *trattoria* were known as much for the dish you always requested as their menu. So while I always asked for the rabbit at Mariposa in Via Bertiera (and Luca, who was usually my companion in that neck of the woods, would order *tortellini pasticciati*) at Leonida it was *pappardelle al cinghiale* – wild boar, seasoned with black pepper – unless it was a Sunday when I would have the *cotoletta alla Bolognese*, washed down with a glass of the excellent local *Lambrusco*. The ladies, however, were somewhat less accustomed to eating out and took their time over the menu.

Alba's eyes lit up. She glanced at the Comandante who was, naturally, paying, then continued looking down the list.

'What have you spotted?' I said.

'Ah, it's just that white truffles are in season . . . but never mind.'

'It's your birthday,' I said. 'You should have what you want.'

'But— '

The Comandante said, 'Please, Alba dear, have what you like.'

'The taglietelle with porcini mushrooms and truffles then,' she said.

'Rose,' I prompted. She looked at me hopefully.

'The same?'

'Go on then,' I said, 'but you'd better eat it up.' She rolled her eyes. The *padróne* looked at Jacopo.

'Just a salad for me,' he said. We all looked at him. 'What?'

'He's becoming a *ciccione*,' said Alba, delightedly. She reached across the table and pinched his cheek. '*Cic-cione.*'

'*Get off.*'

'There's a girl he fancies,' said Rose. Jacopo glared at her.

'Who's *this*, then?' Alba looked as if all her birthday wishes were coming true.

He shook his head. 'She's talking rubbish,' he said.

'*I'm not*,' said Rose. 'She's—' Jacopo's scowl stopped her dead. '*Whatever.* Ooh . . . *look.*' A couple were sitting down at the opposite table, an English bulldog pup settling between their ankles. My heart sank. Rose was already rising, transformed from aspirant young lady to teenage girl. She went over and began petting the puppy while shooting me almost fiendish looks of endearment.

But, cunningly, it wasn't until we had finished our *dolce* (once again, I hadn't needed to look. In fact, this time nobody had – that would be Leonida's famous *Zuppa Inglese* all round) and the couple were getting up to leave that she went over to pet him goodbye, and when she returned to the table mentioned it – to her grandfather.

'Ah,' he said, Lear-like at the head of the table. 'I'm afraid that would be a decision for your father.'

I pretended not to have noticed until she said, 'Dad, Granddad says we can have a bulldog but only if you agree.'

'I said no such thing, young lady,' said the Comandante. 'As well you know. I said it was up to your father to decide. Dogs – they're a big responsibility.'

'Quite right, Giovanni,' I said. 'They need to be walked three times a day, for one thing. It's hard enough getting you out of bed once a day, Rose.'

'I would,' she said. 'If I had something to get out of bed for.'

'What? Like school?'

'You know what I mean. Oh come on, Dad, he was *so* cute, wasn't he. You can't deny it! And it would be patriotic – you know, *British*.'

'He was no more British than . . . I don't know. *Zuppa Inglese*. And, Rose – it is very cruel, to keep a bulldog, or any short-nosed breed come to that. They have terrible problems breathing. They have miserable lives.'

'And they fart a lot,' cut in Jacopo. 'Bulldogs.'

'*Come on*, Dad.'

'It's cruel.'

'It's *cute*.'

I was reminded of something Alessandro had said, which in turn reminded me to check my watch. Was it that time already? I would have to get going.

Rose let out a sigh. 'Okay then,' she said. 'I *suppose* we can get an *ordinary* dog.' Jacopo laughed.

'You "suppose", do you, *tesoro*?' I said, rising. I shook my head. 'I'm sorry, love, but really – no.' I looked around the table. 'And that's final.' Although, as with so much else, it turned out I had once again underestimated Italy's ability to surprise – my daughter would eventually get her dog.

But that's another story.

'An appointment,' I explained. The Comandante frowned, then apparently understood. He gave me an approving nod, although I hadn't told him what I was up to – but, of course, he would have his own sources.

I gave everyone a farewell hug and kiss with the exception of my daughter, who permitted me only a peck on the forehead, and stepped into the afternoon sunshine. I reached for my sunglasses, feeling like a proper Italian.

Along with most Bolognese, I usually avoided the bars around Piazza Maggiore because of the high prices, but this afternoon I made an exception.

I ordered a five-Euro *caffè lungo* and took advantage of one of the few places in this city of porticoes where you could enjoy a coffee outside and feel the sun on your face. I gazed across the piazza and thought about the people who had created this view, who were capable of crafting such beauty out of a world consisting chiefly of wood, iron and stone; the absurdity of considering ourselves their superiors.

A bell finally began to toll. A troop of *carabinieri* in full dress uniform – with their double pointed *lucerna* hats and red-lined capes – mustered in the centre of the square. They drew their glinting swords. Snapped to attention. The tourists sitting around me held up their cameras and phones to capture the spectacle.

From the far corner of the piazza, a hearse began to back up to the bottom of the church steps, then stopped. The undertakers got out and began to unload the coffin containing Sergeant Rodolfo Romano. Some of the tourists lowered their cameras – funerals didn't quite fit vacation memories – and the undertakers passed the coffin to half a dozen *carabinieri*, who began to carry it into the church, step by step.

The great and good, led by Mayor Carlo Manzi and his wife, began to emerge from Palazzo d'Accursio. They put on a good show, the Mayor and his missus, suitably sombre, and no fear of acts of sabotage here either, ringed as they were by cops armed with machine guns and sabres.

Bringing up the rear of the procession were more *carabinieri*, led by none other than Ispettore Alessandro, his grim-set resolve beneath his Napoleonic-era hat leaving little room for doubt that he would not rest until he had found the individual responsible for the murder of his trusted right-hand man.

Dolores came to sit beside me.

'You can wipe that grin off your face,' I said, 'half the uniforms here think you or one of your pals was behind it.'

She did her best to suppress her good cheer and handed me the envelope containing the journal. 'All done,' she said.

I took the book out. 'They didn't probe too deeply?' She shook her head.

'I told them the truth,' she said, 'I came across it when I was cleaning out his place. It looks like they're going to use all the juicy bits.' She thought about it. 'Political ones anyway. I think they might be leaving the dirty ones out.'

'I'm surprised,' I said. 'I thought the readership of the *Carlino* would have found them the most titillating.'

'You want to know what they're going to call it?' she said.
'Tell me.'

'*The Last Testament of Paolo Solitudine*. I think he would
be pleased.'

It would be published a couple of days before the city went
to the polls. A hand grenade hurled out of the past. How much
it would harm Carlo Manzi's chances of re-election I couldn't
say for sure, but it might do the trick. The Bolognese could
overlook a career in radical student politics, even involvement
in terrorism, but Manzi's depiction as a government snitch –
that, they would find harder to forgive.

The pallbearers entered the church. The dignitaries now
began to mount the stairs, led by the Mayor and his wife.

As she reached the final step, Marta Finzi stumbled slightly
in her heels. She reached out for the arm of her husband, but
as soon as she had steadied herself, she let go.

Turn the page for a sneak peek
at Tom Benjamin's next book
The Hunting Season

Chapter 1

There was no hint of murder that morning. On the contrary, it was bright after a weekend of rain. Autumn had arrived late – floods had hit Spain and a string of Italian cities on the west coast, but Bologna had endured the bad weather with her usual equanimity. This was the city of porticoes after all, and built to withstand extremes.

My daughter had already left for school, so I locked up. From our balcony, an undulating wave of terracotta rooftops swept down toward the centre, rose-damp tiles glowing beneath a sheen of steam and throwing the courtyard, indeed the rest of the city below the roofline, into dark contrast.

But like so much else in Italy, there was always sun if you knew where to look. I walked along our little Via Mirasole then onto D'Azelgio, crossing the cobbled road and stepping up to the old orphanage – the *Bastardini* – where warm light flooded between the tall, red brick columns. I slowed along with the other pedestrians to savour every last lick of summer. The church bells, which seemed to keep their own hours, began to peal.

We had arrived at what I liked to think of as our 'English

Summer', when the indomitable Italian heat tapered off and the city became liveable again. Rose might mourn the end of weekends at the beach but I felt like I could finally breathe again, and while for my fellow Bolognese it was a minor tragedy they marked by switching to dark colours, today I stuck to the chinos and linen jacket of British Summertime. On the whole, I didn't like to play the Englishman abroad, but it only felt fair to show my appreciation.

Even the broken lift at our office on Marconi did little to affect my mood and, after climbing four floors, I pushed through the varnished double doors, smiling at Alba, who rose from behind her desk. Her look of discomfit alerted me to the couple sat waiting beneath the large abstract painting that dominated the reception.

'Daniel. Here is the family Lee. They are American.' She sat down, clearly relieved at having delivered a coherent sentence in English.

The couple looked at me the way all parents did – as if I was a rescue vessel upon the horizon. But it was hope married with intense anxiety. Would they be able to attract my attention?

'The Consulate in Florence sent us,' Mr Lee grabbed my hand. 'They said you were the best English detective in Bologna.' I nodded, although I would have taken it as more of a complement if I hadn't been the only English detective in Bologna.

The Lees were of south-east Asian origin. Korean, I guessed from the surname, although they were outfitted in the uniform of middle-class America abroad – chinos and Ralf Lauren polo shirts, blue for him, pink for her. But in my current get-up I could hardly talk

'Tell me,' I said. 'How can I help?'

'It's our son, Ryan,' said Mr Lee. 'He's disappeared.'

That 'English sun' was slicing through the blinds so I pulled them closed. I kept the window behind open: the Comandante's office had had the weekend to rid itself of the old man's cigarette smoke but I knew even though he would refrain from lighting up in deference to the Lees, the legacy of his packet-a-day would reassert itself soon enough if I didn't keep the air circulating.

The couple were sat on the bottle-green Chesterfield sofa. I took a matching armchair opposite, alongside the Comandante. Between us and our would-be clients was a glass-topped art deco coffee table, upon it – a clean crystal ashtray, a couple of rarely opened hardback books on Bolognese architecture and, within a rather beautiful amber-stained Lucite box, fresh tissues. It could have been a gentleman's club or a therapist's office. It sometimes felt like both.

'Ryan,' said Mr Lee. 'Our boy, he's a *supertaster*.' He looked at me as if this explained everything. I looked at the Comandante, who clearly had no clue either. 'It's like perfect pitch,' said Mr Lee, 'only for taste. It means you've got more, literally more taste buds, but also . . . what are they? Smell? Smell buds? Anyway, cells or whatever in your nose, and they combine, and, well, you can taste things other people, no matter how well trained – and actually, he was really well-trained – can. No computer can do that stuff. That's what I said, wasn't it, Mary? No computer's going to be able to do that stuff, so Ryan, our Ryan's going to be just fine.' Now his voice broke. His wife took his hand and placed it in her lap. She began to explain.

Their son was supposed to meet them at the airport. He was often travelling to Europe for work and they had always wanted to visit. This time they thought it would be great to meet up in Bologna and maybe, if Ryan had the time, he could join them on trips to Florence and Venice.

Only, he hadn't been there when they arrived. They had waited, called his cell but it had gone straight to voicemail, sent messages, but he hadn't replied – or opened them, said Mr Lee. They had emailed from their hotel. That was two days ago, and there was still no trace.

'So this wasn't the same hotel Ryan's staying at?' I said.

Mrs Lee shook her head. 'Well, it could have been – but we booked it online, it was an offer. We asked if he was there,' she added. 'Just in case.'

'So you don't know where Ryan is staying?' They looked at each other.

'I know this must seem terrible,' said Mr Lee. Mrs Lee squeezed his hand. 'But we didn't think to. I mean, we just expected him to be at the airport, or get in touch. Ryan travels a lot. He's a freelance, has lots of clients. Always on the move. He comes to Italy a lot, and France, the south of France. His speciality is truffles.'

I checked my notes. 'He's a "supertaster", you say. I guess that's someone who samples food, like they do wine?' They nodded. 'Then his client here . . .' They looked at each other.

'Like I said . . .' Mr Lee managed to look both desperate and ashamed.

'So we don't know his client.' They shook their heads. 'Never mind. Has this kind of thing happened before? I mean, a sudden loss of contact, disappearance, that sort of thing?'

'Never,' said Mrs Lee. 'He usually checks in every day. Calls, or at least sends me a message or email when he's in Manhattan . . . that's his home – we live in the greater Vegas area, where he grew up . . .' She looked at her husband. 'Even when he did the Appalachian Trail, he called every few days and we were able to follow him on Facebook . . .'

'And there's been no activity there, either?' I asked. 'Or on any other social media you're aware of him using?' They shook their heads.

'Not since a couple of days before we set off,' said Mr Lee.

'And that was?'

'A store window,' said Mr Lee. 'Full of truffles, cheese. Those hanging sausages . . .'

'Salami,' said Mrs Lee.

'Did it say where?'

'Hold on.' Mr Lee checked his phone, showed me the post. '*Boscuri.*' I took a note.

'We would like to have access to your social media, if we may. To see if we can find anything . . .'

'Of course,' said Mr Lee.

'And you've contacted friends, family . . .?'

'Nothing,' said Mrs Lee.

I looked down at my notes. 'In your regular calls, he didn't mention anything about the hotel?'

'Only that it was nice, central . . .'

'That he was having any difficulties, problems . . .?' They shook their heads.

'He never said much about his life,' said Mrs Lee. 'He was always asking us about ours.'

'Ryan's an only child?'

'How did you know?'

Daily phone calls. Dutiful son. The sense they had cast all their hopes and dreams into the sole life raft that was Ryan Lee. I shrugged. 'You hadn't mentioned any other siblings. Well, our experts can check online, and in the meantime we will also contact the police – the hotel should have registered him when he arrived. You haven't contacted them yet, I presume?'

'The Consulate said to get in touch with you first,' Mrs Lee said.

The US Consulate was as useless as the UK's, I noted. But their laziness was our gain. 'We'll need his details, photograph, hobbies . . . I take it he wasn't married?' I asked.

Mrs Lee's eye widened. 'I think we'd know.'

'Girlfriend, then?' I left unsaid: boyfriend?

'He had a girlfriend at university,' said Mr Lee. 'But since he moved to New York . . .' He shook his head. 'So, you're saying you can help us?'

I glanced at the Comandante who gave an almost imperceptible nod. 'We'll get straight on it.' Relief swept their faces – if only because something was finally being done, they no longer felt alone.

'I'm sure everything will be fine,' I added, but I was already thinking about hospitals for Alba to ring around. As I led them out, I pictured Ryan in a coma somewhere. Secure mental facilities? He was in his late twenties – the classic age for males to experience their first psychotic episodes. I added homeless shelters to the list. He could simply be sitting babbling and shoeless in a corner somewhere. Or worse. The morgue. She should try morgues first, I decided, if only to rule them out. We were by the lift. I shook their hands.

'Really,' I said. 'Try not to worry. I'm sure it's nothing. Just a mix-up.' It seemed to help Mr Lee in particular. I was 'the best English detective in Bologna', after all.

And kind words cost nothing.

Chapter 2

I knew the Comandante's English language comprehension was excellent but his spoken almost non-existent. I suspected this was not due to a lack of language skills – I had heard him speak impeccable French – but his very lack of impeccability. The importance of *bella figura* – literally cutting a 'beautiful figure', actually making a good impression – was hard-wired into his generation, albeit that the young like his son, my brother-in-law, Jacopo, seemed to harbour few such reservations about ejaculating English as if it consisted wholly of half-heard pop lyrics.

But the Comandante had certainly understood the Lee's well enough and was now surveying me curiously across the table at Epulum, a classic 'old man's' *trattoria* hidden behind a dark door beneath a narrow portico with grimy, frosted glass shielding the clientele from curious passers-by. Beside the entrance, a yellowed menu was barely legible behind a foggy plastic cover, listing the classic 'Bolognese' dishes: primi like *Tortellini in brodo* and *Tagliatelle al ragu*, secondi *Bollito al carrello* (a boiled meat only true Bolognese could stomach) and *Braciola di maiale* (roast pork) and, for the *finale*, a binary choice between *Zuppa Inglese* (a Bolognese chef's rather game punt at Victorian trifle) or 'Meringue'. The original prices in Lire were scribbled out and replaced in biro with figures in Euros slightly above the going rate.

The hunched *padrone*, almost certainly an octogenarian, appeared at our table, notebook at the ready. The only menu in this place was stuck to the wall outside.

'I'll take the *cotoletta*,' said the Comandante. 'With truffles, the white.' The *padrone* nodded approvingly. 'And he will take – pasta right?' I nodded. 'The *tagliolini* with porcini mushrooms, and black.'

Without asking, the *padrone* poured a ruby red *Otello* Lambrusco into the Comandante's glass. I covered mine.

'I've work,' I said. 'And you know, Giovanni, I'm old enough to order my own food, thanks.' An amused smile fluttered behind the curtain of the Comandante's neat grey beard.

'But you like truffles? The white have just come in season, you know.'

'So why, then, did you order me the cheaper black?'

'Well, Alba's always telling us we should make economies.'

'And you thought the white would be wasted on the Englishman. I think that's a little unfair.'

'Can you taste the difference between black and white, then?' the Comandante asked.

'Probably not,' I admitted. 'Can you?' He frowned. How could I even doubt it? 'If you ask me,' I said. 'It's just marketing.'

The Comandante prodded a grissini bread stick toward me. 'And that's precisely why you got black.'

I poured myself a glass of sparkling water. 'So, tell me,' I said. 'To what do I owe this honour?' If he wasn't lunching somewhere like this with one of his old cronies from the *carabinieri* or Polizia di Stato, Giovanni usually liked nothing better than to eat alone accompanied by the latest lengthy comment piece by Ernesto Galli Della Loggia in the *Corriere della Sera*.

'I'm concerned about this young man, Signor Ryan,' he said.

I nodded. 'It doesn't look good.'

'Well, perhaps Alba and Jacopo,' who he had watched me brief before we left, 'will turn something up.'

'Even Dolores,' I said.

'I remain to be convinced.'

'I know.' And I also knew he wasn't talking about *Signor Ryan*. 'Although you could greet her a little less like you want to haul her in for questioning every time you see her.'

'Perhaps I will,' he said. 'When she does something about her ridiculous hair and clothing.'

'The fact that she doesn't look like a private investigator is sort of the point. Jacopo hardly dresses like Sam Spade.'

'Jacopo is my son. And anyway, he works on,' – he made a vague gesture – 'computers. Dolores is your, our, *employee*. And she is, now what is it they say? *Client-facing*.'

You've been gossiping with Alba, I thought, who was also no fan. 'Jacopo is an *employee*, too,' I said brusquely. 'And I employed Dolores because she's bright, energetic, and clearly has an aptitude for our business, as she demonstrated on the Solitudine case.' I sat back as the *cameriere* laid down our meals. 'And we owed her.'

'We paid her back, generously, in my opinion,' said the Comandante. 'By securing her release from gaol.'

'She's a good kid,' I said. 'Your real problem is that she's not a blood relative like Jacopo or Alba.'

The Comandante was leaning over his *cotoletta Bolognese* – breaded veal covered by Prosciutto and smothered in melted Parmesan.

He drew in the apparently refined aroma of additional white truffle, looked up at me. 'Neither are you,' he said, not unkindly, and the whole history of our relationship was conveyed within those steady grey eyes.

I certainly couldn't have got away with addressing any other Italian boss of his age and stature with quite the same licence had he not been my father-in-law, but then, were he not my father-in-law, I wouldn't have been sitting there in the first place.

When I had arrived with my late wife, Lucia, more than a dozen years earlier, I had soon found myself helping out with the family business: first the security side – basically as a bouncer at a homeless shelter (no mean feat for someone of my modest proportions), then playing a more active role in Faidate Investigations, especially after Lucia's death when it had been touch and go whether I would stay. But the Comandante couldn't bear to lose his granddaughter as well as his daughter (having, only a few years previously, also lost a wife) so . . . we remained. In that sense – the work, I mean – I was one of the few lucky ones. The chances for foreigners finding employ outside teaching English or some highly specialised discipline were approximately zero. The phrase *muro di gomma* – wall of rubber – didn't just apply to Italian officialdom's notorious impenetrability but also the labour market. Only that weekend I'd seen a news item lamenting the latest expat survey voting the country one of the West's worst places to live despite, as the reporter had pointed out, remaining one of its favourite tourist destinations. *Was that it?* Had Ryan Lee confused the two? Behaved like a cosseted tourist in Italy when he had crossed the threshold into the tenebrous ecology of *Italia*? This was Giovanni's fear.

'Supertaster,' he said. 'A sort of *food detective*. Specialising in truffles, that most expensive *fungi*. I wonder if the consul would have been quite so relaxed if an American private investigator on the trail of diamonds had gone missing.'

'You noticed that, too,' I said. 'Still – I've heard of "blood diamonds" but never "blood truffles".'

'You smile, my boy, but it is a largely unregulated business notoriously beyond the purview of the taxman. And once you step outside the law . . . well, you are always likely to come across unscrupulous individuals. It is not unknown for truffle hunters to take pot shots at each other, indeed for them to enter the woods and never return. Let us hope this is not one of those occasions.

'Signor Ryan arrived just as white truffles have come into season. For a specialist, that doesn't seem like a coincidence. A few shavings, barely a powdering on my *cotoletta* here, has upped the price by two thirds.' Now he picked up a *pane comune* – an unsalted Bolognese bread shaped like a clam that fit in the palm of his hand. 'Do you have any idea what a white this size would reach?' I googled 'most expensive white truffle'.

'Around two hundred and fifty thousand euros,' I said, looking at the bun as if it really were that precious.

'And they're currently digging them up in the hills around here,' he said. 'If they're *very lucky*. Perhaps Ryan had been called to verify a find.' He shrugged. 'One hypothesis.'

'And something went wrong. He discovered something he shouldn't have.'

'Although experienced, he may have got out of his depth. The weak point of the young,' said the Comandante, 'is confidence. Especially, I imagine, individuals of the calibre of Signor Ryan. Over-confidence – that may be where danger lies.'

'Why are you looking at me like that?' I said. 'I'm hardly a young man anymore, Giovanni.'

'Ah, but if there is one thing we can be sure about,' his eyes twinkled. 'You will always remain considerably younger than me.'

We went to the counter to pay. 'Mr Lee must have been visiting Boscuri for the truffles,' said the Comandante.

'Nothing like the Boscuri white,' said the *padrone*. He gave the Comandante a knowing wink.

'How is the market this year?'

The *padrone* made a satisfied smack of his lips. 'Can't complain.' Giovanni chuckled.

'I bet you can't, you old dog.' He checked his watch. 'As Signor Ryan's photo indicated, they also have some excellent local cheeses. If you leave now, Daniel, you might pick us up a nice piece of truffle-infused *Pecorino* for this evening.'

'Good job I didn't have any wine, then.' I was thinking about the tiring drive across the hills.

'Well,' said the Comandante. 'You did say you had work to do.'

Standing before the till there was a delicate model of a pig, apparently crafted out of a single piece of chocolate brown paper, but without the rigid, automaton-like folds of traditional origami. This may have been down to the more delicate paper, a kind of 'crepe' that creased like tissue, and in consequence the animal appeared much more lifelike. It was quite the work of art.

'Clever,' I said.

The *padrone* shrugged. 'Customer left it.'

Glossary Bolognese

Anarchism – although still clinging on in a sort of final redoubt at Piazza di Porta Santo Stefano, during the 1970s and 1980s Bologna's anarchists ran various *centri sociali* (see below) in cafes, bars and bookshops across the city before being winkled out, property by property. The year we arrived, they reoccupied a building in our street and my enquiries in stumbling Italian were met with a Dolores-level of disdain. Shortly thereafter they were evicted by Carabinieri. See also social and cultural activists *Lábas, XM24, Wu Ming*, etc.

Antonello Ghezzi – Bologna-based conceptual art collective.

August 2 – travellers passing through Bologna's railway station may notice one of the two main clocks upon its façade stopped at 10.25. This was the moment on 2 August 1980 a bomb exploded in the waiting room killing 85 people and injuring a further two hundred. Occurring at the height of the 'Years of Lead', two members of a neo-fascist organisation were subsequently sentenced to life imprisonment, although further probes and parliamentary enquiries have encompassed a range of actors including the Masonic P2 lodge, the CIA, Italian intelligence agencies and Palestinian groups. Every 2nd August the *Associazione tra i familiari delle vittime della strage alla stazione di Bologna del 2 Agosto 1980* holds a memorial concert in Piazza Maggiore. See also *Ustica*.

Blu – pseudonymous Bolognese graffiti artist, 'the Italian Banksy'. Active since 1999, he has achieved worldwide recognition while maintaining strong associations with anarchism and public art, and in 2016 removed all his murals from Bologna in protest at what he saw as the Comune's efforts to profit from them.

Bologna è una regola – Luca Carboni's hit (*Bologna is a rule*) deftly articulates the city's unique status in Italian culture. While other cities may be renowned for their beauty or food (and Bologna is respected for both) it chiefly represents *freedom* to Italians, somewhere to be the person you truly want to be, especially if you don't fit into the mainstream; a city of tolerance and experimentation. While for foreigners, Rome, Venice or Siena might symbolise the romance of Italy, Bologna occupies a special place in the hearts of many Italians and is, arguably, their most loved city. See also *Roxy Bar*.

Brigate Rosse (Red Brigades) – active particularly through the 1970s and 1980s, in 2002, professor Marco Biagi, an economic adviser to the government, was shot dead by Brigate Rosse terrorists in the *Ghetto*, nearby to the piazzetta now named after him.

Centri sociali – self-organised associations of leftists or anarchists often squatting in unused buildings, providing spaces for not-for-profit activities like concerts and advice centres. See also *Lábas, XM24*.

Città del cibo – the Comune's attempt to brand Bologna 'City of Food' has met with some success, drawing increasing numbers of tourists. This has not received universal approval, however. Alongside the usual graffiti, you can occasionally spot (considerately written in English to avoid any misunderstanding): *'Fuck Food City'*.

Compianto sul Cristo morto – created in 1460, the *compianto* by Niccolò dell'Arca resonates to the modern visitor with a naturalism uncommon for the era. A life-size terracotta group hidden in a corner at the Sanctuary of Santa Maria della Vita, the six figures around the corpse of the dead Christ could have been captured by a contemporary photographer such is the immediacy of their grief and horror.

Fighetti – plural of Fighetto. Fashionable, wealthy Bolognese youth – the boys typically sockless, the girls strapless – habitually spotted supping expensive cocktails at the latest hot bars and eateries sprung up to cash in on this new, although often very old, money.

Lábas – political collective that in 2012 occupied an ex-barracks in the city centre, partly in protest against gentrification, and ran social projects with locals. In August 2017, Lábas was 'violently ejected by the forces of law and order'. In September of the same year, 15,000 people marched for the 're-opening of Lábas', as a result of which Lábas was granted Comune property elsewhere 'inside the walls' and continues to pursue its objectives.

Osteria della Luna – inspired by an existing osteria that should be recognisable to most Bolognesi. One of the last surviving traditional osterias, dating back five hundred years to when the wine was cheaper, the company rowdier, and you could smoke indoors.

Piazza Verdi – epicentre of Bologna's student life, drugs trade, and home to the world's first opera house built from public funds, the *Teatro Comunale*, in 1763.

Roxy Bar – legendary bar on Via Rizzoli, referenced in Vasco Rossi's 1980s hit *'Vita Spericolata'* which, roughly translated, means 'life on the edge'. See *Bologna è una regola*.

Spaghetti Bolognese – never ask for spaghetti Bolognese. See *tagliatelle al ragu*.

Tagliatelle al ragu – what to ask for if you want *spaghetti Bolognese*.

Ustica – Via Saliceto in Bolognina is home to the most haunting memorial in the city: Itavia Flight 870, a passenger jet travelling from Bologna to Palermo that in 1980 crashed in mysterious circumstances killing all 81 passengers. Known in Italy as the 'Massacre of Ustica', like the August 2 bombing, the facts are veiled by claim and counter-claim. Enquiries by relatives to government officials met what became known as a 'muro di gomma', literally a rubber wall, because they just bounced back. The recovered parts of the plane's fuselage were returned to Bologna where they were reassembled in an old tram shed, along with objects from the victims, within an installation featuring lamps, mirrors and loudspeakers in which the travellers 'thoughts' can be heard as the visitor moves through the memorial.

XM24 – *centro sociale* on the site of a former market since 2002, including a 'People's Kitchen', 'People's Bike Shop' and 'People's Free Gym'. I ♥ XM24 flags are commonly seen draped from windows throughout the city, although when I first saw them I thought they were plugging a radio station. At dawn on 6 August 2019 riot police raided the site, bulldozing barricades in an attempt to evict those inside. See also *Lábas*.

Wu Ming – Bologna-based, multiple award-winning collective of 'cultural activists' which first enjoyed success with novel *'Q'* (writing as 'Luther Blissett'). Although the four authors appear widely in public, they refuse to be photographed.

Acknowledgements

After turning up for work in the morning at L'Antoniano di Bologna, which provides advice and hot lunches for the homeless, there would be a three-hour wait before we opened the doors to the canteen, and it was then, when I wasn't processing new arrivals or studying Italian, that inspiration for *A Quiet Death* began to come to me – here was a very different side of Italian life, not one most visitors are familiar with, but how could I capture it? It wasn't until I stumbled upon *Naples '44* by Norman Lewis, the writer's account of his experience as a British secret policeman in Italy at the close of the Second World War, that I found my way into the story and began to imagine what it would be like to be an English detective in today's Italy . . .

But it has been a long journey from L'Antoniano and I couldn't have made it on my own. I would like to thank Alex Goodwin at Cornerstones Literary Consultancy for his indispensable support, and my friend Gordon MacMillan for advising me to reach out to professionals in the first place. Yet for all the hard work, I wouldn't be writing this was it not for the faith of my agent, Bill Goodall, and the enthusiasm of Krystyna Green and Hannah Wann at Constable.

I would also like to thank my friends and readers, particularly Michael Atavar, Chris Bailey, Mike Bailey, Nick Cobban, Prue Crane, Nino Giuffrida, Nick Lawrence, Matthew Straddling and Marco Settembrini. It's no small favour to read an unpublished manuscript on top of all of life's other distractions, and is deeply appreciated.

Finally I would like to thank my wife, Lea, my most important audience. Apart from patiently reading – and listening – to repeated drafts and suggesting innumerable improvements, without her this novel would simply not exist.